The Kitchen Dance

Geri G. Taylor

Published by
Melange Books, LLC
White Bear Lake, MN 55110
www.melange-books.com

The Kitchen Dance ~ Copyright © 2013 by Geri G. Taylor

978-1-61235-540-5 Print

Names, characters, and incidents depicted in this book are products of the author's imagination or are used fictitiously. Any resemblance to actual events, locales, organizations, or persons, living or dead, is entirely coincidental and beyond the intent of the author or the publisher. No part of this book may be reproduced or transmitted in any form or by any means, electronic or mechanical, including photocopying, recording, or by any information storage and retrieval system, without permission in writing from the publisher. Published in the United States of America.

Cover Art by Geri G. Taylor

The Kitchen Dance
Geri G. Taylor

According to Rene Descartes, no two bodies can occupy the same space at the same time and any physical motion of a body involves moving other bodies from the space they occupy. In my first work of contemporary fiction, Joule and Allen create their own movements in *THE KITCHEN DANCE.*

To my dear friend, Judy, who shares my dark sense of humor and makes me laugh almost every single day.

To Nancy, my publisher, and Jane, my editor: I am delighted to have met you.

To my family for their support, and to Hero, Dash, and Storm for sitting at my feet or the arm of my chair and keeping me company while I write.

And to all my dear friends who had to hear the abbreviated version of this story, helped me to edit, and suffered my search for validation.

Prologue

Joule

If you had asked me right out of graduate school when a person "found" himself, I would have answered, "Right after graduate school." Twenty plus years later, I am still finding myself.

After graduate school, I moved, with a group of friends, into a twenty thousand square foot warehouse close to an airport where we, all artists of sorts, were going to express ourselves in our various styles. Against zoning laws we turned the massive area into working and living spaces. A combination of tents, plywood structures and one, old over-the-cab camper served as bedrooms. We shared one bathroom with no bathing facility, a living area comprised of second hand sofas and chairs on a large wool carpet, and a makeshift kitchen. It was very Bohemian.

Saul and I shared a twelve by fourteen foot structure built from studs and sheets of plywood in one corner of the warehouse. I, being an interior designer, had given it style. With little heat and no air conditioning, we snuggled during the cold nights, and knocked out two walls for ventilation replacing them with mosquito netting during the long, hot east Texas summers.

There was little privacy and even less discretion among the roommates.

My work space was about a thousand square feet and custom furniture was my specialty. I contracted the framework and focused my time, talent, and limited space on upholstery. Many a fight broke out when I came home to find my roommates and their guests testing out my sofas. I created walls of studs and hog wire around my work area to keep peace in our little commune and kept my finished work in the back of my van.

Geri G. Taylor

Saul was a painter. Although his work was not my particular taste, I loved him for his passion towards his craft and his appetite for lovemaking. He worked in a loft we built over our room, where the light from the windows was better. The smell of oil paint and solvent hung thick in the air. If the recreational drugs did not kill us, the fumes would. We retreated to my parents' cabin (Would I ever be able to call it my own?) whenever we could. There we skinny-dipped in the lake, soaked in the hot tub, and made love on a deck that overlooked the lake.

Victor, my dear friend since college, had not found his style or medium of choice, and was gone more nights than home in his corner of the warehouse. He had fastened a long, thick metal pole across the corner of his space and draped it with musty, red velvet curtains a theater had thrown out. He dropped out of college and traveled Europe for a year. He dabbled in various mediums, including welding, which the other roommates quickly vetoed. He was the life of the party, often arriving home with an interesting assortment of guests. His parties created connections. Connections created opportunities. Opportunities created money.

Camilla, a textile artist, and her husband, Glen, used the old office space in the warehouse for his writing and her sewing projects. They lived in the over-the-cab camper parked near the bay doors. He strummed a guitar and she sang. They played their music loud and made love even louder. They contributed the large dining tent strung with Christmas lights, and a variety of chairs where, around a banquet table that came with the warehouse, we gathered to share our meals, ideas, and plans for our futures.

Daisy was the oldest of our group by eight years. She was a poet and painter of miniatures. Most of her work was no larger than six by nine inches. Why she felt the need to live in a loft, I will never know. She was quiet and kept to herself in a dome-shaped tent where she used large screw eyes embedded in coffee tins filled with cement instead of tent stakes. When she did emerge, it was to cook fabulous meals, and we all gathered in the kitchen to help. It was then and there I learned the kitchen dance, and the true value of relationships.

We all knew this life was as temporary as the tents and draperies, but it was a great place to grow. If pruning creates healthy growth, fate proved my gardener. I came home from my part-time job one evening to find my roommates gathered around the table. Their faces, dimly lit by the Christmas lights, were dull and expressionless. I noticed something or someone was missing. That is when Daisy told me Saul packed up his belongings and left for New York. Three years together and he did not even bother to leave me a note.

The Kitchen Dance

I withdrew to the cabin for a week until my grandfather came down from New Jersey to encourage me to get my life together. Two weeks later, I landed a position with The West Agency, a prestigious architectural firm in the city. I have been there since.

Some friends come and go in a lifetime. Some leave you with their pearls of wisdom or brief recollections, fond memories, and utter disappointments while others have profound effects on the decisions one makes in the future. Sometimes, when I am overwhelmed with my life, I think of these simplistic, yet complicated times. I never heard from Saul again, but occasionally I find myself wondering, what if? Camille and Glen joined the corporate world, Camille in textile imports and Glen, the president of a bank. Daisy moved to Arizona and published three books of her art and poetry.

I see Victor occasionally. He once told me Saul tried to make his mark in New York's art scene but ended up teaching at a high school in Iowa. Still the life of the party, Victor never found his own style. My life, however, took another turn: another pruning.

Chapter One

Joule

"Joule? Honey, you don't have to do this right now," Elaine comforted me in her east Texas drawl as she dragged the empty box past the closet door.

I ran my hand over several hangers of men's suits, some of which still held my husband's scent. "Yes, I do. You said you were here to help, so help."

"Let me in there. You can stand here and sort." Elaine pushed past me in the crowded walk-in closet Daniel and I built to help distinguish the living area from the bedroom of our spacious loft apartment.

I stepped from the closet, over the empty box, and into the bedroom area where piles of multicolored apparel contrasted with the white carpet and walls.

Elaine climbed a small stepladder to get the shoes lining the top shelf. "What's this door for?" Elaine balanced precariously on the flimsy step stool and regarded the access door in the ceiling. "Do you have storage up here?"

"No, it's just a crawl space," I told her, offering her a hand to steady her perch while pointing with the other. "Hand me those shoes first." Elaine reached up and handed down several large shoeboxes containing pairs of men's shoes. That is all they are now, I reminded myself; men's shoes, shoes worn by a man, a man no longer in my life. I took a last look at a few pairs of the shoes before placing them in the larger box. They were expensive, fine-leather, Italian made lace-ups and loafers worn with his suits tailor-made to fit his broad shoulders and long arms and cut to make his thick waist appear slimmer. He was a man who appreciated style and it showed, not only in his fashion sense, but in his work. I sorted through some athletic shoes worn for specific sports; jogging, racquetball, tennis and a pair for basketball. He had twice as many shoes as I, and his casual shirts and slacks spilled over on to the racks and

The Kitchen Dance

shelves considered "my" side of the closet. I opened the only shoebox not in pristine condition. It's worn corners were taped together. It fitted neatly into the stack of other boxes, and now held, instead of shoes, a collection of photos, greeting cards and newspaper clippings. I lifted out several photographs of a handsome man I would never see again; Daniel, my murdered husband.

"Jou-elle? Hel-loo?" Elaine sang as she balanced a few more boxes in her arms. "You're about to lose your helper."

I held up a newspaper article I pulled from the ratty shoebox and exchanged it for the stack Elaine was about to drop. Without looking in the shoeboxes, I added them to the stack rapidly filling the brown moving box.

"Award winning architect shot down in his home." Elaine read the title of the article aloud. She read through the text of the article silently to herself while I shuffled through the contents of the ratty shoebox. "What are you doing?"

"Hand me that scrapbook on the other shelf," I told her as I cleared away a stack of clothes revealing a patch of white carpet.

Elaine reached towards a shelf on the other side of the closet retrieving a thick scrapbook. She climbed down the ladder and joined me on the bedroom floor. "What do you have?" She regarded the box.

"Just some things I culled." I opened the scrapbook and flipped through the pages revealing decorated arrangements of cleverly cropped photos and notations celebrating the best times of my life with my husband, Daniel Parker.

Elaine picked up the shoebox of mementos. "What do you want me to do with this?" She waved the article in my field of vision.

"Throw it away," I replied while flipping through the scrapbook. "I will sort through the box and send the pictures of Daniel to his mother."

Elaine studied the newspaper clipping. "Life isn't a scrapbook, Joule. People can't just sort through their lives picking only the best for a lovely scrapbook to set on their coffee table for all their friends to see pretending that is their life. It would be great if we could put all the bad stuff in a box on a top shelf in the closet. We could keep it hidden away from the world or just toss it in the trash. It doesn't work that way. It is all this hard stuff that makes life real. This is your life, honey!" She thrust the box in my direction. "Don't get rid of Daniel's belongings because you think it will make your bad memories of Daniel just go away," Elaine offered with heartfelt sympathy.

I reached for the article, put it in the shoebox on top of the other items and closed the lid. I set the shoebox on top of the scrapbook and put it back on the shelf, on my side of the closet, next to my dust covered camera bag. I ran my fingers along the camera bag's zipper wanting to take a look at the contents but dismissed the idea and wiped the dust off my fingers on the leg of my jeans. I arched my aching back then bent down, stretching until my fingertips touched my toes.

"Don't quit on me now!" Elaine followed me into the closet and climbed up the ladder handing me more boxes. She quickly emptied the shelves as I loaded the shoes in a new moving box. She stepped down and looked over the remaining clothes in the closet. "What are you going to do with all this space?" She spoke without thinking. "I guess I will take you shopping so you can fill it up again." She folded up the stepladder and set it against a bare wall. "I'm sorry." She realized what she said, patted my shoulder and gave it a little squeeze.

I closed the corrugated box filled with his shoes and retrieved another from the stack in the living room area while Elaine took clothes from the rack in groups of four or five hangers in each hand. She continued to load them in the boxes, without paying any attention to them. What, after all, did they mean to her? She had her rhythm and perhaps her silence was her way of protecting me.

After filling two boxes, and halfway through another, I became aware of the specific clothes going in the box. I broke her flow when I stopped her to pull out a trench coat from the pile. I pulled the coat to my face and smelled it. The spicy scent of his aftershave still lingered in its fibers. "He was wearing this the day we met." I carried the trench coat into the closet.

"Maybe you should keep it?" Elaine suggested.

I clutched it to my breast. "No. It'll do someone else some good." I considered tossing it in the box of clothes when I noticed the stain on the sleeve. "Do you think I should have this cleaned first?" I showed the stain to Elaine.

Elaine examined the faded smudge. "No, Joule. You're giving it to the homeless. I don't think a little stain will matter." She said it in a snooty way which was unusual for Elaine.

I continued to examine the coat until Elaine reached for it. "Give it to me. I will try to get the stain out," she offered without hesitation.

"No." I tossed it in the box instead. "That's okay. You're right. Give me some more clothes." I ended the topic abruptly and bettered my effort to complete the task with no more reminiscing.

We carried the boxes down the steep flight of stairs leading to the warehouse below the loft and piled the boxes by the oversized warehouse doors.

"Where is Roosevelt?" Elaine asked gathering her purse and coat off the top of the box she set atop the others.

I considered the consequences of disturbing my roommate. "He's probably sleeping." I regarded the late hour and combed my hair away from my face with my fingertips. Elaine and I smiled at each other validating our accomplishment

The Kitchen Dance

and embraced. "Thank you so much for helping me." I held her at arm's length. "I have to say, 'I could not have done it without you' because you know; I could not have done it without you."

She laughed and kissed my cheek. "I'm glad to help." She adjusted her handbag on her shoulder. "And you should get that service elevator fixed," she suggested and she pushed through the door leading to street.

"It's on my to-do list 'Laine," I expressed, as if it was not a priority. I waved good-bye. My priorities changed the past year and more than my service elevator was in disrepair. I pulled myself up the staircase railing with one hand while supporting a sore knee with the other. During my ascent, I surveyed the warehouse, stopping at the landing at the top of the stairs. There was still so much to do. A surge of depression hit me so hard I could hardly breathe. I tried to shrug it off as exhaustion but I knew the feeling would follow me like a shadow as it had so many times before. A warm shower and a glass of wine while playing a little solitaire on my laptop would coax me into, I hoped, a dreamless sleep.

* * * *

The next morning, I heard the chuff of an engine battling the cold and checked from my loft's bedroom window to watch the dull white delivery truck's approach. Clouds of smoke coughed from the exhaust as it stopped in front of my warehouse. The obese, burly man I recognized from the soup kitchen extracted himself from the driver's seat, his breath indicating the chill of the early hours. He opened the rear door of the truck. An irritating screech of metal against metal made me shudder as the rear door scraped in its tracks. His partner, a tall scrawny teen with long dull blonde curls, slid gracefully from the passenger's side and immediately began hefting the overstuffed boxes of clothing sitting by the rolling doors at my warehouse dock. He selected a box he could manage and disappeared with it in the truck's cargo area.

Oscar, or Oliver, I could not recall his name, only that it began with an *O*, pushed a large box with the steel toe of his work boot as if the gesture could calculate the parcel's weight. He was more bulk than brawn and his massive arms did not realize the strength they suggested. He squatted before a box, his knees protesting the attempt, and using his hands to brace himself, stood up and returned to his supervisory role. He pulled a pack of cigarettes from the inside pocket of his coat, shook one out, clenched it between his stained teeth and proceeded to light it. He blew out a long stream of smoke that mingled with the moisture in the air.

The thin young man, "Blondie", I spontaneously nicknamed him, returned to the stack of boxes and rubbed his gloveless, chapped hands against his biceps hoping the friction would give him some relief against the cold. Oliver or Oscar kicked a box which the young man immediately understood as a signal to lift. Elaine and I had strained under the weight of the box, lifting then guiding the box, sliding it down the staircase. It resembled a child bumping down a snow covered hill. Blondie managed alone, with little effort, to get it in the truck. This was the heaviest box, filled mostly with slacks; some still crisp from the dry cleaners. There were jeans, rarely worn but purchased faded and frayed as if they had been worn, as was the style.

Blondie picked up another much lighter box. Daniel's shoes, their original boxes discarded at the shelter and soup kitchen and the designer names whose gold imprinted labels would have no more value than the rubber bands used to secure the pairs of shoes for distribution. He handed the lighter box to his supervisor who balanced it on his protruding gut, cigarette dangling from his chapped lips, and hoisted it in the rear of the truck. Blondie, working twice the speed of his boss, completed the task quickly while short bursts of cold puffed from his nose and mouth before his boss even finished his cigarette and with that, Daniel's belongings were cleared away.

When the truck pulled away, I noticed Roosevelt sitting in one of two padded folding chairs on the sidewalk. He offered neither assistance nor suggestions. He simply watched as each box was removed from the stack and vanished in the rear of the truck. A casual observer would assume the old man homeless but he had a home. He lived with me. Roosevelt Graham was an elderly man who never told me his age, but I guessed by his appearance was closing in on eighty. He sat huddled against the cold with the early morning sunlight glinting off his blue-gray eyes, his dry-wrinkled skin, and his frizzy matted hair. He watched the men drive away in the truck. He wore a dark tweed coat over faded slacks and worn but recently polished brown leather lace-up shoes. He watched without offering his opinion. This was unlike Roosevelt who usually sat at his post for hours speaking to everyone who came by.

I waited until after the truck was far enough down the street and the chug of the diesel engine faded before I opened the smaller door beside the large warehouse door. Struggling with my parcels, I was carrying a long dress bag over my arm, my handbag, and a large bag over my other shoulder; I tried not to spill the cup of steaming coffee in my free hand. I handed Roosevelt the cup of coffee but he didn't take it. "Good morning," I offered cheerfully. "Did they just pick up the boxes?" I asked as if I were not aware of the commotion taking place below my loft. Roosevelt did not answer me, instead he continued to watch the traffic picking up on an adjacent street.

"Okay. There is some ham in the fridge and I picked up some eggs last night if you want some breakfast." I set the coffee in the chair next to him. No

The Kitchen Dance

response. "I forgot to get some juice at the store yesterday. Do you want me to get you some juice before I go to work?" I attempted, but still no response. "I won't be home until late. I have a cocktail party after work," I reminded him and yet still no response. "I'll bring you something from Elaine's," I bribed. No response. "Well, it's rather cold so don't stay out too long," I expressed with concern even though he continued to ignore me. I waited. "I'll see you later then," I surrendered but Roosevelt still offered no reply. I adjusted my parcels and walked away.

"I like the mushrooms." Roosevelt, barely audible, mumbled to my backside.

I turned around. "What did you say?" I said even though I clearly heard him.

"I like the mushrooms," he enunciated with enough clarity and volume to be heard over the hum of noise and commotion building as the world came alive on that winter's day. "The ones with the stuffing," he reminded me.

"I'll bring you back some."

"And some cake," he insisted.

"Of course, I wouldn't forget the cake." I could not hold back the smile. I did not have to glance back as I walked away knowing once I cleared the corner, Roosevelt would take the coffee.

I hailed a cab, deciding the expense was justifiable versus the effort and time it would take to warm up the engine of Daniel's car or my old van. I still referred to it as Daniel's car even though my name was now on the title and registration. He bought it despite my protests. I never wanted the sports car and only used it out of necessity but still had not put forth the effort to sell it. The van I usually drove was bulky and difficult to drive through traffic and rarely reliable on winter days, especially those mornings that barely reached above freezing.

I would become accustomed to Daniel's clothes being gone first, see how I felt, then sell the car. I realized the car should have been the first to go. It would probably be easier to let go of the status symbol he believed so necessary in his self-perception of success. At least the clothing still held a faint scent stimulating warm recollections of his vibrant personality but the Jaguar XK8 brought back negative memories of arguments that tore through our marriage like a storm. We were different people in more ways than two people could be. If the saying is true opposites attract, we were clearly an example of that cliché. Attract we did. I could not imagine a man more different from me and unyielding to change. I changed, ever the chameleon. That made our marriage work but it was our careers which held us together.

I waited for the elevator in the lobby of the executive building where my office windows overlooked downtown's busy streets. The antiquated building with its classical Art Deco architectural styling hosted a lobby with chrome accents, black and pale pinks swirling in the granite of the geometric patterns on the wall, and the black and white marble floors. It retained the cold that both visually and physically drafted in past the air lock's rotating door. I adjusted the clothing in my arms, smoothing out the dress I would wear that evening. Then I hugged the bundle closer to my body as other people entered the lobby jostling for positions around the elevator doors.

Philip West, my boss, approached me. He was a man who looked better in his sixties than he did when I first interviewed with him nearly twenty years ago. His once dark hair was now more salt than pepper. His once pale pockmarked skin, now chemically peeled, maintained a subtle tan from the solar bed he and Elaine, his wife and my best friend, kept in their exercise room. The glint in his eyes and his rueful smile reminded me he was the same Philip I had known for years.

"Good morning, Joule," Philip greeted me as we boarded the elevator together. "Elaine wanted me to ask if Roosevelt was speaking to you yet."

"Barely," I answered, "But, we had a breakthrough this morning. He asked for some of Elaine's stuffed mushroom caps from the party tonight." I stepped closer to him allowing three people to get off the elevator on their floor.

Philip smiled and chuckled. "And cake?" He motioned for a young man to press the button for our floor. The young man quickly obliged.

"Of course." I mimicked his soft chuckle and stepped into the void left by the others.

"Of course." He paused as the elevator continued its ascent. "Listen Joule, you did the right thing. Don't let him make this harder on you. You need to move on."

"I'm okay. Roosevelt is just being his usual overprotective self. He'll get over it." I prayed the elevator would stop and more people would board and put an end to this conversation. The elevator did open only to let off more passengers increasing the void until we finally reached our floor. The pregnant pause lasted forever and the remaining young man offered no distraction. I had never been more aware of the creaks and groans the aged mechanisms moaned as they seemingly strained, pulling us to our designated floor. We cheerfully said our good-byes and went our separate directions. Elaine was my dearest friend from a friendship that sparked the instant we met. Philip, her husband, my boss, was not. Our tidbit of lighthearted dialogue I knew was encouraged by Elaine during her attempt to soften her husband but Philip West was all business, a character flaw he shared with my late husband.

I worked incessantly through lunch and all afternoon on some last minute

The Kitchen Dance

changes and finishing touches to an interior design sample board of our latest project. After the long workday, I dressed in the women's executive lounge and loaded the boards in my assistant's car. We drove to the West's luxurious home where we joined the thirty or more people for drinks and hors d'oeuvres. The room was decorated in deep jewel tones with candlelit warmth, sparkling crystal, and an adequate fire in the fireplace bounced yellow light off the richly dressed guests. I followed Philip's instructions and dressed to blend not to attract attention. My dress, cut just above my knees, was a somber shade of dark brown with light green embroidered accents and a glistening light green silk swatch around my neckline attracting light to my green eyes. I wore high heels, a simple, yet elegant gold necklace borrowed from Elaine, dark red painted lips, and broad welcoming smile.

"People," Philip once pointed out to me, "I am not just talking about men, I mean women as well, look at your breasts and don't hear a word you're saying. Wear subtle colors, honey, discreet necklines and dress up that incredible mouth of yours so people watch what you're saying. What you say about the work you do is what we are selling here. I'll have plenty of young ladies to keep the clients entertained in the other area." Philip always walked a thin line between what he referred to as a casual observation and I would deem sexual predation.

I knew this for a fact. The West's parties were notorious for their guests. Elaine confided in me she contacted a local talent agency for young, exceptionally attractive females, and handsome male actor wannabes complete with detailed scripts talking up the newest project. "What happens after the cocktail party is their own business," Elaine explained.

I was not hired for my good looks. I was average on my best days. Average height, average weight, I even wore an average shoe size. Nor was I hired for my capacity to influence clients with my amorous ways. I was hired for my mouth and the words that came out of it, Philip informed me. I had the wisdom of a gifted designer to backup what I said. Thankfully, I had a big smile with straight white teeth and a shapely mouth that, when glossed up, could make the words appear more interesting to watch as this apparent wisdom flowed forth.

Elaine, accompanied by Taylor Prescott and his wife, met me halfway through the crowded room.

"Joule! I want you to meet the Prescotts," Elaine burst out enthusiastically. "Taylor, Elise, this is our interior designer, Joule Dalton."

"Jew-well," Elise mispronounced sarcastically, "as in diamonds?"

"Joule," I corrected her, knowing all too well her type, "as in the famous physicist or unit of energy."

"Oh?" Elise replied, obviously not getting it.

"James Joule," Taylor Prescott intervened. "Actually James Prescott Joule. It appears we have something in common."

Taylor Prescott and I smiled at this clever observation and thus our friendship ignited. However, Elise still did not get it and turned to Elaine for an explanation. "Joule's father was also a physicist but no relation to the famous chemist John Dalton," Elaine, who heard the "Joule" story before offered. "Right, Joule?"

"My father was a college physics professor and yes, no relation to *the* John Dalton," I added for Mr. Prescott's amusement.

"She is head of our interior design team." Elaine continued to support me, "You may recall her work on the G. B. Landon building." She directed this at Mr. Prescott.

"Beautiful work, Ms. Dalton. I hope you will be working on our building," Mr. Prescott encouraged.

"I have some ideas." I selected a glass of champagne from a passing tray, nodded at the server, sipped just enough to give my lips a glisten of the bubbly liquid and slipped into schmooze mode. "I'm still waiting for the architects to finish their final design."

I turned slightly and took the well-rehearsed two steps away from Mr. Prescott who took the cue to follow. We continued the typical cocktail party pleasantries in a more intimate space beside the massive carved marble fireplace mantel where a server was removing drink glasses from recent connections.

Elaine, a graduate from the same school of cocktail party etiquette, gently guided Elise away to mingle with other guests.

"Is she married?" I could hear Elise ask Elaine as they walked away.

"Who?" Elaine asked, feigning distraction.

I glanced their way in time for my eyes to meet with Elise's who was looking back possessively at my conversing with her husband.

"She's a widow. Her husband was one of our top architects. He was killed, murdered, actually. It was about two years ago." Elaine piqued Elise's interest.

"Oh, my goodness," Elise replied. "How sad."

Elaine pulled her away from my earshot and either filled the curious Elise in on the tragic story of "Poor Joule", or distracted her with the introduction to other guests, as was my dear friend's typical way.

"Joule." I felt a cool hand on my arm, startling me with an impolite interruption of my conversation with Mr. Prescott. "I'm not feeling well," whispered Barry, the owner of the cool hand. He brushed his lips gently against my ear. "Do you mind if I cut out early?"

The Kitchen Dance

"Mr. Monroe wanted to show off his new project. Can't you stay a little longer?" I encouraged him.

"I saw the demonstration at the office." He sighed with exhaustion. "I need to get to bed. Do you mind catching a ride or a cab?"

"No," I relented.

"Thanks for understanding." He lightly kissed my temple and patted me on the back. "By the way, your sketches look great on the demo," he offered as compensation for his early departure.

"Husband?" Mr. Prescott asked.

"No," I answered then considering the sudden proximity of Mr. Prescott's body against mine, added, "Boyfriend." I forced a smile.

Barry Stuckey was a handsome man with dark brown hair he custom tinted by a high-end stylist to hide the gray. He wore one of the three tailored suits he owned with a deep purple shirt and a matching tie that would complement a darker skin tone than he possessed. I watched him as he walked out, patting men on their shoulders and ever so gracefully slipping his arms around women's waists, giving them a quick kiss against their jaw line fringing on their earlobe and neck. That was his spot of choice. It was his attempt at subtle affection with a hint of eroticism. He flashed his expensive smile in a way that was as artificial as his porcelain veneers. I dated him out of convenience and to keep Elaine from fixing me up with her "friend of friends".

I knew what would happen next. A young woman would meet Barry outside. They would laugh and flirt with each other leaving the house. Everyone would know they were going home together. Why he thought I didn't know I found more comical than a concern.

Barry, in his mid-forties, just a couple of years older than me, dated me for prestige. He believed it would help him grow as the newest member of our design team. He was recently hired away from a firm that, due to the recession, was filing bankruptcy. I knew he preferred the young girls, the interns, the ones right out of college who were gaining more experience than income. Experience he would give them. He had not advanced as he hoped in his previous firm and was trying to take the fast track to the top on the skirt-tails of the only single woman with any clout in this firm—me. His attempt was as unsuccessful as most of his project ideas, and I feared his continued employment was, perhaps, loosely dependent on his simulated attraction to me.

Elaine encouraged Philip to keep him around for my benefit and I knew one word from me would mean his pink slip. I also knew the same word could lead to a false sexual harassment case of which I wanted no part. I kept Barry at arm's length, but Barry played the part of my boyfriend when it benefited him and now, I played it to benefit me.

Geri G. Taylor

William Monroe called for the attention of our guest. He was our latest client in the development stages of a live-where-you-work housing and retail progressive community that brought back the "town square" feel to the suburbs with a modern twist. The group gathered, passing my display boards for the community center featuring interior construction materials, flooring samples, swatches of fabrics and paint chips, into an audiovisual room and seated themselves in front of a large screen. A computer-generated demonstration began to play with all the special effects of a Hollywood movie, projecting the future utopia. It explained the construction project, solidifying our contract with Mr. Monroe, and impressing our potential client, Mr. Prescott. Mr. Monroe beckoned me to join him and I stood by his side as he introduced me along with the chief architect, whose design was being considered for the project.

"Lovely." Mr. Prescott whispered intimately in my ear as if he were describing me instead of the project. "Lovely work. I'm impressed."

"I believe you will be equally impressed with the presentation we are preparing for you," I returned softly in his ear. I was never a woman of beauty, but I cleaned up good. I suppose I have some essence of attraction, regardless of looks. Perhaps my intelligence, my experience, and my skills as a designer, or it could have been the designer dress I wore. Still, I could hold my own. Philip trusted me with his most valued customers and I played along with the same strategies as a game of chess, calculating my opponents next three moves.

"I'm looking forward to it," Mr. Prescott teased in my ear.

Just as I calculated, I played my defensive move by excusing myself after the presentation, but only after patting Mr. Prescott ever so softly on his forearm. I strolled casually past the group meandering out of the audiovisual room. I rested my hand on the shoulder of people I knew. I gave firm handshakes of introductions while gripping the men's biceps with my other hand. I patted women on the small of their back and spoke softly in their ear over the murmur of the crowd. It was a trick I learned watching the men of my firm. The art of cocktail party interactions included collecting business cards, complimenting women's attire, graciously accepting compliments and name-dropping a clothing designer or two. I slipped business cards into the hands of potential clients from my small purse. I sipped champagne and smiled only slightly, softly, revealing only a bit of teeth to not look overeager, but to appear sincerely interested in what they said and to be very interesting with what I had to say.

I soon found refuge from the game when I located Elaine in the kitchen fussing over hors d'oeuvres and instructing the servers. "It's been a lovely party as always but I need to get home." I spoke apologetically, "And as Philip always says, leave early and leave them wanting more!" I teased.

The Kitchen Dance

"Where is Barry?" Elaine asked distractedly attempting to commit to the conversation.

"He had to leave early." Even though that did not leave me wanting him more. "He said he didn't feel well." I offered some assistance with the trays, working closely with her, our hands toiling together deftly laying out various delicacies in a pattern. Our movements resembled a choreographed dance as we maneuvered in the area between the sink, the refrigerator and the island.

"How are you getting home?" she asked.

"I've called a cab."

"Oh, stay Joule. I need you here." Elaine lied about her need but was honest in her want for my attendance. "Philip will give you a ride home."

I did not have the heart to tell her I did not want Philip to drive me home. Philip was my boss. He was the leader of our team and "as my friend", as he would put it, he did not feel comfortable criticizing my work. I did not mind. In fact, I encouraged his honesty. Elaine was my best friend. I confided my deepest feelings to her knowing full well she, as do most wives, shared them with her husband as I had shared everything with Daniel. I avoided being alone with Philip. I avoided the awkward intimate moments creating the potential for personal conversation. We spoke to each other in code, both knowing everything there was to know about each other, from the secrets of our bedrooms to the torment of my failed attempt to create a family with Daniel. We knew all we needed to know of each other through Elaine. Philip and I practically shared the intimacies of each other's souls without the pleasures of each other's flesh, all to humor Elaine's need for topics to converse. We made quite a foursome when Daniel was alive. Philip and Daniel always wanting to talk shop, while I kept Elaine entertained.

"Okay, now I really must go," I told her as I searched the cabinets.

"In the drawer," Elaine offered. "Another half hour is all I'm asking."

I found two containers and filled one with a few stuffed mushrooms along with tissue-thin sliced meats and cheese hors d'oeuvres. The other I filled with cake and other treats. "Don't put me on the spot 'Laine, I want to get home. I'm taking Roosevelt to the barber shop in the morning." I held up the containers for her acknowledgment. "I'll get these back to you." I gathered a few of the colorful paper napkins and gave Elaine a goodbye peck on the cheek and wiped away the slight, glossy imprint with my thumb.

Chapter Two

Joule

    I slid gingerly into the back seat of the musty cab with the overwhelming scent of cherry air freshener failing to mask the stench of human body odor saturating the cab's interior. I considered changing in one of Elaine's guest rooms, but knew Philip and Mr. Monroe would disapprove of my breaking the enchantment of the party. Seeing me in my work suit may remove the ambiance of celebration and remind the party-goers of the daily grind.

    I looked out the cab's grungy window. I could feel an old familiar wave of depression washing over me again. Tears filled my eyes and I caught a glimpse of their glisten in my reflection in the window. I searched my handbag for a tissue only to come up empty. I dug in the carryall and found my decorative clutch. I pulled a delicate linen handkerchief from my small bag, careful not to disturb the business cards tossed in with the lipstick and breath mints.

    I dabbed at the mascara stinging my eyes. Waterproof, I thought. Tears activated the waxy foundation staining my thin handkerchief.

    "I'll get out up there." I asked the cab driver to stop in front of a well-lit diner a couple of blocks from my loft. The surrounding street and buildings were dark, damp, and a vicious cold settled over the street and steam danced around above the ventilation grates along the sidewalk. I was accustomed to seeing several homeless people who gathered in the alleys and doorways around the diner. Tonight they were few, most having found refuge from the chill elsewhere.

    I knew I looked awkwardly out of place with the hem of my cocktail dress visible beneath my overcoat. I fumbled with my evening purse while balancing the containers of food and my bags from that morning. I fished out some bills

The Kitchen Dance

from the wallet in my handbag and paid the cab driver. I approached two homeless men and offered them something from one of the containers, handing them a colorful napkin from my coat pocket and giving each an appetizer of meat and cheese and piece of cake. I walked farther down the street. I sat on a bench and looked in my carryall for a comfortable pair of shoes. How I thought I could make it home in these heels, I did not know. Suddenly, a young boy grabbed one of the containers and ran. I stood as if I intended to pursue him. "Hey!" I called after the young boy, "I would have given you something." I watched as he slowed, gave me a quick glance and then disappeared into the alley. "At least bring back the container!" I yelled uselessly to the empty sidewalk before me.

Defeated, I sat back down and changed my shoes for my walk home. I should have allowed the cabby to drop me off on the larger street around the corner from the loft. I made it a habit not to get out near the smaller entry door on the narrow and rarely used side street. I preferred in the evening hours to go by the way of the short alley where the rear garage door was located.

I was busy putting on the more sensible pair of shoes and stuffing my haughty stiletto heels in the carryall when I lost track of what was going on around me. Suddenly I sensed someone approaching me. I quickly grabbed for my bags and the other container.

A ragged, fierce looking man stood over me. He slowly extended his ungloved hand, chapped and dirty, cracked by the cold. In his hand was my purse, my delicate glistening evening bag in a filthy hand. I tentatively took the purse from him. "Thank you." I opened the purse and looked inside.

"I didn't take anything, Ma'am," he assured me. "You dropped it back there." He jerked his head back down the street where I exited the cab.

"No, I didn't mean that." I did not intend to insult him. "I just wanted to give you something."

"It's okay." He dismissed my gesture. "I didn't do it expecting something in return."

"This purse was a gift. It means a lot to me." I handed him a twenty, one I kept in the zippered pocket of the small clutch for general mad money purposes.

"No thank you, Ma'am." He hesitated as if he wanted to accept the money.

He stood over me, his face in shadow, as I scrutinized his thin frame, long dingy hair, and scraggly beard. His jeans and work boots looked extremely worn and not in a fashionable way. He was wearing an oversized tan trench coat that I suddenly recognized. I froze, as if my heart jumped into my throat and I coughed to release it. The coat was like an ethereal being taking the form around this thin, pale, scarecrow of a man. I grabbed the sleeve of the coat and found the stain on the sleeve. It was Daniel's trench coat.

"Where did you get this coat?" I blurted out almost accusingly.

The poor man attempted to pull free. "Look lady, I didn't steal it if that's what you think."

"I'm sorry." I stood to face him. He stooped, not much taller than I. "Where did you get it?" I spoke gently, but still hung desperately to the coat.

"There's a soup kitchen a few of blocks over." He did his best to assure me of his innocence. "I just got it from there."

"God, I'm so sorry." I realized I sounded like a lunatic. "It was my husband's. I sent some boxes of his belongings to the soup kitchen just this morning."

"Do you want it back?" the poor man asked.

I was still clutching the sleeve. I released my grip and looked into the frazzled man's face. "Come with me. I want to buy you something to eat." I touched his forearm and turned him towards the diner. At first he hesitated. I was certain by the anxious look on his face he thought I was crazy. Then he relaxed and graciously, like a true gentleman, helped me with my bags and followed me into the diner.

The diner was an architectural interest in itself. Originally home to a fine restaurant with valet parking, the establishment once entertained celebrities. The mid-century modern construction supported rows of neon lights along the top of the single story roofline. Time and urban decay took its toll on the simplistic but lovely structure. John bought the nearly uninhabitable building, refurbishing only the front portion but maintained the large curved window that fitted a circular booth. A maître d' no longer greeted the patrons, instead customers seated themselves. It was common to see a group of policemen from the nearby station having lunch in the round booth but the evenings brought a different crowd. John, the cook and owner of the diner, gave me a disapproving look and motioned for us to sit in a back booth. I exchanged greetings with John by offering him my most pleasant smile to his scowl as I led the man to the booth.

The man set my carryall in the seat of the booth I chose and pulled off his dirty cap, tucking it into the back pocket of his jeans. His eyes, now revealed from their previous shelter of the cap's brim, were a clear bright blue and large for his face, like the proportion of a child's to his thin unshaven face.

Gail, the waitress, appeared with glasses of water, two oily menus, and a superficial smile. She set down the glasses of water in the center of the table, handed me a menu, then set the other in front of my guest. The weary man kept his hands under the table and looked blankly at the closed menu before him.

I handed him my opened menu, and he read it over for a few minutes.

The Kitchen Dance

"What will you have, Joule?" Gail asked impatiently.

The man looked up from his menu at the waitress and met Gail's cool look. He looked to me for kindness. "Ma'am," he directed at me, "this is kind of you, but..."

I took the menu from him. "He'll have today's special and some tea," I told Gail. "Do you want sweet or unsweet?" I asked my guest.

"No tea," he said. "Can I have some milk, instead?"

"Sure." Gail jotted down the order on her tablet. "Joule? Did you want something to eat?"

"No, nothing for me." Then I remembered. "But bring me some pie to go for Roosevelt. Some boy stole his cake."

"Apple or peach?" Gail asked.

"Oh, he loves your peach. Do you want some pie?" I asked the man.

"No, thank you," the man spoke softly as he stared down at the closed menu on the table before him.

Gail snatched the menus from the table. "And for you Joule, how 'bout some hot tea?"

"Just some water for me. Thank you."

Gail tucked the menus under her sweat stained armpit and ripped the page from her tablet as she yelled out the order on her way to the kitchen.

"I'm Joule Dalton." I extended my hand across the table.

"Allen. Allen Brooks," he responded by extending his own grubby hand but pulled it back before I could touch it. He looked around for something or someone in the diner. "Jule, is that short for Julia or something?"

"No. J-O-U-L-E, like a unit of energy," I offered.

"A what?" he asked distractedly.

"Forget it," I laughed. "I've had this conversation already tonight."

"Excuse me a minute." He stood, made a bow-like gesture, and left the table. I noticed how the trench coat draped his body as if it were hanging on a suit hanger as he headed for the men's restroom.

* * * *

Allen

I looked at the weary face reflecting back at me in the bathroom's mirror. The harsh overhead light sucked whatever skin tone I had left out of my complexion, making the grime on my forehead the only color to my face. I pumped the soap dispenser and washed my face in the cold tap water. The cruddy stripes removed easy enough, but the dirt in my fingernails put up a fight. I looked back at a man I hardly recognized and wondered what in the world I was doing.

I proved myself chivalrous by picking up the little purse she dropped. I did not bother to look inside. I knew it was some sort of decorative piece. It didn't look functional as a ladies' handbag. Had it been her handbag or wallet, I may have been tempted to check inside, but I would not have. I could not have lived with myself. I had other opportunities to make the wrong choice but my integrity was all I had left. Sometimes I wonder, if I'd made other choices would I be here now? I think jail or even prison would be better than some of the nights I have spent on these streets.

I took a few paper towels and ran them through the cold water. I checked the lock on the bathroom door. It seemed secure. I slid my pants down and wiped around my genitals and rectum. I could smell my own stench and it nauseated me. I was embarrassed and I did not want my smell to offend this kind woman. I tried some soap to cut down on my own odor even though I knew the harsh detergents in the hand soap would chafe me later. I rinsed and dried myself the best I could. The last paper towel dropped from the holder. I smelled my hands. They held the musky smell of crotch. I washed my hands again covering them with lather like a surgeon and shook off most of the water.

I stepped from the bathroom to hear, "Who is this guy?" coming from the owner or short order cook who slipped up and barked from behind the woman. She jumped startled by his rapid approach. I felt compelled to rush to her aid.

"His name is Allen," she replied. "I dropped my purse and he returned it to me," she told him calmly.

"So you're buying him dinner?" The gruff old man sounded angry.

"He looks hungry," she argued.

"He probably is hungry!" he retorted. "But, you're tempting fate, Joule. You can't trust these people."

The old cook was protecting her. I knew I should just leave, but the thought of a good meal was too tempting. I would keep quiet and be gracious at least until I finished my meal. Then I would thank her and leave.

* * * *

Joule

"Allen, his name is Allen Brooks," I told John more to remind myself. I had to work at remembering names but I spoke his name to remind John this man was somebody.

"I'll just go jot it down in case the police want to know who you were last seen with when something happens to you," John snarled.

Allen returned from the bathroom and slipped back into his seat. John gave

The Kitchen Dance

Allen a sour look as if the bum gave him a bad taste in his mouth.

"Don't worry about him," I assured Allen when John stormed back to the kitchen. "A lot of..." I almost said homeless, "people hang around outside hoping someone will bring them out a sandwich or leftovers." I took in a long breath and blew it out slowly. "So? Where were we?"

Allen pulled several thin paper napkins from the black and chrome dispenser and wiped his clean, damp face and hands dry with them. "Allen, my name is Allen Brooks." He repeated it this time, extending his hand.

I shook his hand but did not reach for his bicep. The reach across the table would have been awkward and, obviously, this was no cocktail party. He held my hand softly, too softly at first, but quickly adjusted his grip to meet my own.

"What kind of business are you in?" Allen held my grip a little longer.

"What makes you think I'm a business woman?" I looked down at my cocktail dress. "Certainly, you don't think I'm a call girl?"

He laughed a deep, hearty laugh, as if it been a long time since he last laughed. "No." He took a sip of the water before him. "I certainly didn't think that."

"Well." I joined in his laughter. "Sometimes I wonder myself. I'm an interior designer. Do I really look like a hooker?" I asked, checking over my, what I considered to be modest, attire.

"No." He settled his laughter down. "You look very pretty. It just seems strange, seeing you around a place like this." He gestured towards John's kitchen. "Excuse the cliché, but what is a nice girl like you doing in place like this?"

I hesitated. "I live here." I took a sip of my own water. "Actually, I live above a warehouse just a couple of blocks from here. And you?"

"This isn't a safe neighborhood." He spoke the obvious.

"No, it isn't," I agreed.

We sat quietly for a moment. I always felt uncomfortable about long pregnant pauses. "Do you have a family?"

"Yeah," he huffed. "Sort of." He studied the chunks of ice in his glass. "Three kids."

"Where are they?"

"With their mothers."

Mothers plural? I thought and waited for more, but he offered nothing. I surrendered to his silence. The awkwardness washed over me. I noticed the faint hum of the ice machine. The muffled voices of John at the grill and the busboy dumping a load of dishes in the kitchen sink. Laughter cracked from another customer responding to one of Gail's comments.

Allen reached for his wallet and handed me two photographs. I smiled before I took them; having learned this was the most respectful way to look at photos of someone's children, hoping they would be attractive children so you could offer a sincere compliment. I smiled genuinely when I saw their sweet faces. One picture was a school portrait of a seven-or eight-year-old boy. I could tell by the front teeth overwhelming his small mouth. It was an older picture, rubbed smooth from being tucked away for many years in a leather wallet. He had the same soft brown hair color with a widow's peak as the grown man sitting before me minus the gray around the temples.

"That's James Allen Brooks III. He's named after me and my father. He used to go by Jimmy," Allen told me. "Since our divorce, his mother started calling him Buddy."

The boy's eyes were clear as glass, perhaps green or blue just like his father's, with creases folding under his eyes when he smiled. Other than his hair color and eyes, it was difficult to say whether the boy resembled the man in front of me. A scraggly beard covered much of his face. His long thinning brown hair was dull and greasy, slicked back from his forehead and pressed flat by the trucker's cap he'd been wearing.

The other, a more recent photograph taken by a cheap camera, a bit grainy and dull, was of two children. The girl appeared older than the boy in the school picture. She stood with her arms around the shoulders of the younger boy. Neither child had their father's large eyes. The color of their eyes was indistinguishable from the distance the subjects were from the photographer. They were noticeably handsome children, nonetheless.

"That's Tracy and Jimmy. Tina wanted to name my youngest son James Allen, too. It's a long story." He left it at that.

I began to ask Allen about this, but Gail, the waitress, returned with his plate of food. "They are beautiful," I told him and I did not have to embellish.

Allen did not hesitate before taking his first bite. He smiled at me to let me know either the food was tasty, or he appreciated the compliment. Regardless, he continued to enjoy his plate full of food, pushing it in with his fork, barely taking the time to taste it. John made up for the lack of taste with vast amounts of salt. Allen chased every other bite with a sip of milk until it ran out, and then followed up the each bite with a gulp of water.

I gently placed the photographs near his elbow. He glanced at them while he ate. I motioned to Gail. I sipped my water and looked out the window at the activity on the street. "It's getting colder," I said absently.

"How is everything?" Gail asked more out of habit than concern. "Would you like some more water?"

I offered her my glass and she refilled it.

"Anything for you, sir?" Gail's sincerity was unconvincing.

The Kitchen Dance

I looked back at Allen enjoying his meal.

"He'll have more milk."

"I'm fine. Thank you." He looked at her name tag. "Gail."

I nodded towards the glass and Gail took the empty milk glass and gave him a quick smile mocking pleasantry, topped off his glass of water, and left us.

"You didn't tell me where you live," I mentioned.

Allen finished chewing his bite and chased it with a drink from the glass of milk Gail quickly returned. "I came to the city to do some construction work. I had a truck." He wiped the milk residue from his scruffy beard and mustache with a thin napkin. "It was stolen. Tools and all. Can't find work without my tools. I had no place to stay or a way to get home. Then I heard about this shelter. They let me stay there for a few days while I did some work for them. That's where I got the coat."

I was startled at first. This was the most I heard him say the entire time. Perhaps the nutrition sparked something in his brain or revved up his blood sugar, either way, he was now quite chatty. "So is that where you're staying tonight?"

"No. My work is done there."

"So, where are you staying?" I was genuinely curious and concerned.

Allen looked up from his plate of food then out the window.

"You can stay at my place," I offered bluntly.

Allen looked back at Gail and John who were keeping their eye on him. "I don't think that is a good idea."

"I won't take no for an answer." The words came from my own mouth unexpectedly but I continued to spit them out with a strange sense of confidence. "So, do you know anything about elevators?"

* * * *

I already decided our trip home would be safe enough. I knew or could recognize most of the homeless people who hung around the streets near my warehouse and they were either annoyed, frustrated, some strangely pleasant or ignored me completely. I usually took the path of least resistance on the nights I would arrive home after dark. Oddly enough, I was not afraid of Allen attempting to mug me. He may have a full belly now, but he had been hungry for many days and perhaps I felt his gratitude was my reason for trust. He stood taller now when he helped me with the door. He was not quite six feet tall and was probably much thinner than his usual physique but I felt I could defend myself if necessary, had I something to defend.

We entered the lower level of the warehouse through the side street. I listened through Roosevelt's door to a small room, a former office, just inside the warehouse by the bay doors. I could hear his television. "Roosevelt, are you awake?" I pressed my ear against the door and could hear the creak of his chair as he stood.

The door opened and Roosevelt looked out.

I handed him the container and the box from the diner. "One of the boys stole your cake so I picked up a piece of pie at John's."

Roosevelt peeked around his door at Allen.

"This is Allen. Allen, this is Roosevelt Graham."

"Hello." Allen offered his hand.

Roosevelt responded by giving me an angry look, taking the containers and closing his door. I gave Allen an obligatory shrug and led him up the steep narrow staircase to the loft.

"Your friends are trying to tell you something. You shouldn't trust someone you don't know," Allen offered from the few steps he maintained behind me.

"I never said I trusted you and I don't always listen to people I know," I assured him as we climbed the steep staircase.

"Wow! That's a long way to fall." Allen looked nervously over the rail of the landing at the top of the stairs.

"Are you afraid of heights?" I looked over the familiar access to my loft and the eighteen foot drop.

"No, just falling from them," he answered.

We entered my loft, and I turned on a few lights. The ambient lighting strategically placed to highlight several relief sculptures crafted from high-density board lined the back wall of the loft. I took the coat Allen wore and examined it only for a moment. It smelled sour, as if it had been away from me for years, taking the form and smell of another man. I hung the coat in the closet next to the entrance.

Allen appeared busy admiring the artwork, stopping to look at each one. "Who is the artist?"

"I did them," I confessed.

"They're good,"

"Thank you," I added out of habit. "It doesn't matter if they are good or not. It was just therapy." I sounded flat and unappreciative. I gathered pillows and linens from another closet in the wall dividing the living area from the sleeping area. "Would you like to shower?" I offered.

"Yeah, that would be great." Allen perked up as if he hoped I would ask.

"It's this way." I showed him to a bathroom in the far corner of the loft. We passed my king-sized bed draped with various soft white linens and the large black and white photographs of interesting angles of local architecture I

The Kitchen Dance

kept hanging above the headboard. I turned back to look at Allen in the same soft glow continuing throughout the loft. I went into the closet and turned on the closet light spilling across the dimly lit space. I could see Allen in profile highlighted by the light of the bathroom against the dim lighting of the room. "I've saved a few of my husband's clothes that might fit you."

I left Allen to look around while I dug in a lower dresser drawer and pulled out some clothes. I fondled the chosen pieces before taking them to Allen in the other room. These particular articles of clothing were a bit harder to let go. They were pieces of Daniel's lounging around the house clothes and they brought back good memories of snuggling on the sofa after a long day at work.

"Here, try these." I handed Allen, who was now standing at the end of my bed, a pair of sweat pants, a golf shirt, and Daniel's college sweatshirt.

"I like the pictures." He studied the collection of framed gelatin silver prints of images taken from street level at obscure angles. "Did you take them?"

"Yes," I answered bluntly.

"More therapy?"

"No." I did not want to go into the whole story about why I lost my passion for photography. "I took those years ago."

Allen took the clothes and went to the bathroom.

I busied myself making up the sofa bed.

"Roosevelt!" I jumped, suddenly startled by a figure standing behind me. "What?"

"Will he be staying the night?" Roosevelt muttered in an exasperated voice.

"Yes," I fumed, still frustrated from being startled. "On the sofa bed. If you are worried...lock your door."

Chapter Three

Allen

 I didn't know such a place existed in this grungy part of town where dilapidated warehouses lined narrow streets with broken asphalt and potholes. The exterior was nothing more than corrugated siding with chipped and peeling paint. The home she created inside took up about a quarter of the building and the rows of windows on the second floor looked over a pitiful view.
 In the bathroom, I checked out the feminine scented bath gels and shampoos on the shelves cut into the shower's slick wall and made my selection. I was surrounded by white, like being in a cloud. I wondered what kind of woman would live in such a sterile, colorless environment. Even her photography was harsh and unfeeling. What worried me more was why this attractive woman, obviously with some money, would live in such a dirty and dangerous part of town? I knew there were some artists and such who fixed up several of the other warehouses. I doubt they compared to this place. Even more of a mystery is why would she offer to bring a homeless man into her home? I picked up her razor and considered shaving but changed my mind.
 That old black man, I thought, how long had he been hanging around here? Who is he to her? It looked as if he'd a place downstairs like he lived here. I wondered if she'd another room downstairs. The warehouse looked huge, probably a hundred by five hundred feet. All I needed was a dry warm corner and I would be happy. A shower and one good night's sleep…if I could get a good's night's sleep.
 After the shower, I stood before the full-length mirror, my body steaming and clean. I wiped the steam from the glass and looked at my whole body at once. I was about half the man I used to be and that wasn't much man to compare. The hum of the vent was not able to circulate the amount of steam my

hot shower made and it quickly fogged over the mirror again. I felt embarrassed. I wondered what she was thinking. Was I going to use up all the hot water? It was a long time since I took a good shower, even at a truck stop, and compared to the shelter's showers, I thought that was as good as it got. Sink baths were a luxury at this point and I was even luckier if the bathroom had hot water. I tore at the tangles in my too long hair with my fingers and combed back my hair with my hands the best I could. The unruly waves and curls sprang up around my neck and face. I did not want to use her comb. What if I had picked up lice? I wiped off the fog again and checked my scalp in the mirror. My hair was thinner than I recalled. The stress, the lack of good food, either way, my years showed in my graying hair and receding hairline but I saw nothing crawling around.

I walked from the bathroom dressed in the clean clothes she gave me. The clothes, like the trench coat, were a bit large. Her husband was probably a taller, heavier man. I held my pile of dirty clothes in my arms, not sure of what to do with them. I used my elbow to slide open the large barn-style door hanging from a track she closed when I went into the bathroom. I saw Joule talking quietly to the old black man, Roosevelt, by the loft's door, like he was either staying or leaving. I knew he did not want me in here with this woman. This woman named "Joule".

* * * *

Joule

Roosevelt was difficult to convince that I knew what I was doing. I had a good feeling about this man. He reminded me I once had good feelings before. I caught an expression in his eyes and turned to see Allen, freshly showered and dressed in Daniel's old sweats. They were my favorite sweats because they reminded me of a more relaxed, comfortable Daniel. He was my Danny in his sweats. I smiled fondly at Allen. Actually, I smiled at the baggy clothes, and the thought of calling him Al.

Suddenly, the moment caught up with me and I realized Allen was standing there looking awkward with his clothes, the dirty clothes he had been wearing, rolled up in his hands. "Let me take these for you." I tentatively approached him and reached for his bundle of soiled clothes. "I'll put them in the wash."

Allen carefully handed me the clothes as if unrolled they would dump dirt on my white rug. I noticed his bare feet, his toes curling in the plush fibers.

"Are your feet cold?" I asked.

"No." Allen became self-conscience of standing on the rug and quickly stepped off.

"I'm sorry. I don't have any socks to fit you." I sensed his embarrassment. "Why don't you just get comfortable?" I pushed Roosevelt ahead of me out the door. "Just make yourself at home."

Roosevelt, not pleased with my hospitality, made it obvious with his facial expressions. I bounded down the stairs ahead of him while he slowly managed them one by one. I took the clothes to the laundry area next to Roosevelt's room and loaded the washer with Allen's clothes. Roosevelt walked in just as I was starting the washer.

"What?" I could feel his eyes following my every movement.

"Nothing." He sighed more than protested.

"It's not 'nothing'. Just say it," I insisted.

"How would you like it if I brought some crack whore in here?" The words "crack whore" sounded out of place coming from his mouth.

"First of all, you wouldn't bring some crack whore in here. Second of all, you know as well as I, that man is no drug user. Finally, you know I don't just bring anyone in off the street."

Roosevelt took a sharp intake of air.

"Stop it!" I yelled, and then realized sound carried up the steel framework of the warehouse and could be heard in the loft. "Daniel hired those men!" I hissed. "That man is cold, he's hungry, he's dirty and he's tired. I've managed to help him with three out of four. Just let him alone."

Roosevelt did not reply. He walked out and I could hear him going to his room and locking his door.

* * * *

Allen

I tried to make myself comfortable but I could not figure out if I should sit on the sofa bed or in the chair. I tried the sofa bed. The foam mattress was firm. Springs held tight between the canvas and frame. Good quality. I ran my hands across the soft sheets: cotton, probably a high count. My first wife liked nice things. Smooth cotton sheets and expensive comforters with lots of pillows. This woman, Joule, was a lot like my first wife whose house was filled with nice things. I wondered if Joule put her husband in credit card debt to keep her in this lifestyle. Everything white. White walls, pickled wood flooring, white cabinets in the kitchen, white sheets and blankets on her bed and now, white sheets stretched across the sofa bed. How could anyone stand this much white? It looked like death. Like the inside of a coffin. I moved to the oversized chair, white leather, soft as a glove, and I sank inside the soft cushion. Feathers, I thought. I remembered the feather filled cushions of my first wife's parents' home.

I thought of the formal living room where I only sat once. It was the first time I had met her parents. They greeted me at the door and led me into their fancy living room just off the foyer. I worked as a framer for the contractor who built their house and hadn't seen it since it was rough. It was a beautiful room filled with expensive furniture and real wood paneling. The paintings hanging on the dark walls probably were chosen to fit the furniture but did not look like they were picked out by the people who lived there.

I walked around the loft. I could hear Joule's voice. I heard the words, "stop it", clear and distinct. The rest ran on in a dull murmur. I stepped lightly from place to place avoiding the creaks and moans of the hardwood floor beneath my feet. I heard Joule at the loft door and quickly settled on the end of the sofa bed.

She came in and went straight to the kitchen area where she turned on another light giving the room a new bright glow. "Can I get you something?" she offered.

I stood up and went to a counter dividing the kitchen from a dining area choosing to keep the bar between us. "Water is fine."

"You can have something stronger," she offered. "I have some beer and I think...," she dug deeper in the refrigerator and retrieved a bottle of wine, "I have some Zinfandel."

"Water is fine." I dared not drink anything stronger.

She returned the bottle to the refrigerator and busied herself preparing two glasses of water.

"I'll wait for the clothes to wash but you can go to bed if you're tired," she informed me handing me a glass of water.

"I'm tired but I'd be glad to do the laundry," I offered, leaning back against the counter.

"That's okay." She laughed, but beneath the laughter, she sounded weary herself.

"I'll stay up with you, then," I insisted, taking a long drink of the cool water to help wake me up. "Who is Roosevelt?"

"He came with the place," she told me. "He was living here when we bought the warehouse. My husband and I fixed up a room out of the former office and remodeled the bath for him."

"Where is your husband?" I didn't see any signs that a man had been around recently.

"He was killed. Almost two years ago. Exactly nineteen months and sixteen days ago." She practically recited as if it were something she reminded herself of daily.

"What happened?" I gave it some thought. "Wait. You don't have to tell me if you don't want to."

"We hired a couple of guys to work for us. They tried to rob us and killed him." She spoke in such a casual emotionless way I felt she could not be the same person who just bought my dinner.

"That must be why Roosevelt doesn't trust me."

"He doesn't trust anyone." She smiled at the thought. "He's usually pleasant. But he isn't too fond of this man I have been seeing. His name is Barry. In fact, he probably wouldn't approve of anyone I dated. Then again, he's a good judge of character." She finished her water then pulled the bottle of wine from the refrigerator and filled her water glass half full. "Barry left from the party tonight with another woman and thought I didn't notice." She sipped the wine as she strolled over to the stereo encased in a white cabinet. She turned on an old compact disc with Linda Ronstadt singing Glenn Miller. *What's New* belted out through the speakers. She turned it down.

The music played softly as she swished from side to side in her slinky cocktail dress. The dark brown was surprisingly somber for a party dress but the light green spiked the highlights in her green eyes. She sat on the back of the sofa and sipped her wine.

Nervously I raked my fingers through my still damp hair.

"That reminds me, I've got to take Roosevelt to the barbershop tomorrow morning. So, I will be getting up early. You can sleep in if you need to." She spoke to me as if I were an old friend who just dropped by to crash at her place for the night.

"I'll probably get up and be out of here before you go." I could think of nothing else to say.

Joule looked disappointed. She took another long sip of her wine. "You said your truck was stolen. Did you report it?"

"I keep calling the police station but they haven't found anything." My legs ached and the soft chair with its matching ottoman was tempting me.

"Come, sit down." Joule pointed to the chair.

I sunk into the soft chair as if cradled in the hand of God. I began to put my feet up on the ottoman but noticed my long, dirty toenails and tucked them under the boxy piece of furniture instead.

"What kind of carpentry work do you do?" she asked.

"I've done all kinds over the years. Now, I mostly do finish work." I could feel the feather cushion sucking the last of my consciousness out of me.

"You know what?" she burst out a little too enthusiastically, "I have a cabin. It needs some work. I haven't been there in ages. Do you think you could ride out with me tomorrow and take a look at it? You could live there and work on it for a while."

I adjusted myself in the chair. "Look, you don't even know me." Perhaps it was the alcohol causing her to make irrational decisions like bringing some homeless guy back to her flat. I wondered if this was a way for her to get back at Barry. "Why would you want me to work on your cabin?"

"I think I'll check the clothes now." She looked at her watch and dashed off unexpectedly.

* * * *

Joule

I knew Roosevelt could hear my footsteps coming down the metal stairs no matter how softly I tried to creep. He peeked out of the door of his room to make sure it was me heading to the laundry room and quickly closed his door. "Go to bed," I warned.

I checked the wash. I turned the dial to short wash but it would still be several minutes before the cycle ended. I sorted through a basket of clean clothes and found one of Roosevelt's shirts. It was one of his nicest shirts, not his church shirt, but the one he liked to wear when I took him to special places like the barber. It was a bit worn around the collar and the cuffs. I would have to convince him he needed a new one. He would argue. He would not see the point of it. I set up the ironing board and turned on the iron. By the time I finished my wine and sorted through the thoughts tumbling in my mind, the iron clicked to remind me it was hot. I ironed the shirt and hung it on the bathroom door knob connecting the laundry to Roosevelt's room. I listened through the door. There were no sounds from the television, only the low tones from the music upstairs resonating through the steel beams.

I pulled Allen's clothes from the washer and tossed in the dryer his underwear, socks, and tee shirt, dingy from being washed with his jeans and dark shirt. I hung up the jeans and dark blue shirt. I could put them in the dryer in the morning so the thumping of clothes tumbling in the dryer would not disturb Roosevelt.

When I returned to the loft, Allen had fallen asleep in the big chair. His feet, still firmly planted on the floor, were tucked beneath the ottoman. I pulled down the covers on the sofa bed and gently coaxed him awake. He woke with a start. "It's okay." I calmed him down. "I just thought you would be more comfortable in the bed." I spoke softly as I guided him to the bed. I turned the music off and climbed into my own bed. I fell asleep to the familiar sounds of traffic and the soft sound of sleep in Allen's breathing.

Chapter Four

Allen

I was startled awake by the sound of someone pounding on a door. I sat up in a tangle of sheets and blankets not knowing where the hell I was.

A woman dashed past the end of the bed where I had spent the night. She was wrapping a robe around her as she ran for the door. "Oh, no! I overslept." she cried out as she passed. "I'm coming! I'm coming, Roosevelt!"

She opened the door to find the old black man, Roosevelt; I remembered his name now, with a sour look on his face. I remembered that face. "I'm sorry. I forgot to turn on my alarm. I overslept," she pleaded for his pardon.

I got out of the bed and headed for the bathroom before I was forced to deal with this cranky old man.

* * * *

Joule

I escorted Roosevelt inside the loft and noticed how he immediately began inspecting the room. I realized Allen was not on the sofa bed. I left Roosevelt standing in the living area and ran back towards the bathroom. "Do we have time for breakfast?" I tossed over my shoulder.

Roosevelt did not answer. The door to the bathroom was locked. I already guessed Allen was there but I needed to go to the bathroom. Resigned, I returned to Roosevelt's undaunted glare. "Do you want some juice? Oh right, we're out of juice. How about some cereal?" I tried to sound cheerful, pacifying Roosevelt while waiting for the bathroom. Roosevelt hovered over me as I opened the refrigerator. We both studied the contents of the refrigerator. Allen finally came out of the bathroom to join us in the kitchen. I slipped past him in the crowded kitchen without so much as a good morning.

* * * *

Allen

I joined Roosevelt who was checking out the stuff in a container from the refrigerator. I looked in several of the stark white cabinets filled with white or clear dishes until I found a glass, then reached past Roosevelt to get at some milk. "Mornin'." I tried to sound chipper and sincere but the old man didn't answer. Not that I expected one. I poured myself a glass of milk.

"I'm keeping my eye on you, boy," Roosevelt growled in low tone resembling an old hound dog.

I did not respond. Instead, I tried to hold back a smile behind the glass of milk I was drinking. Joule came back into the kitchen area hopefully in time to save one or both of us.

"I'll be ready in five minutes," she called out as she took off for the loft's door.

I could hear her footsteps pounding down the metal staircase. I turned to catch Roosevelt smiling and started to laugh myself. We both begin to sincerely laugh. By the time Joule came back, Roosevelt and I were sitting together at the counter eating cereal. We had come to an unspoken truce.

She tossed my neatly folded underwear, tee shirt and rolled up socks at the end of the sofa bed. "Good, you're eating." She stated the obvious before disappearing once again, this time, towards the back of the loft. She returned a few minutes later, her hair combed out and her face freshly washed. She slipped on a leather blazer she pulled from the entry closet over her turtleneck sweater. She wrapped a colorful knitted scarf around her neck and pulled a red wool hat over her hair. She fished a tube of lipstick from the blazer's pocket and spread the color across her lips without looking in a mirror. "See, I'm ready. Let's go," she added as she stuffed her fingers into a pair of thick gloves.

Roosevelt rinsed his empty bowl in the sink and put it in the dishwasher. "You need to run this," he informed her.

"Okay, honey, when I get back." Joule came to the kitchen, adjusted Roosevelt's clothing and straightened the buttons on his starched shirt. I watched her as she fastened his overcoat then took Roosevelt by the arm and led him away from the dishes and to the loft's door. "Allen, your clothes are in the laundry room downstairs. Please don't feel you have to run off. I meant it about the cabin," she reminded me. "At least leave me a note or something. We

The Kitchen Dance

could meet at John's diner later." She grabbed her purse and her cell phone from its charger and they left in a hurry without saying good-bye.

I watched from the upstairs window as Joule led the old man from the warehouse. On the way out the door Joule bent over to pick something up. At first I couldn't make out what it was. Then I discovered it was the container I saw the boy take from her the night before. She picked it up and looked inside. It was empty. She closed it and tossed it into the warehouse before closing the door. They walked down the street in early morning sunlight, their shadows stretched out along the sidewalk. I noticed Joule making a call on her cell phone and her breath puffed out in the icy air just before they turned the corner.

I finished up my cereal and found room in the dishwasher for the bowl, the spoon and my glass. I found the liquid dishwasher detergent below the sink, filled the dispenser, and set the machine to wash. I put on my ratty but clean underwear and slipped Joule's dead husband's clothes, back on. The place looked different in the daylight. The sun coming through the slats of the blinds made the room glow in long vertical stripes. I opened one of the blinds. The room was filled with light like a spot light that was too bright, way too much white. I closed the blinds the way she'd left them and walked down the stairs to the warehouse.

The huge room was filled with stacks of lumber, power tools, equipment, rolls of colorful fabric wrapped in plastic and a variety of incomplete furniture projects. Where her loft lacked in color, this place was the opposite except for the layer of dust and the plastic sheeting covering the scene.

I made my way through the work area and located the elevator. I attempted the door but it was difficult to open. I looked around the work area and found miscellaneous tools and a can of spray lubricant. I worked on the elevator door for close to an hour just to get it to open.

* * * *

Joule

I asked the cab driver to pick Roosevelt and me up around the corner and drive us to his favorite barber. It was in a quiet part of town, just a couple of blocks, from where he used to teach. The barber's father was Roosevelt's barber for over sixty years. Reeves Junior took over his father's shop seven or eight years ago. He refurbished the place removing most of the charm of the old barbershop, but maintained its integrity as an all-male establishment. It was a walk-in and wait shop and there were four other men ahead of him. I checked my watch and let Roosevelt know I would return in about an hour. I needed to run some errands.

The Kitchen Dance

On Saturdays, as was our ritual, I either drove him or accompanied him in the cab to make sure he made it to the barber and back safely. Roosevelt was hardly feeble but he had experienced a mild stroke and had moments of confusion brought on by exhaustion. This and driving him to church on Sundays was all he ever asked of me. All I did out of love. I once asked him why he did not continue to live on the side of town where his daughter and her family still resided. He seemed disturbed by my intrusion in his personal life and the subject was never broached again. I drove him to church and Anna, his daughter, would bring him home after a family dinner. He would take a long nap, as was his ritual, then we would go to John's diner for pie.

The rest of the month were basically hellos and good-byes, brief snatches of conversation, and the occasional note, but I kept an eye on him, whether he liked it or not. I picked up groceries for him and he watched over me like a guardian angel. He was my tall, dark, and fuzzy gray haired angel, with a dull, dark tweed coat.

There was a second-hand shop located just a few blocks from the barber shop. On a good day, when there was time, I would walk there and shop. I especially enjoyed the books. I could always tell the best books by the amount of wear on the spine. I would read a page or two, sometimes a chapter. If I thought about the book during the week, when I returned and the book was still there, I was delighted. Sometimes I would read another chapter. Occasionally, I even purchased the book for fifty cents or a dollar then donated it back the following week.

Sarah, who ran the place, was a thin woman whose limp blonde hair faded into the color of her skin. She smelled of patchouli and always had a kind word to say. I would miss seeing her today and it dawned on me she may think something was wrong if I did not stop by. I had the cab driver go by her shop. She sat at her desk near the front window. I asked the driver to honk his horn. He did so. Sarah, startled at first, waved generously when she recognized me. I waved back hoping she got the message. She was a very intuitive person. Perhaps it was the patchouli.

I jotted down a little note for Sarah basically saying all was well and I had to run an errand while Roosevelt was at the barber. I asked the cab driver to drop it by when he had a chance and tipped him a little extra for his effort. Sometimes, I just have faith in people.

I could not follow my usual routine because today I had a different plan. I asked the cab driver to drop me off at the police station. I would find out something about Allen Brooks. Sometimes, I had faith in people and sometimes, I did not.

Geri G. Taylor

* * * *

It had been almost two hours since Roosevelt and I left the loft. Roosevelt was now clean-shaven. Reeves Junior always gave him a good old fashioned close shave and, every time, I ran the back of my hand against his cheek to feel how smooth and gave him a kiss. He smelled of *Barbasol* with a hint of camphor. He carried his hat in his hand and stroked his trimmed hair with one hand as he walked out of the barber shop. I bid good-bye to Reeves Junior and he gave me a strange look.

"All right. What exactly was the topic of conversation today?"

"Well," Roosevelt answered as he held the cab door open for me, "they prised it out of me."

"Prised my ass!" I laughed. "You couldn't wait to share some juicy news with the boys. Just what all did you say?"

Roosevelt slid into the cab beside me and fixed his hat carefully over his new haircut. "You know I have my worries for you. That's all it was about," he said reluctantly. "I wouldn't go about telling them your business and I'd never say anything against you. But, I live there, too. It just concerned me having some strange man in the place."

"I know." I patted his forearm. "I will take care of it when we get home."

Allen was gone when Roosevelt and I returned from the barber but I found a sticky note on the laundry room door. It simply read that the clothes I loaned him were in the wash and he was grateful and would be in front of John's around six if I would like to meet.

I felt an overwhelming sense of sadness. I climbed the stairs to my loft then straight to the kitchen to find something to eat. In the morning's rush I forgot all about eating breakfast. I heard the loft door and there stood Roosevelt. Knowing I was disappointed, he joined me in the kitchen and made a compassionate gesture by placing his hand on my shoulder.

Suddenly, a startling mechanical sound interrupted the silence. Roosevelt and I both headed for the elevator doorway in the loft. The clanking and groaning continued until Allen appeared in the elevator's opening as it rose from the warehouse. He slid open the gates.

Without as much as a word, I grabbed Roosevelt and pulled him in the elevator with me. Allen closed the gates and the three of us rode the elevator back down.

"You fixed it! Look, Roosevelt, it works!" I exclaimed with perhaps too much enthusiasm. "I was kidding about you fixing it. I thought you were just a carpenter. I had no idea you were mechanically inclined." I switched the lever to ride back up and the elevator shifted into gear and carried us back to the loft.

The Kitchen Dance

"Okay. What was wrong with it?"

"It's simple. One of the doors in the warehouse was jammed and it threw the breaker. I unjammed the door and reset the breaker."

"Is that all?" The elevator stopped on the loft floor but I did not open the gate.

"No. It was more than that. A bolt fell into the track and it jammed the door closed and prevented the motor from starting. I spent most of the morning getting the door open. Then I figured the bolt fell from somewhere. So, I found where it came from and replaced it. I tightened all the bolts and...*Wal-la*."

"Oh, just listen to him, Roosevelt. He even speaks French." I thought it best not to correct him.

"To tell you the truth, I don't even know what *wal-la* means," Allen confessed innocently.

I laughed and set the elevator to take us back down to the warehouse while Roosevelt just held on for the ride. "A successful landing." I opened the gates.

Allen regarded all the confusion in the warehouse. "What is all this for?"

"I used to design and craft furniture for some of my clients." I helped Roosevelt out of the elevator.

Allen ran his finger across the layer of dust. "Doesn't look like you've been down here in a while."

I looked around the room as if I had never seen it before. Everything looked unfamiliar to me now. There were bolts of fabrics I did not recall ordering, sketches I did not remember drawing, and unfinished projects, which I forgot who they were for.

Allen followed me around identifying different saws and power tools. His voice seemed distant and unfamiliar. I looked back to see Roosevelt's discomfort with Allen touching these things and he busied himself replacing the tools back where they were before Allen touched them. I stepped around a large tarpaulin on the floor.

Allen reached down to move it.

"No!" My voice sounded louder and more panicked than I expected.

Roosevelt stepped in to put the tarpaulin back down exactly where it was. "That's where we found Mr. Parker."

Allen knelt down and folded a portion of the tarpaulin back. Faint traces of the outline where dirt collected in the adhesive left from the tape mixed with small pieces of ripped tape remained. A stain deep brown with age, spilled past the line. "This place must hold a lot of bad memories, Joule." Allen replaced the tarpaulin but Roosevelt adjusted it to return it to its exact original position. "Why do you stay here?"

"It's our home." I quickly walked back to the elevator. Allen ran to help me with the elevator's gate. I looked back at Roosevelt who stood motionless over the tarpaulin. The image froze in my mind taking me back to another time fewer than two years ago—

Roosevelt stood over me, like the guardian angel he always was, but he could not protect me then. I cried desperately as I cradled Daniel dying of a gunshot wound in his chest—

The elevator jolted and climbed to the loft.

"Are you okay?" Allen asked me.

I could not tell him. I was not ready to talk about it again. It was better when, like the stain under the tarpaulin, it remained covered up.

"Do you want to check out the cabin?" I made the effort to change the subject.

"Sure." Allen attempted to go with the flow. "Are we taking Roosevelt?"

"No." I went to the kitchen. "He doesn't like to go anywhere except the barber, the diner and church," I responded as I began grabbing an assortment of food items and stacking them on the counter.

Allen followed me to my bedroom and leaned against the door jamb as I pulled a change of clothes from a dresser. I went into the bathroom where I picked out some toiletries. "Can I help you with anything?" he offered with some hesitation as he followed me into the living room.

"Hand me that bag." I pointed to a duffel bag on the top shelf in the entry closet. He did, and I quickly stuffed the armload of items in the bag. I picked out some keys from a drawer in a thin table by the elevator.

Allen took the trench coat from the closet and put it on. He went back to the kitchen and searched the lower cabinet for a bag to put the groceries in. Successful in his search, he came from the kitchen carrying two recycled bags filled with the deli meat, cheese, bread, and condiments I pulled from the refrigerator.

I stopped my erratic behavior long enough to catch my breath and looked at Allen wearing Daniel's coat. Allen appeared to be an unusually patient man, nothing like Daniel, who would have been in a larger uproar than I was, attempting to rush out of the loft as if it were on fire.

We rode the elevator back down. Roosevelt was no longer standing in the warehouse. I pushed the door control on the wall and up went the rear overhead door revealing the garage where I kept my van and Daniel's sports car. I pushed another control on the wall inside the garage opening an exterior door leading to the alley. I opened the sliding door on the white Ford van and tossed my handbag and the duffel bag in the back. Allen joined me. He set the two bags of groceries beside the duffel and closed the sliding door. I climbed in the driver's side and started the van. It coughed in protest of being disturbed on such a cold

The Kitchen Dance

day, but with time, the engine would warm up. I adjusted the radio and prepared for the wait.

"Should we say good-bye to Roosevelt?" Allen suggested.

"Give him a minute." Before the words left my mouth Roosevelt appeared in the garage opening to the warehouse.

"We're heading to the cabin. Do you want to come?" I yelled from inside the van.

Roosevelt shook his head no as he approached my window.

"Be careful," he offered as I rolled down my window.

"I will be home this evening. I just wanted Allen to take a look."

"Are you sure you're not taking on too much?" Roosevelt asked.

"I'll be fine," I assured him and rolled my window back up.

Allen waved at Roosevelt who in turn raised his hand in a slight effortless wave while mouthing the words "Good-bye."

* * * *

Allen

I did not know what to say to her. Her actions may have seemed irrational if I didn't know what provoked them. I could only guess that her husband's death still caused her a great deal of grief. I believed she would tell me if she felt I needed to know. The drive was quiet and I didn't know where we were going except that we were traveling northeast and there was a big lake northeast of the city.

I thought about my wife. I realized I never told Joule about my second wife. I wondered if it mattered. I hadn't spoken to my wife since a few days after my truck was stolen. I asked her to wire me some money so I could come home. I waited at the Western Union office for several hours until their office closed. She never sent the money. I called my home but there was no answer. I called the next day and spoke to my kids. My daughter told me their mother was not at home and did not know where she was. I did not know what to do. I thumbed a ride twenty seven miles outside the city but crossed the interstate and thumbed the twenty seven miles back in. It would probably be better for me on the streets; better for everyone.

I regarded the stain on the trench coat sleeve. "This stain was here when I got the coat." I finally broke the silence.

"Yes, I know. I did that," she admitted.

"Looks like grease."

"From a car door. You know that part on the side of the door where the lock is?" Her voice remained flat. She reached forward and turned down the music on the radio.

*　*　*　*

Joule

"It was raining—*pouring*, and, of course, I forgot to bring a raincoat or umbrella. I called for a cab to run me to a meeting with a client across town. Thinking I could dash from the building to the cab was a huge miscalculation. I would have been soaked. The cab driver was honking at me and I stood there like a kid who would not jump into the deep end of the pool. Daniel had just returned to the office from a lunch meeting and ran from the street to get under the awning with me. He offered me this trench coat. I barely knew Daniel, then. He worked with a different team in our agency and I always thought he was a jerk." I laughed.

"I guess chivalry is not dead," Allen joined in.

"I guess not. Of course, I was thinking, that's just like him, trying to get in my pants by loaning me his trench coat." I gave the comment some thought. Perhaps I should not have been so casual with Allen. "Anyway, the coat was huge and heavy. I'm certain I looked awkward and childlike running to the cab with the coat over my head."

"I'm sure he thought you looked adorable," Allen added.

I gave the image he must have conjured of me some thought as well. That was the encounter that started our relationship. Perhaps he saw me as something resembling adorable. I smiled. "I made it to the cab but the portfolio with all my sketches slipped from under my arm and landed in a puddle by the curb. I reached from the cab door for it and it looks as if I drug the coat sleeve against this greasy protrusion. I guess it was where the door locks into the door frame. Whatever it was, the cab driver screamed at me to shut the door. That is when Daniel ran from under the awning to help. Now he was soaked." I laughed again. I looked back at the stained sleeve and recalled Daniel standing by the cab with my portfolio, both soaked with rain.

"I just knew the rain had ruined my sample board. I handed him back his coat thinking maybe the rain would let up but by the time I made my meeting. I was all wet anyway." I recalled Daniel covering his head and shoulders with his soggy trench coat and waving me on. I could not smile again.

"Sounds like a bad day."

"I've had worse. Much worse," I considered. "We never kept cash in the loft. No jewelry, nothing worth pawning off. Most of the equipment is too heavy to move. We had nothing of value to steal." I made it a point to stop thinking about that day. The images and the order of events had faded and lost

The Kitchen Dance

their continuity. "We walked in on them."

Allen caught on quickly. "Did he put up a fight or something?"

"No. He was just trying to talk to them." I thought of how I would tell Allen the story and if I should tell him the story. "Daniel told them to take it easy. He was trying to calm them down. He was standing with his hands in the air. I was just a few feet behind him. There were two of them. They were young. Just kids. Teenagers. One was holding a gun. Daniel told them we did not have any money in the warehouse. We were working on the loft, but we were not finished with it. 'Let's go upstairs,' he told them. 'I will give you all the money I have.' I think he wanted to give me the chance to get away."

"Did you have any money upstairs in the loft?" Allen asked when I trailed off.

"No. Just what was in his wallet or my handbag." I remembered. "The kid without the gun thought it was a trick and began yelling at his friend to send me. 'Send the wife!' Then the one with the gun told me to go upstairs and get the cash. He called me Mrs. Parker. I kept my last name, Dalton, when I married Daniel. The guy didn't know that. He warned me not to call the police. If I did he would shoot Daniel. Daniel turned to face me and gave me the okay to go. I ran up the stairs to the loft. I found about seventy dollars in my purse and I looked everywhere but I could not find Daniel's wallet. I looked in the kitchen. I searched the bedroom. I could hear one of the men, the one with the gun, I think. I could hear him yelling what the fuck is she doing? I could not hear what Daniel said. Then I heard the other guy yelling it was bullshit and that I was calling the cops." I paused. The rest of the story was too hard to tell. I told it to the police for their report and I tried to remember the words I used.

"It's okay if you don't want to talk about it," Allen assured me. "I think I know the rest of the story."

"I heard the gunshot then ran back down the stairs." I spoke in monotone, as if I were reading the police report. "Both men were running out of the warehouse through the open garage and down the alley."

"Where was Roosevelt?"

"Sitting outside. He came in through the front entrance when he heard the gunshot. I almost ran over him at the foot of the stairs." I remembered running to my husband and falling on my knees in front of him. I lifted him into my lap. "Roosevelt grabbed the portable phone and dialed 911." I paused. "We waited for them to come while Daniel's life slipped away."

I could not share with Allen the words I cried out pleading with God to save Daniel. I begged Daniel to stay alive but the bullet in his chest had more power than my prayers. His life, like his warm blood, pumped out with each heartbeat.

Chapter Five

Allen

At the end of a long, dirt road tucked in a massive clump of trees; Joule and I came to this very large cedar slat home she referred to as a cabin. I always thought of a cabin as a small wood house with a few rooms and a fireplace. This place was much larger than I thought it would be. Joule pulled the van close to the front porch. The bushes were trimmed around the cabin and the front porch and walkway swept clean. I climbed from the van and admired the large covered porch, the dark green metal roof and the stone foundation.

Joule was taking her time entering the cabin and opened the front door but blocked my entry as she looked at the neatly arranged furniture and freshly swept floors. It looked as if she had just returned home from a run to the market. She stepped clear of the door to the cabin. I walked inside and noticed how clean everything was.

Joule seemed to stare in disbelief. "Wow! The Fuhrmans have taken good care of this place." She exhaled a long held breath.

I followed Joule into the room and looked around nodding my head impressively. "Not quite what I'd expected," I admitted. "You made it sound like some ramshackled hut. This is like a mansion."

Joule walked to the kitchen and read a note left on the counter. I joined her in the kitchen and briefly looked over her shoulder at the note then checked out the view of the lake from the window while she loaded the refrigerator with the groceries she brought from her flat.

"I called the Fuhrmans this morning and they came over to spruce the place up. They live just up the road," Joule filled me in. "Mr. Fuhrman has been the caretaker of our cabin since my parents bought it about forty years ago.

The Kitchen Dance

He's handy with small jobs. Daniel and I were in the middle of adding on a master bedroom and bath on the back side of the cabin."

"So, your parents lived here?" I gathered.

"They lived in the city. This was their vacation home." She sounded almost apologetic. "They left it to me."

I sensed her loss and quickly changed the subject. "What did you have in mind?"

Joule led me down the hallway.

The first bedroom of the three had the typical bed and other furniture. A dark quilt covered the bed. Across the hall was a bathroom. Fluffy towels, a new roll of toilet paper and the scent of air freshener reminding me of a fancy hotel.

A sheet of dull plastic was tacked across the hallway. We stepped through the makeshift curtain separating the front room from the two back rooms. The second bedroom on the front of the house was filled with woodworking tools and lumber piled against the wall. I lifted a stud from the pile and sighted down the board to check its straightness then put it back on the pile. I wiped a layer of dust off the skill saw. This place looked a lot like her warehouse. Abandoned.

The third bedroom was the one under construction. The wall facing the lake was removed. Beyond that was the partially finished addition. Plywood was nailed up over the two by fours of the unfinished exterior walls and roof. Nearly two years of exposure took its toll on the huge room. It took me a moment to take it all in. Joule then led me through a door to a large bathroom featuring a whirlpool tub filled with dust and construction debris. I checked out the damages while Joule watched me closely. "I can do it. But, it may take me a month or so."

"I've put aside this part of my life for so long, I guess another month or more won't matter." She added, "If you need any more materials I can take you into town."

She led me through the French door that opened from the new construction's bath to a deck that extended the length of the house. The cabin perched high on a steep hillside that overlooked the lake. "We planned to extend the deck out here," she informed me as she pointed to the weathered joists and beams jutting away from the house.

I followed her through the living room to the opposite side of the house. On the other side of the huge wall, with the stone fireplace and handcrafted bookcases, was another room. It was a smaller room; sort of a den or sitting room, with two leather arm chairs in front of another fireplace that must share the same chimney shaft with the living room. A dark oak roll top desk sat against the wall with an oak and leather desk chair. I bet her father or mother sat at the desk and looked out over the tree shaded hillside to the lake below. This end of the house and the way it nestled in the treetops made it look like a tree house but the trees, though bare from the winter's cold, could use a few limbs pruned to improve the view.

I found pictures of Joule and her parents on the bookcase by the fireplace. Joule was much younger in one picture. In another, she was a high school graduate with a parent on either side. Another picture showed her father playing a guitar. His dark hair was longer than I expected and combed back straight. He sported a van dyke and appeared to be in his forties. Joule looked a lot like her father; minus the beard. He was wearing a bright blue shirt with a tiger climbing over the shoulder. He was quite the hippy in his day. Someone took a beautiful black and white photograph of who I guessed was Joule's mother, obviously nude holding who could have been Joule as a baby.

"That's my mother and me. My father took it," Joule mentioned as I held the picture. "That's me." She pointed to the baby like I would think the other woman was her.

"Beautiful. Both of you."

Joule smiled. "Her name was Kathy with a K. Not Katherine or Kathleen. Just Kathy. My dad's name was James. Like you and your son. He only went by James; not Jimmy or Jim."

"Was he a photographer?" I asked.

"Physics professor." She told me, "Photography was his hobby."

"What happened to them?" I replaced the photograph on the shelf.

"Car wreck." She headed for another door off the den. "Leaving here. About ten miles from the city. I pass it every time I drive out here." She opened the door and showed me another bedroom filled with furniture. Some pieces looked to have come from the other bedrooms.

"This was my parents' end of the house." She explained, "We thought it would make a nice guest quarters. Plus, the view from the back bedroom is better."

I agreed. The property jutted into the lake like the finger of a big hand and the new design of the back bedroom had a grand view of the open lake.

We stepped around the furniture. Joule opened the vertical blinds and we stepped out on the deck. A portable hot tub sat under a vinyl roof built across the deck, damaged from age and where a limb may have fallen on it. I lifted the lid of the drained hot tub. It was similar to the type my first wife, bought or charged, of course. Maybe I would fill it with water. Check it out. See if it was working. This entire place needed a lot of work. "Once you've gone, how will I get around?"

"Come on. I'll show you."

The Kitchen Dance

I followed Joule to a massive garage/workshop tucked in the woods down a narrow drive practically hidden by trees and undergrowth. She unlocked and opened the large wooden doors to reveal an old 1977 Ford Bronco Ranger. She opened the door to the burnt orange classic and slid into the oyster white vinyl upholstered seat. I tapped on the white roof. "Does it run?"

"It has its moments." She reached for the keys under the seat and after a few attempts cranked it up and put the standard transmission in gear. After a few jumps and stalls she backed it out of the garage and cranked down the window. "Want to go for a ride?"

I leaned in the driver's window and checked out the ride. The rear seat had been removed probably to haul cargo.

"Mr. Fuhrman has been taking care of old Clifford, too. I named the Bronco Clifford when my dad first brought him home. I was fifteen then. I thought it was cute. I learned to drive in that beast and I loved every mile I put on him."

Joule slid over to let me drive. I climbed in and put the Bronco in gear. It stalled out immediately. We laughed as she tried to instruct me on the old Bronco's temperamental personality. I was finally able to get the beast moving in the direction of the Fuhrmans' house about a half mile away.

When we arrived at the Fuhrmans' house, Mr. Fuhrman came out of his home to greet us. He was a healthy man in his early seventies. After struggling to get the door open, Joule jumped out of the Bronco to greet him with a hug. She was busy thanking him for the great job he did taking care of the place when I got out of the Bronco, and stood by it until Joule introduced us. I walked forward extending my hand. After a few minutes Mrs. Fuhrman joined us. Joule and Mrs. Fuhrman, a heavy woman in her late sixties, greeted each other with more hugs.

"I want you to meet Allen." Joule reached for my upper arm and pulled me towards her. "He'll be doing some work on the cabin and staying there for a while."

"Well, come in. Come right on in," Mrs. Fuhrman insisted.

I felt a strange sense of belonging. Showered and with clean clothes, I don't think I looked the homeless bum that it seemed I'd become. These people were kind to me. Even Joule seemed more familiar, like we were friends.

I followed Joule and the older couple into their home. It was a smaller, split-level ranch that made good use of the hillside. The older woman had hung heavy drapes over the huge windows that looked out over the lake. I guessed keeping the cold out was better than letting the view in. I pulled back the curtain and looked out over the back of the house. A series of decks and staircases provided access to the lake. It was an ideal piece of property for the young but I wondered how an older couple with failing joints could manage such a place.

"Come on over here." Mrs. Fuhrman pulled me away from the window, and I let the curtain fall back into place. "Have you two had lunch?"

I checked my watch. Of course, the watch was gone. I hocked it for a twenty that barely covered two days' worth of meals. "Joule?" I would leave the decision to her.

"Oh." Joule checked her sporty watch, probably a designer, something expensive. "It is lunch time. I haven't even eaten breakfast."

"Then you'll stay for soup?" Mrs. Fuhrman insisted more than asked.

"I brought some sandwich fixings." Joule tried to bow out.

"Sandwiches!" Mrs. Fuhrman exclaimed, "You need something hot on a day like this! Come on, honey." She pulled Joule towards the kitchen. "Help me heat up this soup. If you want some sandwiches we can make grilled cheese."

Joule gave me a defeated look and I was happy to be able to read her expression. I smiled and shrugged to answer.

Mr. Fuhrman took me downstairs to his den. The dark knotty pine paneling made walking down the stairs like descending into a cave. The walkout basement had sliding glass doors that opened out to a covered patio. Mr. Fuhrman chose not to close the heavy curtains in his domain and the chill in the air was obvious. He stoked the fire in a smoky wood burning stove and took his seat beside it.

"Sit down, boy." He spoke to me like I was some teenager dating his daughter.

I chose a seat on the plaid sofa, sinking into the old foam cushions.

Mr. Fuhrman turned up the golf game on his television as if the commentary would make the action more exciting. "Play golf, son?"

"No, sir." My God, I was sounding like a teenager. I looked around at the trophies proudly displayed on the wall. Mr. Fuhrman was not only an avid golfer but also a fisherman. This is probably why he lived in a lake house.

"I caught that one right out here." He pointed at the largemouth bass mounted on a piece of cypress I was admiring. "You fish?"

"Yes, sir, I do fish."

"Good. You'll have to come by. I'll take you out in my boat when the weather warms up."

I considered the next month of working on Joule's lake house. "Yes, sir. We could have a warm spell in a week or two."

"Allen?" Joule called from the top of the stairs.

"Yeah?" I craned my head to listen over the golf announcer.

Her legs appeared on the steps with dark brown boots with a high heel

The Kitchen Dance

under dark blue jeans. She bent slightly and looked down through the banister. "Did you want a grilled cheese sandwich?" She smiled a curious smile that made me think we may be here for quite a while.

"No, thanks," I played along. "Soup is plenty."

* * * *

Joule

The soup was boiling hot and could not be eaten quickly. Allen and I sat at the mercy of our captors. I passed on the sandwich but now I wished I had something to munch on while the soup cooled. I was starving. Allen was great. He answered the barrage of questions thrown at him from both sides of the table. Mr. and Mrs. Fuhrman filled the time between questions with their own stories, usually pertaining to the question they just asked.

"What was your last name, son?" Mr. Fuhrman asked.

"Brooks."

"Your family from around here?" Mr. Fuhrman continued with the usual line of interrogation.

"No, sir, Mississippi."

"I knew a Brooks in the Marines. He was from Mississippi, or was it Alabama. Old Miss. Yes, he graduated from Old Miss. Did you go to Old Miss?"

"Yes, sir, I did. A couple of years." Allen attempted a sip of the scalding soup.

I was learning something about Allen and I was enjoying their exchange.

"I'm an Aggie myself," Mr. Fuhrman bragged, "Met Mary there. Not at A&M. College Station." He smiled at Mrs. Fuhrman and she smiled back as if they shared a secret. "Joule, here, went to Baylor on scholarship."

I agreed with a flick of my eyebrows and a nod while I blew intently on my spoonful of vegetable soup.

"Interior design." Mrs. Fuhrman beamed. "But I bet you knew that, Allen."

"I knew that she was a designer." He smiled at me as if we shared a secret. "A very good one."

I stirred my soup and blew on the entire bowl. "My goodness, Mary. Do you think we got this soup hot enough?" I looked up to see Allen braving another spoonful.

"Let me get some ice," Mrs. Fuhrman offered.

"I will." Allen excused himself.

"He's a pleasant young man," Mr. Fuhrman confided. "A bit scruffy, but I suppose that's the style these days."

Mrs. Fuhrman joined in, "I'm sure there's a good looking man under all that hair."

Allen returned with the ice. I looked up at his clear blue eyes. Perhaps Mary was right. I put a couple of ice cubes in my soup and after a few stirs was finally able to eat it.

We left the Fuhrmans and still managed to save the afternoon. We took the van through the tree-lined road that led to the highway. I decided we would go to the small town nearby that thrived on the small population of locals and the weekenders. I parked in front of a shop that sold hardware and lumber. We entered the store and Allen went straight over to the tools while I spoke with Mr. Austin, the owner, who knew me since I was twelve. I explained to him that Allen might need a few building supplies and if I could just start an account I would pay for it the next weekend. Mr. Austin looked at Allen and gave me a nod. He punched in my name on his fancy new computer system and my old account came up. Allen picked up a roll of plastic sheeting and I put it on the account.

Allen hefted the roll on his shoulder while I opened the back of the van. "I have a couple more stops," I mentioned. "I didn't ask you before, about driving and all, but do you have a valid driver's license?"

"Yeah." He set the plastic sheeting in the back of the van. He pulled his wallet from his pocket and flipped it open to the sleeve that held his license. "It's not a good picture." He handed me the driver's license.

I looked at the picture. He looked different with short hair and without the scruffy beard, but the eyes were definitely his. I did not bother to check the date of expiration before handing it back. "I'll show you a bad picture." I dug in my handbag and pulled out my wallet. "Here." I handed him my open wallet.

He examined the picture behind the vinyl sleeve as he climbed in the passenger seat. "Ha! You don't weigh that much!" He laughed.

I snatched the wallet from his hand. "You are not supposed to read that part! Comments were for picture quality only."

"In that case..." He reached for the wallet.

"What?" I handed it back to him.

He examined my photo closer. "Poor lighting. A bit out of focus. And you should have tilted your head to the side like this." He tilted his head slightly and smiled a put on smile.

"So you're a photographer, too," I quipped. "You are a real Renaissance man."

Allen handed the wallet back. "I like to be well-rounded." He smirked.

* * * *

The Kitchen Dance

Allen

I followed Joule around the small grocery store while she selected some groceries and loaded them into a basket. When the basket got too heavy, she handed it to me to carry. I carried the basket of food to the counter where a man, nearly as old as Mr. Fuhrman, with clean-cut white hair, wearing a crisp shirt and a four-in-hand tie, greeted her fondly. He eyed me with my long hair and scraggly beard with some concern.

I suddenly felt this strange feeling like I woke up in some kind of an alternate universe. It was like something out of *The Twilight Zone*. One moment I felt comfortable being around Joule. Acceptable. Now I was back in reality. The trip back and forth was a bit disturbing.

"Mr. Davison, this is my friend, Allen. He's going to be working at the cabin. If he needs anything, just let him charge it. I will take care of it when I come back next weekend."

"W-w-well, J-Joule," Mr. Davison stammered. "I-I-I don't have ch-ch-charge accounts anymore. Ha-Haven't had 'em in y-years."

"Okay, then." She hesitated.

"You c-can get one of these." He held up something resembling a credit card. "It's a pre-pre-"

"Prepaid?" I asked.

Joule cut me a quick look and I think I got the meaning of it.

"Yes," Mr. Davison said with a bit of spit foaming in the corners of his mouth. "Prepaid debit card." He nodded his head to push the words out. "You can p-p-put some money on it n-n-now."

"I'll do that." Joule cut off his 'now'. "Do you think fifty will be enough?" She turned to me.

"Yeah, plenty." I looked at the basket filled with more food than I had eaten in the past month. I thought of my kids. I wondered if Tina was making sure they'd enough to eat. Certainly the money we had left in savings could get her and the kids by for a year or more.

Mr. Davison cut another steely gray-eyed look at me as he rang up our purchases. Joule charged it. I thought of my first wife. Everything on the credit card as if there was no limit. It took me years to get out of that debt. Certainly Joule wasn't setting herself up for the same downfall.

She handed me the card. "Oh, I forgot!" She checked her watch. "Damn!"

"What is it?" I was afraid I caused her to miss something.

"What time does The Dollar Store close?" she asked Mr. Davison.

"The Dollar Store?" Mr. Davison asked. "The Dollar Store c-c-closed over a y-year ago. Wal-Marts is p-p-puttin' most of us out of business," Mr. Davison added.

"I hate to drive all the way back to Wal-Mart," Joule complained. "Do you know where I can get some men's underwear?" Maybe Joule was concerned about embarrassing me because she followed the question quickly with, "Roosevelt wanted me to pick some up for him."

"Old R-R-Roosevelt is still around?" Mr. Davison asked as he bagged the last of the groceries.

"You remember Roosevelt?" She smiled. "I brought Roosevelt out to the cabin before we started the renovations," she let me know. "He's doing just fine."

"You should b-bring him b-back out." Mr. Davison grinned, his teeth or dentures, an unnatural shade of white. "You c-c-can p-pick up some men's sundries at the drugstore."

"Okay, thanks. We'll check there." She picked up a bag and handed it to me. Mostly cans of soup, beans and fruit. She picked up the bag with tea bags, crackers and bread. She balanced my load with a bag of milk, cheese and meats and carried the eggs herself. "Do you want to drive?" She balanced her bags to find the keys in her handbag. "It may help you get to know the area." She handed me the keys then waited for me to open her door. No women's libber here.

I glanced over at Joule occasionally as I drove. She looked different. Healthier. Her cheeks and nose were pink from the cold and she looked nicer than she did with the dark make-up she wore on her face the night before. Her fancy hairdo was all combed out but there was still some curls flipping out in uneven directions. Her hair was shiny brown. Not like the dull brown of my first wife, probably from all the bottles of dye she put on it. I wondered how Joule kept her hair so shiny.

* * * *

Joule

I prepared sandwiches for an early dinner. I wanted to be on the road before dark. I turned on some music since I'd canceled the satellite service years ago and there was not much for entertainment. I sang softly to an old Lyle Lovett compact disc, his soft husky voice made me want a beer.

Allen built a fire after inspecting the chimney and it appeared to be functioning properly. Now he was checking out the back bedroom to get a better idea of what was in store for him. He returned from the back wiping his hands on a rag. He pulled a sheet of folded paper from his back pocket and showed me a list of supplies by holding it up to my face while I rinsed the

The Kitchen Dance

dishes. I read the list, nodded and returned to the dishes. Allen offered to dry.

"What are all these vases, plates, and bowls you've got?" Allen asked about the collection of similar pottery that lined a shelf three quarters of the way up the paneled wall in the dining area and scattered among the books on the bookcases.

"It's called Fulper Pottery. It was manufactured in New Jersey where my mother grew up. Most of the pieces belonged to my Grammy but my mother hunted down pieces for years." I picked up a small green vase not more than six inches tall and showed Allen the mark. "It was produced around the turn of the century until the nineteen-twenties. The plant in Flemington burned down in the late twenties and after that the name was changed to Stangl. My mother only collected the Fulper though," I told him.

Allen admired the solid green dishes and picked up a thin vase about a foot tall with a faded paper label that read, "Yellow Flambe." Mixed with the dishes along the shelf were more vases, pitchers, and a pair of candlesticks with a flat dull glaze.

I led Allen back into the living area where a collection of trinket boxes were kept behind a cabinet with glass doors. I pointed out several vases and bowls with a shiny glaze. "These are Fulper as well."

* * * *

The sun was getting low and we were so busy the entire day that I never walked down to the pier at the lakeshore. I took Allen down the long steep stairway with several landings to break up what seemed like a lengthy trek to a pier stretched out over the lake. I pointed out damaged steps on the way.

Allen looked back at the house perched on the hill above. "Looks like the house is about to come down this hill."

"Maybe." I looked back at the addition jutting out over the hill. "Thirty years of erosion has changed the landscape."

"Aren't you concerned about building a home on such a foundation?" Allen asked, markedly concerned.

"No. It hasn't fallen yet," I responded curtly. "Don't worry," I assured him. "We had engineers take a look at it before we started the new construction. It's a cantilever system." I tried to convince him. "It will hold. It's like I told Elaine—just because something looks precarious doesn't mean it's not sturdy."

Allen looked dubious.

"It should be fine if it's maintained." I patted him on the shoulder. It was always a good way to work a man.

We walked all the way down the stairs and stood together on the pier beside the boathouse to admire the lake. It was cold, crystal clear, and smooth as silk sparkling with the help of the setting sun.

It was almost dark when I finally got in the van ready to leave. It was much later than I intended. I wished I could stay. It was almost two years of my rarely allowing me to even think about the cabin and now, I did not want to leave.

"I have to take Roosevelt to church in the morning. Are you going to be all right here alone?" I asked.

"Sure."

"If you need anything the Fuhrmans will help you out," I reminded him.

"Good." His responses came quick. I imagined that he was tired or eager to be alone.

"Get me some figures, an estimate of how much I'll owe you for your labor." I did not want him to think I forgot.

"Joule? I should say Ms. Dalton. It sounds more businesslike, more professional. Don't you think?"

"It does." I could feel my brow furrow. "What?"

"You won't owe me anything. I mean, I expect for you to consider my room and board in the payment."

"Allen. Excuse me, Mr. Brooks. You have family you need to take care of. I insist on being fair. You just give me a price." I had a clear idea of what a project like this would cost and something told me he knew what a place like this would rent for a month. "And Mr. Brooks, just so you know, there is very little you can do to hurt me. You can steal everything I have. You can burn down my cabin and destroy my warehouse. It's just stuff. The most important things in the world to me are already gone. And as far as the Fuhrmans go. He's got a shotgun and he won't hesitate using it, if you give them any trouble."

"Look, Ms. Dalton." Allen sounded offended as I hoped he would. "If you're not okay with this…"

"No, it's not that. I want good stuff to happen. I want it for everyone. But I don't want to be devastated when they don't." I could tell I made him even more agitated.

"W-w-well…" He stammered like old Mr. Davison. "I'll try not to devastate you."

"I didn't intend to leave on this note…so please, forgive me, but I think we've been skirting around the elephant in the room all day. I'm just going through this, this, 'thing'." I hoped he'd understood. "Anyway, the work needs to be done and—"

"Look." He stopped me. "If you need references I can give you plenty."

"You're fine, Allen." We stood awkwardly in silence for a moment. "I want to trust you." I looked into his startling blue eyes catching the light from

The Kitchen Dance

the porch. "I have to. It is all part of that 'thing' I'm going through." I told him good-bye and he did the same for me, tapping his flat hand on the side of the van, as if it would guarantee me a safe ride home.

Chapter Six

Joule

I was in the loft's kitchen with Roosevelt cleaning up after our breakfast. He dressed in his nice dark blue suit that I just picked up from the cleaners a few days before. I wiped down the counters picking up his well-worn Bible with the dark brown cover and the frayed binding. "If you're not going to bring it up, I will."

Roosevelt remained without comment as he washed the breakfast dishes. I maneuvered around him.

"Do you think I should be worried?"

Roosevelt turned to give me a disappointed look and a little grunt for an answer.

"At least take your coat off." I observed his damp sleeve. "I just had that cleaned."

He pushed up his suit coat sleeves.

"Would you like to drive out there with me tomorrow?" I offered knowing the answer. "I could call in sick or just take a personal day. We could even do some fishing."

"My old bones just can't handle that long ride in the van." Roosevelt gave his usual response. "Besides, it's too cold to fish."

"The Jag has comfortable seats." I smiled. "We could park it on the pier down at the landing. I could keep the heater on and we can fish out the windows."

"Oh, you know I'm not going anywhere in that machine." He laughed his deep graveled laugh. "Not even fishing."

"One day!" I warned him, "I'm going to get you in that car!"

The Kitchen Dance

I dropped Roosevelt off at his church and spoke briefly with Anna. His daughter would have him home a little later than usual. "It appears we'll miss out on our pie at John's," I told Roosevelt.

"You could always pick some up for later," he suggested.

I would gladly do that for him. Roosevelt did not like his routine interrupted. I knew it would make Anna's plans for his day go much smoother if he knew he had some pie waiting for him. "I'll do just that."

I dressed comfortably for the day, I needed to because today, every fourth Sunday, I did volunteer work. I walked into the soup kitchen filled with the less fortunate. I greeted a few familiar faces before going into the kitchen where I grabbed an apron, a hair net, and some gloves. Other volunteers carried on with their duties. I tucked my hair in the net, put on the apron, washed my hands, and put on the thin plastic gloves. I joined the kitchen dance of other volunteers as they moved gracefully around helping to serve the food. After saying hello to some of the other food handlers and greeting some of the people we were serving I positioned myself in line next to the director.

"Della, do you remember a homeless guy doing some work around here last week?" I asked as I put out the first tray of warmed rolls.

"No, why?" Della opened a box of apples. I felt my eyebrows furrow and Della noticed my sudden look of concern. "What's up?" she asked.

"I met this guy who said you were letting him stay here while he did some work around the place," I told her.

"No, not likely." Della piled handfuls of apples in a large metal bowl. "I can't let anybody sleep over, Joule, fire codes you know."

"He said he did some work here."

"Not here." Della insisted, "I can only hire bonded workers. Why?"

"No, reason." I began to hand out rolls to the long line of hungry people.

* * * *

I pulled my van into the garage, exhausted from my day at the soup kitchen. I grabbed the bag containing two Styrofoam containers of pie, both peach, and stepped in the elevator for a ride to the loft. Truly, it was a waste of electricity, but I was exhausted. The elevator came to its abrupt halt and I pulled open the gates. It was good to be back in my stark white, uncomplicated loft. I stayed longer to help clean knowing Roosevelt would not be here waiting for me. Instead, I found Barry had made himself comfortable on the sofa. Beside him was the neatly folded stack of linens and a pillow that I failed to put away the day before. "What are you doing in here?" I asked impatiently.

"Your doorman let me in." Barry smirked as he sipped a Samuel Adams Boston Lager, from my refrigerator no doubt.

"Very funny." I took the pie to the kitchen and looked for something in the refrigerator. I found a carton of juice and I had no idea how it got here. I poured a glass of the orange juice and remained in the kitchen area to drink it. Barry entered the kitchen and attempted to embrace me. I shrugged him off and put my glass in the sink.

"So, where were you yesterday?" Barry asked.

"I went to the cabin."

"When are you going to take me to the cabin?" He made another attempt to cuddle.

"Never." I pushed him away again.

"What's wrong with you today, Joule?" Barry seemed genuinely confused.

"I know about your little friend at Elaine's party. I noticed she left right before you did. Was she waiting for you?" I confronted him.

"No, Joule, it's nothing. I was just talking to her," he tried to convince me.

"It doesn't matter. I don't want to be seeing anyone right now, Barry. I guess I'm just looking for an excuse."

"Are you sure about this?" Barry asked.

Suddenly, I became aware of the problems he may cause at work.

"Yes." I put my arms around him. "It's not you. You're great. I just don't think I can give you everything you need right now." I shifted my hands around to his stomach and pushed him gently out of the kitchen.

Barry took the cue to leave but stopped to point out the bed linens. "I see you had some company last night. Who was he?"

"Just some homeless man I picked up on the street." I gave a sardonic smirk.

Barry laughed. "Knowing you it probably was."

I returned with a sarcastic laugh.

Barry started down the steep stairs.

"Barry, wait." I called out after him, "Did you say my doorman let you in?"

"Yeah. Roosevelt," he answered.

I came down the stairs with Barry and showed him out.

"Roosevelt?" I knocked on his door. "Are you in there?"

Roosevelt was still in his suit when he came to the door.

"Hey. What happened? I thought you wouldn't be home until later."

"I told Anna I needed to get on back home." He sounded sad.

"Oh, honey. Come on upstairs. We'll have some pie."

"Is it peach?"

"Yes." I reached for his hand and we walked towards the elevator.

"You know, I don't like to be back in this part of the warehouse,"

The Kitchen Dance

Roosevelt said.

"I know. I'll get it cleaned out and maybe put up a wall or something."

"Blocking it off won't change what happened," Roosevelt reminded me.

"No," I agreed. "Nothing will change what happened but we can paint the wall a bright color, hang some art on it, and give ourselves something else to focus on."

Roosevelt and I sat quietly at the table picking at our pieces of pie. "What are you building?" Roosevelt sliced through the silence. It was an expression he used when I appeared lost in my thoughts.

"Nothing. I was just thinking about Barry—maybe Daniel as well." I pushed the last bits of salty piecrust away. "Why do I—did I fall for their games?"

"Well," Roosevelt chortled, "I know Barry is no damn good and Daniel was a bit of an egotist, not to speak ill of the dead," he finished his last bite of pie. "Do you think this Allen character is playing games with you?"

"No. I don't believe so." Even though the thought of Allen telling me he worked for Della highly concerned me, I dared not tell Roosevelt. He could be tenacious and his propensity for 'I told you *so*' ran rampant, but in a fatherly way.

* * * *

I sat at my desk working on my computer. The workspace I shared with my design team was large, roomy, and well-organized. I liked being at my office usually more than my own loft. The drone of chatter was a pleasant comforting sound. Elaine tapped on the window to the reception area with the view to the massive atrium. She waved and mouthed the words, "Are you busy?" and let herself in my door before I could answer.

"I'm taking Philip to lunch. Do you want to join us?" Elaine asked.

"Just a minute, I need to finish some notes."

Elaine took a seat and dug in her purse more for entertainment than purpose. I finished typing some information on my computer while the idea was fresh then saved it. "Where are we eating?" I stood up and smoothed the stylish skirt Elaine picked out for me on our last shopping trip. "Well?"

"Upstairs." She finally looked up and noticed the skirt. "How lovely! It looks great on you."

"Thanks. I like it." I swished it around and grabbed my suit jacket.

"I told you, you would. You look all businesslike and successful with just enough flirt." Elaine gathered herself and we walked out of my office.

Elaine and I met Philip and rode the elevator upstairs to a very elegant restaurant overlooking the city. We ordered our meals without inspecting the menu. We all had our favorites. I was sitting across from Philip who seemed rather distracted while Elaine carried on about shopping, more about my skirt, and an upcoming party. Philip took a call on his cell phone.

"So Lucille Benton is having a big cocktail party next Friday, a reception for some new artist she wants to exploit," Elaine rambled. "Do you remember her, Joule? She hired your friend Victor to do over her house."

"I designed a sofa for her living room," I recalled.

"Really? Then you must come! You and Barry should have dinner with us afterwards. I was thinking of the new restaurant that opened last month. What was the name of that place Philip?" Elaine continued.

"Da Vinci's." Philip broke away from his phone conversation to answer.

"Yes. Da Vinci's. I just love Italian. So, what do you think?"

"Barry and I broke up."

"Oh? Why didn't you tell me?"

"I'm telling you now." I took a sip of my water with its lemon twist.

"Was it that girl from the party?" Elaine pressed.

"You knew about the girl at the party?" I almost choked on the water.

"Jou-elle," Elaine imparted.

"Oh? Why didn't you tell me?" I mimicked Elaine dramatically.

"I'm telling you now, honey, everyone knew about the girl at the party. We knew about all the girls at all the parties." She patted Philip's forearm for confirmation.

"It wasn't that." I studied the lemon seeds at the bottom of my glass of water. "It wasn't going anywhere."

"Then I have to fix you up with this great guy. What's his name, Philip?"

"Stephen Croft." Philip broke away from his phone conversation again.

"Stephen Croft," she exclaimed as if she just recalled his name herself. "He's perfect for you! I cannot wait for you two to meet."

"That is exactly what you said about Barry," I reminded her.

Elaine looked flustered.

"I know you try, 'Laine. Maybe I'll go to the party and dinner with him but I'm just not interested in dating anyone right now."

"Okay...change the subject." Elaine laughed. "What did you do yesterday?"

"I went to my cabin."

"Really?" Elaine seemed speechless. She sipped her water. "And?" she finally added.

I knew I would regret this. "I took a homeless man out there to live in it while he fixes it up." I said it anyway.

"Is he good-looking?" Elaine did not miss a beat.

The Kitchen Dance

"No," I mused. "And that was not the response I was expecting."

Philip turned off his phone. "You did what?"

"Now this was the response I was expecting."

"I didn't think you were listening," Elaine told Philip.

"I always listen to you two." Philip suddenly sounded paternal. "What did you say about some homeless guy at the cabin?"

"I met this man Friday night after the party. He was in front of John's diner, you know, the one over near my loft. I bought him some dinner. He does some construction work." I took a cautious sip of water. "He repaired my elevator Saturday morning. It actually works!" I fidgeted with my cutlery. "So I took him to the cabin to finish up that construction Daniel and I started."

The table was quiet and I was suddenly aware that both Philip and Elaine were giving me a hard look.

"You said he is homeless?" Philip reiterated more than asked.

"He was temporarily without residence. He is now living at the cabin...for a while."

"Joule! Have you lost your mind? I don't want to say you should know better, but damn it, you should know better. I can't believe this!" Philip chastised.

"Did he have references?" Elaine asked. "Is he licensed and bonded?"

"Yes, he has references, and you know, I didn't ask if he is licensed and bonded."

"What were you thinking?" Philip continued.

"I was thinking I was helping out someone less fortunate."

"Oh, Joule." Elaine added, "You and your little hobby."

"My hobby?"

"Charity cases."

"It's not a hobby! You're starting to sound just like Daniel. I want to do this. It helps me."

"Oh, I'm sorry. Let's not argue about this." Elaine sounded genuinely remorseful. She wasn't one to start an argument, especially in an expensive restaurant.

"What can I say, Philip, I'm taking a chance. I want to believe this man is different."

"Different from those men who killed Daniel?"

"Yes," I hoped. "I think so." I wiggled my fingers over the centerpiece like a gypsy reading a crystal ball. "It was like the spirit of Daniel spoke to me and told me to help this man."

The waiter brought us our salad.

I fussed over my croutons for a moment. "Besides…" I looked up at Elaine. "He was wearing Daniel's coat."

"The trench coat?" Elaine almost choked on her bite of salad. "The one with the stain on the sleeve?"

"That's the one!" I speared a piece of lettuce and red onion.

"Then it's fate!" Elaine pointed out with her fork.

"In a way." I chewed.

"But he's not good-looking?" Elaine reminded me.

"Not really."

"What a shame."

I thought of his driver's license photo. "He is not bad looking. He has interesting eyes. Big blue eyes."

"You two are unbelievable," Philip joined in.

Elaine and I snickered like two teenagers. Philip's phone rang again and he took the call in between bites of his salad.

"Seriously, Joule. At least take Philip and me with you the next time you go to the cabin. We haven't seen the place since, well, you know." Elaine suggested, "Why don't you let Philip check out his work?"

"I can tell you, I will think about it if you'll drop it for now." I poked around my salad.

Somewhat defeated, Elaine returned her interest to her lunch.

Chapter Seven

Joule

I left work early on Friday and pulled up to the cabin in my van just before sunset. The cold spell gave us a break. I went inside the cabin but there was no sign of Allen. I walked back to the master bedroom. The addition was well underway. I examined the work and was happy with the progress. I checked out the bathroom. All of the fixtures were installed, and some of the tile work completed. I stepped out on the new deck off the master bedroom and could see a figure down on the pier. I took the steps down but, as I approached the figure that I expected to be Allen, I grew nervous. He did not look familiar. "Allen?"

He was wearing the headset to an old portable compact disc player and could not hear me. I walked up to him and tapped him on the shoulder. "Allen."

Startled, Allen turned to me quickly, almost losing the rod and reel he held in his hand. He pulled the headset off. He looked amazingly different.

"I'm sorry. Do I know you?" I joked.

Allen laughed and stroked his clean-shaven face. His hair was cut in a short neat style that left soft waves brushed back from his forehead. I was wrong when I told Elaine he was not good-looking. He was very handsome, wearing a new pair of jeans, along with a familiar, and a bit too large, leather jacket.

"Yeah, I thought I would clean up some. This jacket was in the closet. I hope you don't mind."

"Not at all. Who cut your hair?" I was tempted to run my finger across the stray strand on his forehead.

"One of the barbers down past the hardware store." He brushed it away instead.

"Did he take the debit card? I should have left you some cash."

"That's okay. I did some work for Mr. Fuhrman. I bought these jeans and a few other things I needed." Allen reeled the remaining line in.

"Really?" I was impressed. "You look great. Had I not seen your driver's license photo before I may not have recognized you now."

"I hope I look a little better than that photo." He laughed. "Here, want to cast a few?" He handed me the rod and reel.

"It's been a while." I made a feeble cast and quickly reeled it in. "I can do better." I made a more promising cast and slowly worked the lure in. "I like what you have done with the place. I see you found the tile in the garage."

"I wasn't sure if you still wanted to use it. That's why I stopped."

"Daniel picked it out." I never cared for it at the store. "It looks great."

"Do you mind helping me? I could use an extra hand." He smiled at me and I realized without the mustache that had covered most of his mouth he had an attractive smile.

"Sure." I smiled back and tried a few more casts.

Allen regarded me in a gentle way as the glistening of the sun bounced off the ripples in the water and danced in his eyes. I did not see anything that resembled treachery or deceit; however I did not put it past anyone to conjure up a little white lie to give them a leg up. I was never one for confrontation nor did I want to bring it up in the midst of such a tranquil moment. As I cast a final time, I decided on a way I could work the topic of his working at the kitchen casually into a conversation perhaps while setting tile.

* * * *

Allen

Joule prepared fish for dinner. Not fresh fish from the lake but Mahi-Mahi she'd picked up at a supermarket. She poured wine into the sauce and some herbs and sautéed vegetables. I'd never had anything like it. I usually ate my fish fried. We sat around the table after dinner finishing up the French bread she picked up at a bakery on the way to the lake and the bottle of wine that read Sauvignon Blanc on the bottle. She told me it came from a wine shop near her office downtown. The little shop called The Wine Seller, she spelled out the word "seller", was a place she'd designed and she and Daniel had shopped there a lot. They planned on adding a wine cooler in this condominium they were building and she still had some bottles he'd bought right before he died. I guess she didn't want to say murdered, especially since we were having such a fancy meal.

She told me stories of how her parents would stop by this bakery in town

The Kitchen Dance

to pick up a loaf of French bread, and a loaf of cinnamon bread with sugary glaze, every time they came to the lake. She passed on the cinnamon bread this time but now she wished she hadn't. Joule went on to tell me about how she and Daniel sold their townhouse and were busy fixing up the place in the loft to live there while the condominiums were under construction. It was this massive complex east of town, and because their firm designed it, she and Daniel were able to get in early and bought a place on the top floor.

"It was no place to raise a family," she admitted. "I always wanted children. Daniel had other plans. He told me we could always start a family in the condo. We could use the guest room for a nursery. In a few years we could sell the condo and probably double our money. He considered it a good investment."

"Why did you marry him?" I asked.

"He was the only one to ever ask me." She cocked her brow and finished off her glass of wine. "I sold the condo interest a month after he died. The first phase was almost complete but I had no interest in living there. He was right. I doubled the money we already invested in it." She poured herself half a glass of wine and finished off the bottle in my glass.

I regretted having that last glass of wine. We moved to the pit group by the fireplace. She stretched out on one side and I took the other. "I could get used to this," I blurted out without thinking.

"I guess it's quite a change from the streets." Joule smirked.

She looked good in the firelight. She wore a little makeup. I could tell because her eyelashes were darker and longer than before. Her hair was smooth and straight. She had changed into her dark blue jeans after work. I didn't think she wore them to work. She took off the boots and put on some leather moccasins that I had seen in the bedroom closet.

"If I'd known you were coming, I would have washed the sheets," I told her.

"I'm not going to run you out of your bed." She yawned. "I'll be fine on the couch." She leaned forward and pulled a blanket and pillow from inside the pit group's matching ottoman. "I've slept out here plenty of times. Something about the fire."

"You could still add a fireplace to the new bedroom," I suggested.

"I wanted one." She yawned again. "But Daniel didn't. He didn't like the smell." She snuggled down in her pillow.

"I'll let you get to sleep."

"No, we can talk." She sat back up.

"We've got a full day ahead of us." I checked the fire, turning a log over, kicking up sparks and increasing the flame. She looked warm and comfortable and the wine was making me feel drowsy. I wanted to join her on the sofa but deep inside I knew better.

* * * *

Joule

Allen worked me like a man. I guess I gave him the impression somewhere that I was one. He had me schlepping boxes of tile from the garage and mixing thin set. Exhausted by noon, I did not offer to make him a sandwich. Instead, I threw the condiments, deli meat, and cheese on the counter while he washed the lettuce and sliced a hothouse tomato. We worked together assembling sandwiches with the same ease we worked to finish the bathroom.

After a hard day's work we relaxed on the pier. I knew the chances of catching a fish were slim. We chose the sunny pier on the west side of the house because it was warmer. Allen squinted at the sun glistening across the cove towards the Fuhrman's home.

"If the weather holds, I'll have to stop by to see if Bob wants to do some fishing."

"Oh, he won't fish unless they're biting. Believe me. He knows when they're biting." I cast my lure out over the placid water. I did it more for the meditative trance created by the clicking sound of the reel and light thump of water splashing against pilings than the catching of fish. I even pinched down the barbs of all the lures. I wondered if Allen noticed.

The sun was sinking behind the houses across the lake and I knew it was time to leave. Mrs. Fuhrman had brought over some chili so that Allen and I could have a quick meal before I headed back to the city. Allen started a fire while I heated up the chili and cooked corn muffins from a boxed mix. Dinner sat heavy in my stomach, combined with the crackling fire and tiredness from a good days work, luring me to stay the night. I fought the temptation and won.

"We got a lot done." Allen opened the driver's side door for me.

"We sure did." I sighed dragging my tired body into the driver's seat. "I'm sorry to rush off, but Roosevelt will be mad at me if he misses church."

"We can't have Roosevelt mad at you," Allen replied.

"I guess I'll see you next weekend if you think you need some help." I started the van.

"Sure." Allen smiled. "I'll get the job done faster this way."

"I guess you will." I had a sudden feeling of him gone, out of my life, and I did not like it. "Look, I don't mean for that to sound like I'm trying to rush you."

"No, really. I enjoy the company."

The Kitchen Dance

"You can still stay here for a while until you get another job and a place to live," I offered.

"Thanks."

"Okay, then." I reached for the door. "I guess I'll see you."

"Yeah. Bye."

I closed the door but opened the window while the van warmed up. "Okay. Bye." For some reason I could not pull away.

Allen leaned in the open window and I felt my heart leap into my throat. I leaned back in my seat.

"I was just making sure you have enough gas." He checked my gauges.

"I've got plenty."

Allen stepped back and patted on the hood as he walked away. "See you next weekend."

I watched him walk up the porch step where he leaned against a post and gave me a little wave, then I finally drove away.

Chapter Eight

Joule

    I could not wait to get back to the cabin the following weekend. I thought about it practically every minute I was awake and dreamed about it at night. How did a place whose familiarity I ignored for so long now haunt me so? I canceled my appointments and renegotiated a deadline in order to take Friday off. I left right from work Thursday afternoon. When I arrived at the cabin, it was empty and the Bronco was gone. I pulled my van into the garage then made myself busy by clearing out some sweet gum balls that accumulated in a flowerbed in front of the cabin. I could hear the sound of an automobile's engine humming up the long drive to the cabin. At first, I thought it might be Allen but the engine lacked the thumps made by the old Bronco's cranky disposition. A black Suburban came into view and pulled up in front of the cabin. A tall good-looking man climbed out of the driver's side.

"Hello." His voice was deep. "Is this your place?"

"Yes."

"I'm Travis Dunn." He extended his large hand. "Your husband did some work for me."

I instinctively reached for his hand. "He did?"

He engulfed my hand with his warm, strong handshake.

"Yes. I do a lot of construction around the lake. Is your husband home?"

"My husband died almost two years ago." I felt my hand go limp in his.

"Wait a minute." He released my hand gently. "Then who is the guy working for me?"

"Allen? Allen Brooks?"

"Yes. That's his name." The man held his breath as if he had seen a ghost.

The Kitchen Dance

"He's not my husband."

He exhaled a sigh of relief.

"He's doing some work for me and living here at my cabin," I informed him, "Did he say we are married?"

"No, he didn't. I just assumed. I'm sorry. This is embarrassing." The man's tan weathered skin showed visible signs of blushing.

"No, that's all right. I'm Joule Dalton." I shook his hand again as if to start all over. "Allen isn't here right now. I don't know when to expect him back. Do you mind if I ask what you need him for?"

"I came by to see if he got his Bronco running."

"Oh, no." I shook my head fully aware of Clifford's personality.

"I gave him a ride home yesterday. He said he would probably have to work on it today but should be back at the site on Friday. He does some good work. I would like for him to do some more if you can spare him."

"I'm not in a hurry. I know he could use the work. But I was hoping to take him back to the city with me on Friday night. I'm going to a cocktail party. I'm hoping I can drag him along."

"Well, if he won't go, I may be available," he flirted.

"Really?" I flirted back. "Maybe I should take you up on that."

He handed me his business card. I smiled as I read the card. "Travis Dunn." I tucked the card in my pocket. "Would you like to see the work Allen is doing in the cabin?"

Allen had cleaned up the mess we left in the bathroom and finished with the grout. I discovered a stack of sheetrock replaced the pile of studs in the second bedroom. He'd almost finished hanging the sheetrock. Our voices in the bedroom sounded muffled, insulated, and intimate when I told Travis Dunn an edited version of how I met Allen.

I took Travis outside on the deck Allen had completed. Travis leaned against his broad hands on the deck's rail. I noticed no signs of a ring on his weathered hands. I smiled to myself. He expressed the usual compliments as he admired the cabin, Allen's work, and the property. It was getting dark, and although tempted to invite him to stay for drinks, I did not want to appear too eager. It was a little after seven when he finally left.

Allen had still not returned.

I was getting drowsy sitting by the fire listening to a Nancy Griffith compact disc and reading a romance novel. It was an old bodice-ripper my mother kept because she met the author. I wrapped myself up in a quilt and stepped out on the screened back porch of the cabin hoping the cold air would wake me up. I did not want to be asleep when or if Allen returned. Then I heard the sound of the Bronco driving up the road followed by another vehicle. I heard the Bronco door close and then another, a more solid sounding car door, closed. I got up and walked inside the cabin.

Allen held the door open as a young woman entered ahead of him. He turned to find me standing in the living room and a startled look sprang on his face.

"Hey! What are you doing here?" He sounded more perturbed than surprised. "I didn't expect you until Friday."

"Who is she?" The young woman with streaks of blonde in her dark hair asked suspiciously.

"This is Joule. Joule, this is..." His speech sounded slurred.

"Is she your wife?" the woman asked.

"No. She's..." Allen gave his explanation some thought. "She's, like...my boss."

"Maybe this isn't a good idea," she said as she adjusted her jacket for the cold night's air. "I'll see you later."

"You don't have to leave on my account." I cocked my brow at her and then answered Allen's previous question. "I took a Friday off. I thought I would come see if you needed a hand."

Allen stammered, "Well, uh, I-I-"

"Come on in, Allen." I motioned to the pit group. "Bring your friend."

"That's okay. I need to go anyway. I'll see you later, Allen."

"Yeah, let me walk you to your car." Allen could not wait to get away from me.

He walked the young woman out while I waited in the cabin. I could hear the car door open and close and eventually the car drove off. I went to the kitchen and searched the refrigerator, more for distraction than purpose. The refrigerator. now stocked with eggs, milk, juice, fruit, deli meat, and a jar of mayonnaise, suggested Allen was eating better.

Allen walked in and joined me in the kitchen. The refrigerator door provided a barrier between us. I handed him a beer over the door even though he'd obviously had enough. I got one for me and looked in a drawer for the opener. He took the bottle, opened it by hand, and handed it back to me and then opened his own.

I headed for the living area, turned on an old *Eagles* compact disc and sat in the center of the pit group. Allen followed me but sat on the hearth to poke at the fire. He never spoke a word. The fire and the light from the kitchen cast a soft light over the living room. I sipped my beer and let the soothing music and fire's glow settle my unexpected anger.

Allen quickly downed the rest of his beer and subdued a belch. "I want you to know that I haven't been drinking and driving your Bronco. I did not

The Kitchen Dance

intend to tonight, either. I suppose I should have asked you if I could take it out or something." The beer worked up another belch and he tried not to be rude. "I'm sorry." He thumped his chest. "Excuse me. I paid for the gas."

"Look, I'm not going to interrogate you. But don't you ever do that to my Bronco again! If you wrecked him," I shook my head and took a drink of my beer. "I don't know why, but I just didn't think about you out socializing."

"I haven't been with…out…with," he corrected himself, "a woman in a long time," he uncomfortably confessed. "Mr. Fuhrman drove me up to the auto parts store in town. She, that lady…" He struggled to recall her name. "Laura works there. She asked me out. I wanted to test-drive the Bronco after I repaired it so I met her in town. Look, I'm sorry. This is your place and I shouldn't have brought her out here."

"I don't know what to say. I want you to be comfortable here. I shouldn't have surprised you the way I did. I just wasn't expecting you to show up with a date."

Allen got up to get another beer. He signaled if I wanted one. I declined.

"This may be bad timing but I wanted to ask you if you would like to go to a cocktail party with me tomorrow night." I tore at the paper around my beer bottle.

Allen twisted the top off another beer and took a long drink. "Well, now, let's see. I've been asked out twice in the same day. I will have to check my social calendar."

He sat at the end of the pit group.

"I'm not one for fancy parties, Joule. I don't have anything to wear."

"I can take care of that." I sipped my beer.

"I'm sorry. I just don't think I will be any good for you at one of those uppity high society engagements."

I suddenly remembered the man I met earlier. I fished the card out of my pocket. I read the name and handed the card to Allen. "Oh, this man, Travis Dunn, he came by today."

He looked at the business card as if he had never seen one before.

"He says he wants to hire you to do some more work for him."

"Really? Great." Allen appeared delighted. "Don't worry. I'll still be able to work on your place, too."

"Why don't you work for him during the week and I can come help you here on weekends."

"That'd be great." He paused to think and turned to a drink of beer for courage. "But, I want to see my kids again. I thought I could do that some weekends."

"Oh, I'm sorry." I almost forgot about his children. He had not mentioned his family since that night at the diner. "Of course you do."

"But the thing is, I called Tina, my…" He hesitated, "My ex-wife, while I was in town. She told me she has a court order that says I can't see my kids until I pay her some child support. If I go to work for Travis I can pay off some of the back child support. Then I can see my kids."

"Allen, if you need the money, I can pay you for the work you've done."

"No, Joule, letting me stay here is enough but it might take me longer to finish here."

"That's okay. Did you want to see your kids this weekend?"

"No. Tina's pregnant and—"

"You never told me you were having another baby." I was shocked by the news. "Shouldn't you be home for that?"

"It's not mine." Allen looked into the fire.

"Oh? Did she remarry already?" Damn it! The words came out before I could think. He must think I'm so naïve.

"No, the guy is just living with her and my kids in our trailer." Allen finished another beer. He got up and walked to the kitchen.

"Was she seeing him while you were still married?" I tried to remove my foot from my mouth but I felt it tickling the back of my throat.

"I don't want to talk about this. I'm sure your husband was this super guy and you had this terrific marriage and everything in the world you wanted and no one can ever replace him."

"No. It wasn't perfect. Daniel was a workaholic and he expected me to be a workaholic, too. He never took time to relax. Not even here. He was so busy trying to be a success that he never had time for me." I slid to my favorite side of the pit group and plumped up my pillow and relaxed on the sofa. "Everybody has troubles. Please don't think I lived in some perfect world and suddenly the rug was pulled out from under me and I landed flat on my back. I put a few of my dreams off but I have enjoyed being with my friends and doing my volunteer work, something Daniel hated by the way, because I wasn't getting paid to do it. He couldn't see why I would waste my time doing something that wasn't advancing my career." I caught my breath. I rambled on from pent up aggression. I finished my beer. "Now it's time to finish the cabin and do something with the warehouse." I looked over the back of the couch and motioned for Allen to join me. "Come here. Let me tell you what I want to do someday."

He sat on the opposite side of the pit group with a new beer. He handed it to me. I accepted simply because I believed he may have had too many already.

"One of these days I want to sell the warehouse and move out here to live. I would clear part of the woods by the garage and build a bigger shop. Not as

The Kitchen Dance

big as the warehouse, but one that tucks back into the woods and is just big enough for my equipment and tools to build some furniture. Since I do all my drafting on my computer now, maybe I can do more of my work out here and just go into the city for meetings."

"Why don't you do that now?"

"Roosevelt would never come out here. He likes the warehouse."

"Why are you doing that for Roosevelt?"

"Because he's happy where he is and I want him to be happy."

"What about your happiness?"

"I'm fine." I sipped the cold beer. "Anyway, I'm happiest when I think I've helped someone else be happy."

"That's a blessing and a curse. Doesn't he have any family?"

"His wife died but he has two children. They can't take him. Neither of them has the room. Besides, he won't go. He likes where he is."

"Is he...?" Allen searched for words.

"He's not crazy or mentally ill, if that's what you mean. He's just old. Maybe a little senile." I thought about Roosevelt sitting in his chair with an empty chair next to him, and the variety of people who passed by. Several share greetings with him, shake hands, say a few words, and some sit for a while and share stories with him. "He was a high school history teacher. He told me that a few years after he retired he sold his home and banked the money. Then he started wandering around staying in cheap hotels. He spent all day just sitting and watching people. Sometimes he would talk with them. They would tell him all these stories. At first he would go to different places like the park, or the bus station, or the malls, or the library just to watch or talk to people." I looked over at Allen to see if he was still with me. He was.

"He told me that one day he was walking past the warehouse when he noticed all the homeless people. He liked sitting by the warehouse because it sits at an intersection where the small shops and diners end and the warehouses begin. It is sort of a transition in people too." I watched Allen as his blue eyes flickered with the light from the fire.

I remembered one of the times I came out of the warehouse and sat next to Roosevelt. "I've sat out there with him for hours watching the flow of people and lots of them know Roosevelt and stop to talk to him. The former owner of the warehouse gave him a key. He let him live there because he liked having him around. He was sort of a watchdog. "When Daniel and I bought the warehouse, we let Roosevelt stay. He's kind of like a pet. We were building the loft because I was spending a lot of time there crafting my furniture. Then we sold our town house and..." I felt the story could finish itself.

Allen sat quietly, taking it all in. I thought he was tired or the beer kicked in, so I stretched, signaling I was ready to go to sleep.

"I'll sleep on the couch if you'd rather…" Allen offered.

"No. I want to. I want to watch the fire for a while."

Allen was holding back an almost embarrassed smile.

"What?" I asked with the same teased smile.

"I washed the sheets." He stifled a snicker.

I didn't get the joke at first but then it dawned on me. "Oh. So you hoped to get a little action," I confirmed.

Allen blushed and I noticed his blue eyes were rimmed with a darker pink and his eyes were becoming blood shot.

I stood and offered him a hand. "I don't think that's going to happen for you tonight, Casanova." I pulled him from the pit group with all the effort I could muster. The old set had a way of sucking you in.

* * * *

Allen

I woke before Joule and started the day with a splitting headache. I'd not had that much beer in, well…I couldn't recall the last time I'd been drunk. I found some old aspirin in the bathroom's medicine cabinet. They were expired but I took two anyway. I washed my face and rinsed out my mouth with a handful of tap water. I doubted I could get much work done today.

Joule was curled up on what seemed to be her side of the pit group. I did not want to wake her up but I needed some coffee. The grinder caused her to stir. "I'm sorry." I spoke over the noise. "Want some coffee?"

Joule sat up and ran her hands through her hair. "No." Her voice was graveled. "I'll fix myself some tea."

"I'll make breakfast," I volunteered before I realized how bad I felt.

Joule propped her arm on the back of the pit group and looked at me. "You don't look to be in any condition to stand over a skillet of eggs."

I agreed. My stomach was churning as I fumbled with the coffee filter.

"I'll make it," she offered.

"If you insist."

Joule dug her cell phone from her handbag hanging on a hallstand hook by the front door. She made a call, wrapped herself up in her quilt then stepped outside. I saw her come around the house looking for better reception more than privacy and walk down the rotten steps towards the lake. I would have to get on those repairs I thought. When she finished the call, she came inside and handed me the phone.

"Here. Call your kids." She turned on the coffee pot. Apparently, this is a

The Kitchen Dance

very important step in the coffee making process that I seemed to have forgotten. She took the quilt from her shoulders and draped it over mine.

I took the phone and the quilt and went to the back porch. Joule watched from the living room waiting for me to turn. She pointed down towards the lake. I did as she suggested and found the call was much clearer as I stood on the pier overlooking the main lake. The quilt was nice but I wished I was wearing a jacket.

* * * *

Joule

I watched as Allen smiled and laughed while talking to his children. When he walked towards the lake, I wished I could follow. He spoke little of his children. Now I knew why. He must miss them madly. I selfishly wanted to share in this happy moment. I wanted to stand on the pier with him to watch his face and the lines around his eyes crinkle when he smiled and to hear the joy in his voice as he interacted with his kids. I thought about taking him Daniel's leather jacket. It was freezing out there on the lake and he looked rather pathetic huddled under my grandmother's old log cabin quilt.

I decided to start making breakfast instead. I found some ham slices, eggs, and a tube of biscuits in the refrigerator. I preheated the oven and scrambled some eggs in a bowl. A shadow crossed the kitchen window and I glanced out.

The sliding glass door opened in the dining area and in walked Allen. I saw the look on his face was no longer jovial. It was serious.

"Tina told me I could see the kids next weekend." He walked into the kitchen and handed me the phone. I would have thought this to be happy news. "Do you mind if I take the Bronco?"

"No, Allen. Of course I don't mind." I turned the heat off under the ham. "But I think you should take the van. Old Clifford's not that reliable. You can drive me back to the loft this afternoon and take…"

"That's okay. I should probably just catch the bus. Tina wouldn't appreciate my driving up in another woman's vehicle."

Awkwardness hung like a cloud over us the rest of the day. We worked in separate areas of the house. Allen finished taping and floating the drywall in the new addition while I cleaned out the second bedroom. I would start painting it the next time I came to the cabin. I would not be seeing Allen for a couple of weeks and I battled with myself on why that bothered me. He, after all, chose a complete stranger to go out with knowing that I was available. I did tell him I was available, didn't I? I thought I may have mentioned Barry. Yes, he knew I was available. Clearly I was of no interest to him. I was just an opportunity for employment. Damn him, I thought to myself as I chucked scrap lumber and sheetrock into a large trash can.

"You okay in there?" Allen finally acknowledged my existence.

"Yes." I strained through clenched teeth as I dragged the overfilled container into the hallway.

"Need some help with that?" He stood in the doorway with a drywall taping knife in one hand and a pan of mud in the other.

"No." I gave him a fake smile and could feel the grit from the sheetrock dust on my teeth.

Chapter Nine

Joule

It was a relief to get back to my home at the loft and wash off the dust. I was pleased with the job I did cleaning up the room but now it was time to switch hats. I slipped into a dark green dress that was hemmed just above my knee with a vintage styled jacket accented with seed beads.

When I arrived at the party, I was immediately greeted by Elaine and Philip. They introduced me to Stephen Croft. He was an attractive man with dark hair cropped short to fight the unruly curls, with a silver streak that started in a cowlick just off center on his forehead. He had brown eyes and a pleasant smile. He was immediately interested in speaking with me. I enjoyed our brief encounter. We covered the formalities and the typical introductory topics, but I had other plans. I lingered near the door until Travis arrived.

I had asked him to meet me here. I wanted a few minutes to warm Elaine up to the idea. I squelched her growing concern for me and the men I was picking up off the street as she put it.

Travis walked in. He stood tall, a good head taller than most of the guests.

Elaine was first to see him. "Joule, I believe your date is here." She patted my arm as she passed me for the door and motioned for Travis to join us.

His tall lean body moved effortlessly through the groups. He probably was towheaded as a child and his soft wavy blonde hair mingled with gray glowed above the crowd. He winked at me the minute he located me and his hazel eyes sparkled from the chandelier's glow.

"Joule, he's fabulous," Elaine hissed in my ear. "Where did you say you met him?"

"He just pulled up in my front yard." I smiled and waved at Travis who joined us and was immediately swept up in our conversation. I took him to see the sofa I designed and built for the homeowner over which hung a huge atrocious painting.

Victor Harris approached with Missy, the event planner of this little soirée. "Joule!" He kissed me full on the lips and embraced me enthusiastically. I wiped a smudge of lipstick from the side of his mouth, a shade not my own, and introduced him to Travis as my dear friend since our rudimentary drawing class we took our freshman year in college, to explain away the sloppy kiss. Victor gave Travis a seductive once over and quickly yanked a passing woman into the conversation. "Look, Lucy, it's our Joule."

Lucy's last name escaped me just as I was trying to introduce her to Travis because it changed as often as her assortment of ex-husbands. She wore her usual garish colors that washed out her pale skin and pure white coif. She embraced me tentatively, as not to smear her dramatically made up face. "Joule!" she exclaimed as if she wanted the entire room to be aware of my presence.

I complimented her on her home, her selection of a caterer, and marveled, albeit insincerely, on her selection of guests until Victor cut me off. "He's divine!" Victor's breath was hot against my neck as he regarded Travis in a volume that was less than intimate. Victor kept his thinning dark hair clean shaven, and looked and spoke gayer than most homosexual stereotypes, but was as straight as an arrow. He held in reserve a bevy of beautiful women that would make Hugh Hefner envious. He had long, dark lashes and thick eyebrows that he kept neatly shaped to add to his metrosexual appearance. He groomed a little soul patch beneath his thick lips, and the dark hair made his large teeth look whiter when he smiled. He was not much taller than me but made up for his short stature with a personality larger than life. "Don't you just love the painting?" he gushed while making a gagging gesture behind Lucy's back.

I heard rumors of Victor's little gift to women, or should I say big package. I often thought that if I ever felt the urge for a wild fling I would call Victor and lure him to an art museum where we would slip behind a particularly large sculpture. A girl can fantasize can't she? "It's fascinating." I smiled mockingly as I searched for words. "Very emotional."

"Oh Joule, you must meet the artist." Lucy wrapped her bejewel fingers around my arm and tugged me away.

Travis and I exchanged cringes as she called across the crowd in her shrill voice to the artist and motioned for him to join us.

A surprisingly plain looking man emerged from the crowd. He was simply yet neatly dressed, and was in total contrast to the artwork he created.

The Kitchen Dance

He joined our group and the five of us enjoyed a long conversation about art and name dropped the other artists we all had met. It was clearly a case of not judging a book by its cover. The artist's unassuming nature reminded me of Allen, and I wondered what Allen was doing and, whether or not, he would enjoy such a gathering. My thoughts quickly diverted to Travis who wanted to mingle and I introduced him to Philip who worked him into the group he was involved with. I watched Travis from a distance. He was smooth. He blended in seamlessly and several times I saw business cards exchanged. Good for you, I thought for his sake. I did not want to pull him away but the crowd was thinning and I always hated to linger until the end, and I wanted a few minutes with him all to myself.

Travis offered to take me to dinner. I accepted, as the valet service Missy arranged for the party brought my car around the circular drive. Travis was chatting on about the party and the people he met, but fell speechless when the Jaguar pulled to a stop and the valet stepped out. I slid into the driver's seat and adjusted my dress.

"It was my husband's," I told him. "I'm considering selling it. Do you know anyone looking for a Jag?"

"It looks pretty damn good on you." He smiled a sexy smile. "You should keep it."

I shrugged and adjusted my seatbelt. "I'm more of a Bronco girl myself," I joked even though I drove that old full-sized, no-frills delivery van most days. Another valet pulled up in Travis's Suburban. "I guess I'll see you at the restaurant."

"Da Vinci's, right?" he confirmed.

We enjoyed pleasant conversation and a delicious Italian meal. He went for the lasagna which came in a heap on his plate and I enjoyed eggplant parmesan that was crisp but rather heavy on the sauce. After dinner he followed me back to the warehouse. I let us in the garage access but decided against the elevator. It was late and I was afraid the noise would wake up Roosevelt. He peeked out of his door when we passed his room anyway. I gave quick introductions then Travis and I climbed the steep staircase.

"This is my loft." I invited him in. Travis was a talker and we enjoyed another hour or more of intimate conversation on my sofa. The hour was late, more like early in the morning, when I walked him back down.

"My crew started a new home on the lake this week. I should be around next weekend. Will you be at your cabin?"

"Yes. I can be there." Allen would not, so I would have the place to myself.

"Why don't we meet somewhere for dinner?" he suggested.

"That sounds good." I did not want a repeat of this night. Travis was a difficult man to get rid of, not that I wanted to. The cabin's fireplace and that comfortable pit group would make it impossible.

Travis whispered he would call and gave me a soft kiss on the cheek. He got in his Suburban and opened the window. "Joule, I don't think you should say anything to your friend, Allen, about us. He might be uncomfortable with you seeing his boss. I don't want anything disrupting his work."

"He won't be there next weekend, anyway. He's going to see his children."

"So I can meet you at the cabin then?" Travis suggested.

"Let's just meet for dinner first." I smiled.

"Okay. I'll call you."

As Travis drove away I noticed a homeless man urinating just down the alley from my warehouse. Disgusted, I went back in and checked the locks on my doors.

* * * *

Allen

I was working on the railing of a staircase in the entry of a new construction when an attractive woman appeared at the doorway, backlit by the sun. She made quite a silhouette and I noticed some of the other guys stopped working to check her out. She carried a container of food in a sack from a local diner.

"Excuse me." She came directly to me. "I'm looking for Travis. Have you seen him?"

"Hey, have you seen Mr. Dunn?" I asked one of the painters.

"Hey, Mrs. Dunn." The cabinetmaker walked in. "I think he went over to the new site. Wait, I see him driving up."

Travis pulled up in his Suburban talking on his cell phone.

The cabinetmaker leaned against the door jamb and watched her walk away until the painter pitched a fit. "Damn it, Earl. I just painted that." Earl checked his sleeve and wiped at the stripe of paint on it. The painter, who was either just a teenager or looked young for his age, huffed and slapped another coat on the door jamb.

"That boy ain't right," Earl spoke out the side of his mouth and wiggled his fingers in a faggish way, just because the young man was not gawking over Mr. Dunn's wife.

When the dust settled, I could see Mr. Dunn getting out of his truck and greeting his approaching wife. He gave her a kiss as she handed him his lunch. He opened the passenger door for her and then joined her on the driver's side. I could not help but notice them through the front doorway as I finished some work on the staircase before I ate my own lunch.

I thought of Joule when I looked out the window and saw my boss enjoying his lunch companion. I thought of Joule instead of Tina because I thought that Joule might be the type who'd come to see me at work and bring me lunch. I took a bite of the turkey and cheese sandwich I packed and popped open the lid of a thermos I found in the cabin's pantry. Mrs. Fuhrman brought over some vegetable soup and I saved some for my lunch. I sipped the broth as I looked out at the Suburban. Mr. Dunn caught me in my trance.

* * * *

Joule

My dinner with Travis was just what I needed. We had a light dinner; I picked at a salad and he shared with me part of his huge fried shrimp Po'boy. It had been a long while since I had been with someone who really seemed to enjoy my company without my having to play some game to sell him on a project. On the drive to the cabin I had a long quiet thought similar to those when Roosevelt would ask what I was building. I had this unusual feeling of excitement and I could not recall the last time I felt that way. I had been functioning on autopilot for so long that I had forgotten what it was like to embrace the moment and truly enjoy my life. Things were really turning around for me. I felt that somehow meeting Allen and helping him out had opened a door like Dorothy after her tornado nightmare stepping out of her dingy gray farmhouse into the Technicolor wonderful world of Oz.

I enjoyed my newfound motivation to get the cabin finished and looked forward to going there on a regular basis. I could have an open house once the addition was complete and invite Victor who always knew the appropriate people to bring to any occasion. I would get back in touch with Daisy, Glen and Camille. We could have a reunion. I smiled at the thought. I could even invite Saul. The loft had sheltered me like a sterile incubator in the midst of a chaotic world but now the cabin and its warmth and natural surroundings beckoned my return. I felt the cabin drawing me back as a haven of respite instead of a dwelling for ghosts. I had Allen to thank for that. I glanced up at the headlights bouncing off my rearview mirror and I hoped that Allen would continue to work for Travis and that he would do very well for himself and his children.

I waited for Travis to join me on the front porch before I opened the door to my dark cabin. Sounds bounced across the lake bringing back childhood memories of evenings bundled in my quilt on the back porch with my parents as we listened for the waterfowl that called out as they came to roost in the cypress trees along the shore. Travis guided me inside and his large hand felt warm against the small of my back. I turned on a small lamp on the table in the entryway. Travis followed me in then pulled me into his long arms and I felt enveloped in his heat. I giggled like a silly girl and let him kiss me. Then I stretched my arms around his neck, stood on my toes, and kissed him back.

* * * *

Allen

I was standing in the bathroom with the water running in the sink. I thought I heard something. I turned the water off. I did hear something. I heard someone laughing in the living room. Joule was not supposed to be here this weekend and that did not sound at all like her. Too giddy. I slowly pulled the light chain over the medicine cabinet and opened the door. It was quiet now but I noticed a light coming from the entry. Did I leave that on? I grabbed a towel and wrapped it around me. No, I never turned that lamp on. I walked down the dark hallway. I could hear breathing. I turned on the bright overhead kitchen light and surprised the two people making out in the living room.

"Allen!" Joule cried out, "God, you scared me to death!" She tried to catch her breath. "I thought you were going to see your kids?"

"Tina canceled on me." I could hardly say the words as I watched Travis turn away from me as if I wouldn't recognize him.

"I didn't see the Bronco," Joule continued.

"I took it to the shop again. Mr. Fuhrman gave me a ride back." I adjusted the towel on my waist. I was still damp from my shower and the cool air was getting to me.

"Joule, I need to be going," Travis Dunn cut in.

"No, wait. We can tell Allen. I think he'll be okay with us seeing each other."

"I'll just let you talk to him right now. I'll call you later." Travis slipped his coat on.

"Okay." Joule hesitated. She gave me a worried look then walked him back to the door.

I waited in the kitchen for her to come back. I didn't care that I was still in my towel in the bright kitchen.

"Perhaps we need a signal like leaving the porch light on?" Joule came in joking about the situation.

I leaned against a counter and crossed my arms. I was not joking.

"You know—" Joule looked like I was making her uncomfortable.

The Kitchen Dance

"No, I don't. I don't know you at all." I stood my ground.

"What is wrong with you?" Her eyebrows came together creating a broken V between them. Apparently she did not know why I would be angry.

"You are no better than that son of a bitch that is living with Tina. Don't you have any respect for marriage? For a family? I guess you think your money, your job and your fancy friends can get you any man you want."

"What?" She was shocked by my attack on her. "What are you talking about?"

"He's married, Joule."

"He's divorced, Allen," Joule returned. "Just like you."

Oh, damn, I thought. Does she know I haven't signed the divorce papers? "Well then, Mr. Dunn and his ex-wife are awfully friendly. I've seen her all week bringing him lunch to the house I've been working on."

"Allen, he told me he was divorced and I believed him. I had no idea." She walked right up to me and got in my face. Her eyes were misting with anger and I could tell she was disappointed both in the news and the way I went about telling her. She clearly didn't know.

"And what are you accusing me of? Do you think I would intentionally go after a married man? You are right, Allen, you don't know me. No one does. Everyone expects me to move on, to start seeing other people. But, until I met..." She stopped herself and I don't know why. "I don't want to see anyone. I hate dating. I really hate this." She gestured like she was talking about something between us.

She tried to walk away from me but I grabbed her.

"I liked him. I thought he liked me." She began crying and I wanted so much to pull her in my arms. "You know what? Barry didn't want me. He wanted my money. He wanted my friends and the parties. And he wanted my husband's sports car. I wish someone wanted just me."

"God, Joule, I'm sorry." I could not let go of her arm. I still wanted to hold her but she pulled away and stood by the kitchen entrance leaning against the opposite counter. "Look, I was still upset about Tina. I took it out on you." My excuse sounded feeble.

"I don't believe you. You really do think those things about me don't you?" She crossed her arms and looked at the floor.

"It's just easier for you. You can always use your money to fix things or take care of things." My explanation was only making me mad again. "That's why you like Travis Dunn. He's got money. You two are the same. Not like me, anyway. I have always worked hard for what I want. Only I don't get paid the big bucks because I never got the fancy college degrees. I worked for years to save up and pay my own way through college. I didn't have a rich daddy to put me through school."

"I had a scholarship," Joule reminded me.

I leaned towards her and my towel began to slip. "But I quit school when I married my first wife." I tried to fix it but it was just not cooperating. "I worked to support our family. But I couldn't make enough money to keep her happy so she took our son and left." I held the towel closed instead. "You know what our big difference is Joule?" I pointed the finger of my free hand at her. "You told me your husband wanted you to work all the time."

Joule stood her ground.

"Tina, my second wife, didn't want me to work at all. Especially out of town. She wanted me home helping with the kids. Hey, I love my kids. Don't get me wrong. And I loved Tina. I only took local jobs and there were few of those. But if I couldn't work I couldn't make any money." I trailed off then walked past Joule, out of the kitchen and down the hall.

Joule followed me. "So what happened?"

I stopped in the bathroom, Joule right on my heels. I picked up my dirty clothes from the floor and pushed past Joule in the bathroom doorway. I walked towards the first bedroom. Joule followed. "Do you mind?" I asked her. I walked in the bedroom and closed the door behind me.

"You're not getting out of this that easy," Joule yelled through the door.

I stepped out of the bedroom wearing my clean pair of jeans and still pulling on my t-shirt. I walked past Joule, who decided to block the hallway now, to the kitchen. She followed.

"I took a job in the city. I couldn't afford to rent an apartment or a motel. I lived in the camper on the back of my truck. I sent Tina all the money I could. It was just for a few months and I tried to get home on weekends. But Tina didn't like to be alone. That's when she started seeing this guy, Joe. I didn't want a divorce. I told her I wanted to work it out. I kept working. The money was good. I thought it would help." I took two beers from the refrigerator, opened one and handed it to Joule. Our close proximity in the small kitchen suddenly made me uncomfortable. I tipped my beer bottle towards the living room and she got the message. Joule took her spot in the pit group and I sat on the hearth. I opened my beer and took a long drink.

"Then Tina tells me she's pregnant and it's not mine."

"So you gave her the divorce."

I took a long draw on my beer. I needed time to think. I needed a way to word this. I couldn't. "I didn't even think about my kids. Who would get custody and all that?" I got up to start a fire. "So, I went back to my city job. My truck and tools got stolen. I was broke. I couldn't find work without my

The Kitchen Dance

tools and I didn't have a place to live so..." I finished my beer. "I think we're up-to-date."

Chapter Ten

Joule

    Everything became terribly awkward between us. I slept fitfully and left early the next morning before Allen was even out of bed. We both needed a chance to cool off. I was not ready to let this end. I felt we had some unfinished business. I knew I had.
    A call I was waiting for finally came on my cell phone during my drive to work Monday morning. I drove straight to the police station downtown after work.
    "Looks like we have the truck you are looking for." The detective was shorter than me but his ego was at least a foot taller. He adjusted the waist of his slacks to accommodate his paunch when he took his seat behind his desk. "It was picked up as an abandoned vehicle in the next county a couple of months ago. They called the number that's here on the report. His wife answered. She said he didn't live there anymore. The detective asked her if she could give him a message."
    "As far as I know she didn't," I supposed.
    The detective pulled the file from a stack of about a dozen on his desk. He slid on a pair of reading glasses and checked papers in the file. "I see here your friend called in about a week before we located it but didn't leave another number where we could reach him. Good thing you came in and left your number," The police detective informed me. "I'm sorry it took me this long to get back to you, especially since it's been here for so long."
    I held back a comment.
    The detective escorted me to the impound lot surrounded by cyclone fencing. We walked past several vehicles finally arriving at the truck. It was an

The Kitchen Dance

old, burgundy Ford pickup, probably mid-eighties. I was never good at identifying makes of vehicles let alone the year they were built but I recognized the truck style because I once dated a guy that bought one new shortly after grad school. This one had an old Challenger camper in the bed that extended over the cab. I knew this from the graphic "allenger" on the driver's side of shell. The "C" and "h" were hidden beneath an access panel. I walked completely around the vehicle to discover the entire word on the opposite side.

The detective pulled down the folding steps and opened the previously pried open door of the camper. A wretched stench wafted from the camper's interior that suggested the toilet was used to its full capacity and the black water tank never emptied. The detective scratched his balding scalp as if the stimulation would help him think of a plan. He grunted as he climbed inside. How he could or why he felt compelled to go inside the camper I have no idea. I could barely tolerate the odor standing outside the entrance. In his career, I have no doubt he had seen worse.

There was a soiled mattress pulled from the bed area above the cab. The detective stuffed it back into its cubby hole. He pulled a white handkerchief from his back pocket and placed it over his nose. The filter bought him some more time to look around the camper.

I held my breath and looked inside the doorway. I dared not go any farther. I stepped back to catch my breath.

"Looks like he lived in here." The detective stated the obvious, his voice muffled by the handkerchief. "At least someone's been living in here. The report says he had some tools and clothes. This is how it came to us." He informed me as if he believed I thought he was somehow to blame for its condition. Then he stepped out of the camper. His face was blotched with red.

"Are you all right?" I stepped back and held my arms out to help him exit.

"Yes." He stepped away from the camper and inhaled the fresh air. "That camper needs to be taken to the dump." He attempted to blow into his handkerchief some of the odor particles that accumulated in his nostrils.

"Does it still run?" I asked about the truck.

"I don't know. It was towed in. Probably no gas." He walked around the pickup and pulled open the unlocked door and looked in the cab. "No key. But you could have one made. I have the name of a guy at my desk. When can he pick it up?"

"Mmm." I thought about it a moment. "I've got a preview tomorrow afternoon. I can't get out of that. But I should be able to pick him up tomorrow night. We can be here Wednesday morning." I felt confident I could make it happen.

"That'll be good." He closed up the cab and camper doors. "We didn't get enough information to find anyone on the assault complaint, though."

"What assault complaint?" I wanted to know.

"Your friend was beaten up." The detective handed me the file he was carrying under his arm.

I looked at the images in the file. Allen was photographed wearing a hospital gown. His face was badly beaten. His overgrown hair was damp and slipped back behind his ears. One eye was practically swollen shut, his bottom lip was slit and I could see dark red welts around his clean shaven jaw. The other photos showed bruising on his ribs and marks on his back. I traced my finger along the side of his face in the picture. "He never told me about this."

* * * *

The Prescott preview went exceptionally and Philip signed off on all the plans. It would go on to the media department for the full presentation. My assistant and the rest of the team were excited and wanted to celebrate. I was more interested in picking up Allen. I left work early in order to beat the traffic and I hoped to get back to the loft before dark. I took the Jaguar.

When I arrived at the cabin, I found Allen cleaning some brushes at a faucet on the side of the cabin. He walked around the cabin when he heard me pull up.

"You painted the trim?" I asked excitedly.

"Yes," he replied curtly not at all pleased to see me.

"You didn't go to work for Travis today, did you?"

"Yeah. I finished up the staircase before noon. Then I told Travis I was done. I thought I should finish up here before I took on any extra work."

"Allen, you didn't quit because of me did you?"

"I did." He was blatantly honest.

I didn't know what to say.

"What are you doing here? And why are you driving that?" Allen still seemed aggravated with me.

"I have a surprise for you." I tried to lift his mood. "I want to take you back to the city. The police found your truck."

"Yeah?" Allen began walking away. "How did you manage to find out about my truck?"

"I went by the police station and met with the detective you spoke to and gave him my phone number in case he found something."

"I guess my tools were gone." He walked back around the house to finish cleaning the brushes.

I followed him to the water faucet. "Yes. The keys were gone too. Do you have the keys?"

The Kitchen Dance

"No."

"I have the phone number of a man who can make you a new key. I thought we could leave tonight. You can stay with me at the loft again and we'll go to the police station first thing tomorrow."

Allen squatted down and continued to wash out the brushes acting as if I told him nothing.

"Allen, why didn't you tell me about the assault?"

Allen stopped cleaning the brushes. "I didn't think I had to." He stood up and shook the water out of the brushes. "What are we doing here, Joule? I'm not going to cry in my beer because some bad things have happened to me. You said it yourself. Sometimes you just have to move on."

"Sorry I asked."

Allen squatted down to rinse the brushes again.

I went inside the cabin completely confused by his behavior.

Allen walked in a few minutes later. "Do I have time to shower?"

"Yes." I gave up my hope of getting home before dark.

When Allen finished his shower, he found me waiting by the car. Without a word to me he tossed a plastic grocery bag with his change of clothes in the backseat on the passenger's side.

"Do you want to drive?" I asked hopefully, but instead he got in the passenger seat and fastened his seat belt.

I hesitated, wondering if we should work this out before we sat cramped in that tight car. Then again, I hoped the close proximity would encourage him to talk. I got into the driver's seat. "Okay, Allen. Do you want to do this or not?"

"Yeah. I want to go get my truck."

"Have I done something?"

"I could have taken care of this. I don't need your help with everything."

I could feel the tears stinging my eyes. "Would you prefer to find your own way back to the city, or would you like to ride with me?"

"I'll ride with you."

"Do you think my life has been easy just because I have money? My parents died when I was twenty. They weren't there for my college graduation or my wedding. Which, by the way, we eloped, just in case you're judging me because you assume I had some elaborate wedding with five hundred guests! A wedding loses its appeal if you don't have your mother there to help you pick your wedding dress or your father there to give you away! I buried my husband just when we were trying to start a family. Yes, I have money, I have a home, and I have a job. Damn it, Allen, I don't judge you because you had some hard times, so stop judging me because I had some good times."

"I do appreciate your help, but there are some things you just can't fix."

I started the car and pulled away from the cabin. "The detective called your house when they found the truck. They asked Tina to give you the message. Did she ever tell you?"

"No." Allen propped his forearm on the window frame and looked out the window.

* * * *

Allen

We did not talk for the rest of the ride home. I noticed the road sign that read we were twelve miles from the city. I thought about Joule's parents. We were twelve miles from the center of town. I looked over at Joule and watched her from the corner of my eye. There it was; the look. I turned to her to see if she recognized the area of the median where the car accident might have taken place. She never said a word. I just knew. I wondered if she ever put out one of those crosses or wreaths with plastic flowers there where her parents souls left the earth. I felt bad for her and wanted to reach for her hand and hold it but she held the steering wheel with her right hand.

The first night back at the loft was rough. Joule and I barely spoke. She turned on her stereo and the music cut through the silence. She went to bed early and I stayed awake on the sofa bed for hours before I finally drifted off.

The next morning went better. Joule made the coffee and I whipped up some breakfast while she got dressed. She took the day off to help me out. I told her it wasn't necessary. I could catch the bus.

"Maybe we could meet downtown for lunch," Joule offered as she munched on a buttered and toasted English muffin.

I scraped at the last of my fried egg yolks on my plate. "I'm afraid I might be too busy with the truck. Why don't I give you a call at your office?"

"Okay." Joule drank the last of her juice and wrote down her office phone number on a notepad. "I should be taking a break anywhere between eleven thirty to one." She tore off the sheet and handed me the paper.

I stuck the number in my jeans pocket then carried our breakfast dishes to the sink and began rinsing and loading them in her dishwasher. She scraped the bacon grease from the skillet along with the coffee filter into the trash can she kept under the sink. She buzzed around me like a horsefly and I finally stopped with the dishes and told her I would finish up.

"Just let me wipe off the counters and I will be out of your way." She could have felt the same anxiousness that I felt. She threw the eggshells in the trash and quickly wiped off the counters and stovetop.

I wanted to stop her in her tracks and pull her to me and thank her for

The Kitchen Dance

everything she'd done for me but I was afraid I could not stop at a hug.

* * * *

Joule left for work and I left to meet the detective at the police station around nine. I took care of some administration fees before they released my truck. Joule prepared me for that. She insisted I take the cash from her. She said she owed me for all the work I did on the cabin. I told her I would take it but only as a loan.

The detective took me to the impound lot where we met the locksmith. It was much worse than I imagined. Joule warned me but there was no way to describe the smell without the use of a lot of curse words that I guess Joule did not want to use. If there was ever the reason to cuss, this was it. I felt vomit rise in my throat. I fought off the urge and cried instead. The whole night came back to me. I sat on the parking lot's cold black top to clear my head.

The detective was cool about the whole thing. The locksmith avoided me and just kept working on the keys.

"Hey, man. I understand." The detective leaned against the camper beside me. "Your truck and all. Look. I did a little research for you. I found the numbers and directions to a couple of campgrounds where you dump the tanks. Clean the camper up a little." He handed me a slip of notepad paper.

I took the list and thanked him as he pulled me up from the black top. I heard the sound of a key turning in the ignition. The locksmith finished making the key and was checking his work. The key fit but all the ignition could offer was a soft clicking sound.

"Let's see what we need to do to get this out of here." The detective smiled, probably glad to be rid of the old wreck.

The truck just wouldn't start. The battery was dead. Probably just needed a charge or a jump. The locksmith pulled jumper cables from a metal toolbox in the back of his truck. I checked the oil and fluids. Joule warned me about the empty tank so I bought a gas can, some gas, and a quart of oil at a station down the street from the precinct. I finally got the truck running. I paid the locksmith for the key and his extra trouble with the cash Joule lent me.

I knew I needed to call her. She asked me before she left that if we couldn't meet for lunch to at least come back to the loft. She told me I could use her garage in the warehouse if I needed to do some work on the truck. She had a few tools there but I knew I would probably find everything I needed at the cabin. I could tell she still wanted me around. Even after everything I said. How crappy I treated her. She still wanted to help me out and I knew that the truck did need some work before I took it out on the road.

I called her from the front desk of the KOA campground where I once stayed for many months. I dumped the black water and flushed out the tanks. I cleaned out the camper as best I could. "I tossed the mattresses and the dinette cushions. They smelled as bad as the bathroom," I told her.

"So what are your plans?" she asked. "It's only a quarter after twelve. We still have time to meet for lunch."

"I'm a mess. Besides, I'm out here at the KOA and I don't think I can make it back in time." I hoped she would not be too disappointed. "I thought I could stop by your loft and clean it up some more."

"Will you still be there when I get back?"

"I was planning on it." I hoped that would put her in a better mood. "Listen, Joule. Even if Tina let me know about the truck, there was nothing I could have done about it. I would not have had the money to get it back or even put gas in it. And if I got my truck back…" I wanted to add, I may not have met you, but left it off. "What I want to say is that I'm grateful that things have turned out like they did and I want to thank you."

"You can thank me by finishing my cabin and letting me pay you something for your labor." I could tell she was smiling when she said it. Her Texas accent came out when she smiled and talked at the same time.

"I can do that," I let her know. "I'll see you after work, then."

"I'll pick up something special for dinner." I could tell she was still smiling.

Chapter Eleven

Joule

When I got back to the loft, I stopped to check on the boys in the garage. Allen was elbow deep in grime and Roosevelt in suds, working as a team cleaning Allen's truck. I parked the van in the alley and took the elevator up to the loft, carrying the groceries I had picked up on the way home. Allen was an experienced mechanic, having learned from maintaining his truck for many years. Roosevelt was braving the camper with a bandana over his nose and mouth, rubber gloves, and a bucket of diluted Lysol mixed with dishwashing soap.

I preheated the oven and set the frozen pizzas on the counter. They weren't just any frozen pizzas. I ordered them from Da Vinci's take home and bake menu. I decided to ice down a six-pack of beer in one side of the kitchen sink. I pulled the ice container out of the refrigerator and dumped the contents over the Amber Bocks. When I tried to slide the ice container back in the freezer, it lodged on something. I pulled out the container and found the culprit. I reached past the boxes of frozen meals and found a small Plano container usually used to hold fishing lures filled with six rolls of 35mm film. I dumped the film from the container and checked out the three rolls of Kodak TMAX 100 black and white film and three rolls of Fujifilm 100 ISO color print. Every roll had expired over a year ago.

I set up the stepladder and climbed up in my closet and pulled out the Nikon EM my father bought me for my high school graduation. I loaded a roll of the old film in the camera. I heard the oven beep but continued to add the light attachment and lens. The weight of the camera felt unfamiliar in my hands. I snapped a picture. No flash. I carried the camera to the kitchen and dug in the junk drawer for new batteries. I opened the flash and found corrosion in the battery chamber. I put the camera away not knowing I would not touch it for years.

I heard footsteps coming up the staircase to the loft. Allen walked in the door liked he lived here. He smiled at me and I felt suddenly weak at my knees. He came to me in the kitchen. His arms were scrubbed clean and he smelled of citrus. "What are you up to?"

I felt my cheeks quiver under the strain of a nervous smile. I felt like I was on the verge of tears. I handed him the camera and pointed out the corrosion. "I ruined my flash." My eyes watered.

"Oh. I can clean this up." He looked into my damp eyes. "It'll be just like new." He thought I was getting emotional about the camera. The oven beeped its third or fourth reminder. "What's cooking?"

I pulled the pizzas from their boxes. "Da Vinci's pizza. I ate dinner there the other night with Travis Dunn. I guess I can say one good thing came out of that experience." I laughed as a distraction. "But it was Elaine who told me about the restaurant. She could take the credit I suppose." I smirked. I slid both pizzas in on the oven rack and wiped my eyes dry with the back of my oven mitts.

Allen found an emery board in the junk drawer and sanded away part of the corrosion. "Yeah. I can get this off. He took my camera and we both rode the elevator back down to the warehouse.

Allen used the rotary tool and a little WD-40 to clean out the battery case, put in fresh batteries, and checked the camera and the flash by snapping a picture of Roosevelt and me by the truck. The warehouse looked brighter this evening. I had not seen it with all the overhead lights turned on in a couple of years. It was then that I noticed the tarpaulin was no longer on the floor. Roosevelt may have cleaned up the stain. I could smell the bleach and still see faint traces of water on the floor. The tarpaulin was folded up and stored on the top shelf of a metal shelving unit. Roosevelt was never one to throw anything useful in the trash.

This day was sitting heavy on my heart and I felt my tear ducts deceive me once again. "Everything looks great." I was being honest. "But, I need to keep an eye on that pizza." I was as cheerful as I could muster. I dared not face them as I made my way to the staircase.

Allen took the elevator up. I knew Roosevelt would pass on dinner. He always preferred to eat his dinner alone in front of his television. We created a little kitchenette in his space not much larger than the one in the camper.

"That Roosevelt is a hard worker," Allen told me right after he closed the elevator's gates. "I kept telling him not to bother but I think he was enjoying it."

"He enjoys a good project now and then." I set two plates on the table. Allen met me back in the kitchen and slipped on the oven mitts to remove the pizzas.

"I did not know what you liked on your pizza so I picked up one with everything and the classic cheese just in case. You can always take off what you like from the one with everything and pile it on a slice of the cheese." I handed him a thin cookie sheet to slide under the pizza's crust.

"And that is why they pay you the big bucks!" he joked as he pointed a mitt covered hand at me. "You're pretty and smart." He removed the pizza from the oven rack.

"Here." I opened one of the take home boxes. "Just slide it in here."

Allen slid each pizza from the rack into each box and used the rolling cutter I set out on the counter to cut the pizzas in eight even slices.

"If it was just about pizzas you might be right." I carried two ice cold beers to the table. I always preferred bottles over a chilled glass.

Allen set the two boxes of pizza on the table. "Just like take out."

I chose a piece of each, inhaling the intoxicating aroma. "Only better. These are piping hot." I blew on my piece of cheese pizza but burned the roof of my mouth anyway. Even the cold beer could not prevent the thin layer of skin from sloughing off. What is pizza without a little skin?

* * * *

Allen

Joule and I stuffed ourselves with pizza and a couple of beers. We took the last of the beer to the garage and drank them in the cab of my truck. I had removed the dirt encrusted seat cover and had Roosevelt wipe down the seats. The gray upholstery still looked pretty good. I used a shop cloth and wiped off the dashboard while we talked.

"This is nice." Joule smiled.

"Nice, how?" I asked.

"Nice. As in just sitting here, talking, drinking a beer. You know, nice." She seemed relaxed as if this was as hard a day on her as it was for me and she was glad it was almost over.

"Just what do you do at your job?" I asked her.

"I look at the architect's designs and choose some of the main areas and a few of the office spaces to detail. Then I create a three-dimensional presentation with design software. I create a presentation board of fabric swatches, wood stains, paint chips, carpet and flooring samples. Kind of a touchy feely thing. It makes the clients happy if they can feel things."

"And that takes what?" I asked. "I mean what type of education?"

"A master's in design and a lot of letters after your name." She offered her bottle for a toast and I clinked my bottle against hers. "You mentioned you went to Ole Miss?"

"A couple of years."

"What was your major?" she wanted to know. Most women were like that.

"Nothing really. Business Management, I guess. Never got past basics. I dropped out and got married when Cheryl, my first wife, got pregnant."

"Oh, your son must be…?" She looked to be calculating his age.

"No, we lost that baby. She miscarried. But I already quit school and started working. Her father got me a job in the oil field. I worked offshore as a roustabout for a few years until he retired. He helped me start up my construction business. By then Cheryl was pregnant with James. He's in college now."

"Oh. That was the boy in the school picture." She nodded her head like she was remembering the photos I showed her the night we met.

"When Big Roy, Cheryl's father, had his heart attack, I had two families to support and I pretty much ran the company into the ground. I knew a lot about carpentry but not enough about running a business." I didn't want to admit to the credit card debts and filing for bankruptcy. "When the company went under, so did my marriage." I took a long drink of the dark beer. "I haven't seen much of my son over the years. They stayed in Mississippi. I moved home with my parents."

"Tell me about your parents."

"They're still alive. Both in their seventies now. My Dad had an asphalt business but sold his share by the time I moved back home. I didn't particularly want to go into the asphalt business anyway. I started picking up carpentry jobs here and there. I owed a lot of money and I lived with my parents for years until I paid it off. It was okay. We all got along fine." I tipped my beer and took a sip. "Eventually I was getting regular work from this one contractor. That's when I met Tina. She was young. Very young. I moved out of my parents' house into a new double wide I bought and put in a nice new trailer park. Well, it was nice then. It had big lots with a little convenience store, a community center and pool. Tina was awfully impressed. I thought it would be temporary until I could find some property and a build my own house. She's still living there. Not a very uplifting conversation." I finished my beer. "While we're on such a depressing subject, I guess you want to know about the police report." I rolled the lid of the beer bottle around on my fingertips.

She drank the rest of her beer and started tearing off the paper wrapper.

The Kitchen Dance

"We don't have to do this tonight if you don't want to."

"No. I think we should get all this bad stuff behind us."

Joule turned in her seat and leaned against the door to face me. "Okay. Seeing that I know you lived through it all. I think I can take it."

"Good grief. It's not that gory." I laughed. "I'd been staying out at the KOA campground for several months while I worked here in the city. I was on a tight budget, sending most of my earnings home to Tina. I was coming back in one Sunday night late and thought I could save the twenty five bucks a night and just sleep in a parking lot. That's where I was jumped. A couple of white guys, stoned most likely, pried open the camper door and yanked me out of the back. They both pounded on me until I couldn't fight back any more. One searched my pockets and took my keys and the cash and credits cards out of my wallet, while the other held me down. It all happened in a matter of minutes. Luckily, I was still dressed, because the clothes I had on was all that I had left."

"I'm sorry." She slowly leaned forward like she wanted to hug me and I would have let her. I wanted to hold her but I knew better than to let it go there.

"Thanks." I patted her on her knee. "You know, it's getting late and you've got work in the morning."

* * * *

Joule

I took photographs of Allen already hard at work on his truck in the warehouse garage before I left for work. I planned to wrap up work at the office and bring back a set of plans to work on at home. When I got back to the loft, Allen took me on a test drive in his repaired, but noisy, old truck. I could feel the camper causing the truck to sway precariously on turns. It was nothing like riding in the road hugging Jaguar. I brought my camera with me and took more photographs of subjects we found interesting. When we got back to the loft, I took photographs of Allen sitting on the sidewalk next to Roosevelt watching traffic and people.

Allen and I decided to go to John's for dinner.

"Good evening, Joule." Gail brought glasses of water and two menus to our booth. "Who's your friend?"

"I think I've already introduced him to you before, Gail."

"Mmm." Gail tapped her pen against her teeth, and then her eyes grew wide with recognition as soon as Allen's clear blue eyes met hers. "You're that guy she bought dinner for a while back. Yeah. Hey, John," Gail called over her shoulder. "Joule's cleaned up her friend here."

John waved a spatula at us from the kitchen.

"What was your name again?" Gail asked. "I'm sorry. We just get all kinds in here. You can just never tell. And Joule here…"

"Allen Brooks," Allen interrupted. "My name is Allen."

"Well then, Allen. I'll let the two of you look over the menu. Chicken fried steak is our special tonight." She smiled her best waitress-y smile.

"I'll have that." Allen smiled up at Gail. "And a glass of milk."

"How's the chicken salad?" Joule asked.

Gail leaned forward enough for her cleavage to be at our eye level and whispered, "Left over from yesterday."

"I'll take a BLT then," I whispered back. "Tell John that I like my bacon crisp." I grinned.

"If I tell John how you want your food cooked, he'll spit in it." Gail laughed.

Allen piped in, "I just want to thank you, Joule, for bringing me to such a classy joint!"

We all laughed loud enough that John poked his head out of the pick-up window and yelled, "Hey. What's going on out there?" He rang his little bell out of habit. "Order up, Gail."

"Do you want your usual onion rings?" Gail cocked her brow with a saucy expression.

"Yes." I grimaced with guilt and with that, Gail winked at me and went back to her waitressing duties.

Allen looked out the window at the people walking up and down the street. I followed his gaze towards an elderly woman I'd seen several times before as she strolled by with her baby carriage filled with bags of her belongings. Her hair was pulled back in a tight ponytail. Tangles embedded her long mane. She was probably my age.

"I was there just a month ago." Allen turned back to me. "I'm grateful to you, Joule."

"Why didn't you get help from your parents?" I asked.

"I just couldn't go back to them again. I kept thinking that I would get my truck back. I could just take it from there. I could not show up at my parents' house again with my hat in my hand."

"So, they don't know?"

"They know all right. I know for sure that Tina has called them for money."

I felt that Allen was trying to prove to me, or perhaps himself, that he was a better man than his circumstances suggested. I felt an overwhelming eagerness to fix everything I could for him but I knew I could not. Helping him would instead satisfy some need in me. I believe he knew that as well.

The Kitchen Dance

I felt that I genuinely liked him, but had not established why. Physically, he was very appealing. His light blue eyes and brown wavy hair with touches of silver gray glinting around his temples and forehead would appeal to any woman. He had a charming smile and a better diet returned him to a healthier color, weight, and physique. We shared little that would seal our friendship. There was no common background, and no long list of similar likes and dislikes. Nothing bound us together.

I knew that my role in his life was as his employer. He kept me at arm's length the same way I did Barry. I tried to remain there. He wasn't interested in me. Clearly, I was not his type. I don't know if the woman from town, whose name I already forgot, was his type, and I had little knowledge of his ex-wives. Considering everything, I doubted he was even my type. He was at such a pitiable low when I met him and I appeared to be at the top of my game, yet I was not happy. I was feeling lonely, betrayed by Barry, and trapped in a life of either being manipulated or practicing the art of manipulating others. Perhaps I just chose to help him because I felt I could manipulate him.

When I saw him that day on the pier with his hair cut and his face clean shaven, I saw him in a way I did not expect. Then there was the evening he came in with the girl from town. I could not believe I was feeling jealousy. But it was the evening he was wearing only a towel, his eyes flashing with such anger and intensity, which disturbed and aroused me the most.

Perhaps Allen was just pacifying me long enough to get the job done, get paid, and leave. I played that role many times with clients and saw Daniel do the same. He would mock the million dollar clients as if they were just some rich old woman having her kitchen remodeled. He would be so kind and considerate to his client's face and then trash them in the company of his peers. I did not want to fall into that category of the humored client. Yet I was torn between wanting to do something to help out a fellow man and wanting to get credit for it.

"Hey,"

I was looking out the window, lost in my own thoughts, when I felt something hit my chest.

"You still with me?" Allen asked as he picked up the balled up napkin that bounced off me and landed on the table. He rolled it around in his weathered hands. His nails were now much cleaner than the last time we were here.

"I'm just hungry," I lied. "I start to zone out when I get hungry." It was only a half lie. I did zone out. I was just not that hungry.

"I thought maybe—" He quit mid-sentence.

"What?"

"I don't mean to sound pathetic." He tore bits of napkin away from the ball and made a tiny pile. "I guess you've never had money problems."

"No." I slid a few of the torn pieces to my side of the table and created a horizontal line between us. "I did have a period of time when…"

Gail set the plates on the table causing a draft that blew the thin torn paper line across the table. "Did you want anything else?"

"No, we're fine," Allen alleged. "Joule?"

"I'm fine."

Allen looked over his plate. "What were you saying?"

I picked up one fourth of the diagonally cross cut sandwich. "It was nothing." I took a bite off the corner.

"You're not getting off that easy." Allen cut off a piece of the battered steak smothered with gravy and popped it in his mouth.

"After my parents died," I began, taking a sip of water to wash down the bite of dry toast and salty bacon, "my grandfather, my mother's dad, insisted on running my finances. I inherited the cabin, my parents' house, their bank accounts, and a pretty hefty life insurance policy." I wiped the mayonnaise from the side of my mouth that Allen delicately pointed out. "He forced me into some decisions I didn't want to make." I recalled the long lectures, usually under the topic that I was a young woman and that money was a huge responsibility.

"He told me I needed to sell either the house where I grew up or the cabin. I was in college at the time. What did I need with so much real estate? He pushed me to sell the cabin. I chose the house. I have better memories from the cabin. He was hateful about my choice. He bought the house for my parents. Ha!" I almost choked on the dry bread crumbs. "He bought the house for my mother. My father's name was not even on the deed. My father put the down payment on the cabin with his summer salary he received from his research grant from the Department of Energy." I smiled and repositioned the tomato in my sandwich. "There was still a mortgage on the cabin. My grandfather was aggravated with me. He was a bully to my father and continued his wrath against me." I took another bite of the sandwich and let that mull over in Allen's mind.

"Did he handle your investments or what?"

"Oh." I positioned the bite of sandwich in my cheek and covered my mouth with my hand. "Everything. I got an allowance until I finished grad school."

"Did he make good investments?" Allen asked.

I shrugged, nodded my head and smiled. I finished my bite as Allen cut off more of the meat and ate eagerly. It was easier not to talk. I doubted talking about my grandfather would connect us in any way but it was a new topic.

The Kitchen Dance

"Is your Grandfather still alive?" he asked between bites of green beans.

I shook my head no. "They are all gone. My grandfather died about a year after I married Daniel. He liked Daniel. Trusted him, I guess. He thought I made a good choice. My grandfather died peacefully in his sleep. I lost my grandmother three and half years before that to lung cancer. She was a sweetie, but she smoked like an old furnace. She's lucky she lasted that long. My Dad's father died in the military when my Dad was a boy. I lost my Grammy, Dad's mother, just before I got married. She had Alzheimer's. I moved her to a specialized care facility close to my work and fed her lunch three times a week. She thought I was Alice, her daughter. I played along. My Aunt Alice was living in New York at the time and never came to see her. My Grammy practically raised me from infancy and she died having no idea who I was. She never met Daniel. I did not see the point in introducing them."

"So you have an aunt?" he asked.

"Yes. Aunts, uncles, cousins. We're just not the family reunion type." I gingerly chewed on an onion ring dipped in ranch dressing. "Want one?" I offered the steaming hot plate of fried onion rings to him.

"I'm going to be stuffed." He accepted a small one.

And stuffed we were. I finished off my sandwich and onion rings and picked at his leftover steak and potatoes.

I fought the cobwebs filling my head as I helped Allen make up the sofa bed. I could hear Allen already snoring in the other room when my head finally found my pillow.

Chapter Twelve

Allen

Saturday was a good day. I went with Joule in her van when she took Roosevelt to get his haircut. She took me by a junk shop and I met her friend that owned it. Joule looked at books while I checked out some old tools. She bought a couple of books and offered to buy me the hammer I was flipping around and catching by the handle. I told her that I wasn't doing it as a subtle hint, but to impress her with my hammer juggling skill.

We hit the grocery store after we picked up Roosevelt and ran a few other errands after we dropped him off at the warehouse. Once we settled back at the loft I spent time cleaning up the shop and organizing the tools while Joule worked on some drawings for her job. I missed the cabin, but this wasn't bad either. I fell into step with Joule and I liked how it all felt but I also hated the way it felt. I knew it could not last.

"Allen," Joule called to me from the entrance to the loft.

I walked to the stairs and looked up at her standing on the landing. "Yeah?"

She tossed down her portable phone. "You should call your kids."

I caught the phone. "Thanks."

"You don't have to ask," she assured me. "You can always pay me back if you're worried about the cost."

"I appreciate this." I waved the phone at her. I called my home but Tina would not let me speak to the kids.

* * * *

On Sunday, Joule let me drive the Jaguar. She told Roosevelt it was the only way he would get to church, and after much complaining, Roosevelt finally gave in. Joule curled up in the cramped backseat while Roosevelt fastened himself in the front passenger seat, his worn out Bible squeezed against his chest.

I revved the engine while keeping a sideways glance at Roosevelt. His eyes were as big as Ping Pong balls with little gray-brown dots. He looked like a surprised Muppet. I smiled in the rear view mirror where I could see Joule watching the old man from her seat behind me. I eased the car out of the garage and drove it slowly all the way to the church so I wouldn't give the old man a heart attack or something.

"See." I helped Joule climb out of the backseat and helped Roosevelt get out. "That wasn't so bad now was it?"

"Next time, we're taking the van." Roosevelt acted none too happy but I have a feeling he enjoyed himself.

"Do you go to church?" I asked Joule.

"Not lately," Joule admitted. "Daniel and I used to go almost every weekend. He liked the image it created." She settled in her seat. "I can't say I lost my faith. I still believe in God. I just don't worship him right now. What about you?"

"I enjoy going to church. I just hope Tina's still taking the kids."

"You need to go home, Allen. Is there something I can do?"

"I'll get there. I'll see them in a couple of weeks. Anyway, you said you had something for me to do today."

"I'm taking you someplace special for lunch but we need to change cars first."

We dropped the Jag off at the warehouse and started up the van. I knew we weren't going anywhere too special. We were too casually dressed for a nice restaurant, and too nicely dressed for construction work.

"What's this place?" I asked as we passed another warehouse with what at first looked like a store front with large windows and double glass doors. Instead of fancy clothes or stuff for sale, there were grungy looking people standing around drinking from plastic cups, and it looked like they were waiting for something. Some of the people even lined up around the double doors that led to the back of the warehouse. We walked under the awning and down the alley beside the warehouse to a back door. The scene looked all too familiar.

"You don't know this place?" She sounded surprised.

"No. Should I?"

"You told me you did some work here."

"Not here."

"But I sent those clothes here. You know the coat? Daniel's trench coat?" she reminded me. "This is where I do my volunteer work."

"I got the coat at a different place, closer to downtown."

Joule and I went into the kitchen with the other volunteers. She began dressing me with an apron, some gloves and tried to put a hairnet on me. I dodged that and asked if it was necessary. She introduced me to some of the other workers. She joined in with the movements of the other volunteers while I, not familiar with the ebb and flow, bumped into some of the other workers. I was making my way to her when another volunteer jostled me, pushing me into Joule. "Would you like to dance?" I asked.

Joule laughed at my joke, shrugged, and held out her hands like she was taking me seriously. I pulled her into a Tango position as we parted the crowd and danced right into one serious looking woman.

"Hey! You two get back to work!" she barked.

Joule and I separated with guilty expressions.

"Della. Have you met my friend, Allen?"

"No. Allen, it's nice to meet you," Della replied without breaking a smile. "I hope you like onions." She handed me a huge bag of onions. "And you need a hairnet."

"See?" Joule teased. "What do you do with the clothing that gets donated to the kitchen?" I heard Joule whispering to Della while I adjusted the flimsy hairnet.

"We don't have much room for donations so we take a lot of it to the downtown mission or the Salvation Army." I heard Della say. "Why?"

"Nothing." Joule smiled, grabbed some carrots and came over to stand next to me while I chopped.

Joule and I both stood there with our eyes watering over the onions. She reached up and brushed a piece of onion skin off my brow and ran her fingers across the horizontal lines in my brow like she was reading Braille. I lifted my brows making the creases deeper and she smiled.

"You need to cut 'em smaller," Della warned me about the onions as she passed us. "They'll cook faster."

Joule sidestepped away from me. The onion juice squirting in her eyes was becoming too much for her. She picked up her pace of carrot peeling and tossing them to a thin black man who was dicing them like a professional chef.

"You thought I lied about the coat," I finally said.

"What?" She raked the pile of carrot shavings into a trash can.

"I heard you talking to Della about the clothes."

"I never thought you were lying, Allen. I donated Daniel's clothes to this shelter. I had no idea what they did with the donated clothes." She scraped the carrot's skin like she was pissed. "Anyway," she said, pointing the peeler at me, "I already asked Della if you did some work around here for her and she told me you didn't. That was a month ago and I never asked you about it. I just forgot to ask her about what happened to the clothes."

I watched as she went back to hacking away at the carrots. Her eyes were still watering, but this time it was not because of the onions, these tears were real. "Hey." I set down my knife and stepped closer to her. "I'm sorry. I shouldn't have said it that way."

"But you thought it. You thought I didn't trust you." She sniffed.

"I guess those onions are just too much for you." Della laughed to ease the tension. "Allen. It was Allen, right?"

"Yes."

"Why don't you go help Owen with the tables?" Della suggested as she pointed to a big hairy man.

"Owen," I heard Joule say as she turned around to see the same man I was looking at. "I thought his name was Oscar or Oliver."

"Owen," Della reminded her.

"He was the one who picked up the clothes. Who is his helper?" Joule continued to peel the carrots as she talked. "He's that skinny blonde teenager."

"Randy," Della informed me just as the scrawny teen walked in the warehouse pulling a cart full of tables from a storage closet.

* * * *

Joule

Allen, after an afternoon spent preparing and serving food at the soup kitchen, decided to prepare dinner at my loft. Roosevelt was sitting on a barstool waiting to see what Allen was making for dinner to determine whether he would invite himself or not. I talked to Elaine on the phone in my bedroom before coming into the kitchen to witness the comical sight.

"Yes, I guess I like canapés but I thought you wanted to do something different for the Prescott party," I told Elaine over the phone. "No, I don't have a date." I leaned against the counter beside Roosevelt and sniffed the vegetables and seasonings being sautéed in the pan. "Allen, do you want to go to a party Friday night?"

Allen looked over at Roosevelt. "Do we have any plans?"

Roosevelt let out a low hoarse laugh and shook his head.

"Looks like I'm free." Allen turned back to his cooking.

"Did you hear that, Elaine?" I laughed, "He says he's free."

"Joule!" Elaine declared over the phone, "You're not going to bring that homeless man are you?"

I walked into the kitchen and picked at the food Allen was cooking. He shooed me out of his way. I continued laughing and talking on the phone, blocking Allen from the kitchen sink.

"Don't worry," I told Elaine. "He cleans up good."

Allen turned to face me, put his hands on my hips and walked me out of the kitchen in a way that resembled a ten-year-old boy at his first slow dance. "You're going to make me burn dinner," he warned me.

Roosevelt was absolutely drooling when Allen dropped potatoes in with the onions and red bell peppers and covered the skillet with a lid. He checked the meat under the broiler then began slathering butter on a loaf of French bread. "Now that's a man's meal," Roosevelt observed.

"You stayin' for dinner?" Allen asked him.

"I think I got some room for a bite or two," Roosevelt half-committed.

"Leave some room for pie," I reminded him. I was surprised Roosevelt would even consider a break in his routine.

"What pie?" Elaine asked over the phone. "Who is having pie?"

"Allen is cooking dinner for us." I filled her in on the rest and let her go so that I could free my hands to set the table for dinner.

* * * *

Although stuffed on Allen's broiled T-bone steaks, vegetables, and bread, Roosevelt still found room for some of John's pie. Strolling back from the diner, I took his hand as I always did. I reached over for Allen's with my other and he took it. It was a pleasant evening. The weather was growing warmer and none of us wore gloves. Roosevelt's hand was cool and I could feel his bones beneath his thin skin. Allen's hand was firm and warm wrapped around mine. If nothing else, I wanted Allen to feel that he was a part of my unusual family.

After leaving Roosevelt in his room, Allen joined me in the loft. I already set up the sofa bed and was relaxing in the club chair when he returned.

"I was looking for the right time to hand this to you." He offered me a slip of paper.

I read over what I owed him for his work. Below the total of hours he worked and wages he charged was a list of expenses he incurred. He subtracted rent on the cabin, the money I lent him, use of the Bronco, including the groceries I bought him and the fifty dollars on the debit card.

"I called a realtor on the lake who told me a cabin like yours could rent for around twenty-five hundred a month. I asked her what a one bedroom apartment or house would run in town and did some figuring on what gas would run back and forth and came up with this price." He pointed to the

The Kitchen Dance

amount he deducted for rent. "I hope that's okay with you."

"Yes. It's okay, but Allen, it is Sunday, and I don't keep this kind of cash on me," I informed him even though it was a meager amount.

"Well, I was wondering if you could just send a check to Tina instead." He handed me an addressed envelope with a letter already folded and tucked inside.

"Sure, I can. No problem. Can you hand me my checkbook? It's in my purse." I smiled and batted my eyes, too lazy to pull myself from my comfortable chair.

Allen appeared uneasy as he dug inside my purse for the checkbook. He returned to me with the checkbook and a pen. "I appreciate this." He handed me the items.

"It's not like I'm giving you a handout Allen. You worked hard for this." I wrote the check and handed it to him. "I appreciate everything you've done for me. You believe me, don't you?"

Allen accepted the check, and without glancing at it, stuck it in the envelope. He slid his tongue across the old gummy strip. It was, most likely, from an older stationary set at the cabin. He sealed the envelope and set it on the kitchen counter with two bills I planned to drop in the mail on Monday.

* * * *

Allen left for the cabin at the same time I left for work that Monday morning. It was an awkward moment, not sure of how we should depart, interrupted when Roosevelt approached. "Will you be back Friday?" he asked Allen.

"Why? You gonna miss me?" Allen laughed.

Roosevelt laughed his hoarse laugh.

"Yes. It looks like I've got a date with Joule," Allen finally answered.

I looked up at Roosevelt, slipped my arm around his thin waist and the two of us waved Allen off.

* * * *

The week went by quietly. I was caught up in the Prescott presentation at work and exhausted by the time I got home. I looked forward to the evenings spent alone in my loft.

I arrived at the party early on Friday night to help Elaine in her kitchen with last minute preparations.

"Look who I found." Philip joined us in the kitchen.

Philip pushed back the swinging kitchen door to reveal Allen who was dressed in an attractive sports coat and slacks that fit him nicely. Allen stood with his coat open and his hands awkwardly tucked in the pocket of his slacks.

"Elaine, this is Allen." I was surprised by his outfit and very pleased to see him.

"Allen, it is good of you to come." Elaine drawled her words out and formally extended her hand.

Allen accepted her hand cautiously. "I don't get invited to many executive cocktail parties."

"I'm sure you don't," Elaine commented slyly.

"Be nice," I mouthed to Elaine from behind Allen.

"Can I fix you a drink, Allen?" Philip piped in.

"Do you have any beer?" Allen asked.

"Of course we have beer!" Philip slapped his hand on Allen's back and led him from the kitchen.

"He is quite handsome," Elaine admitted. "That's good," she uttered absently.

"What are you really saying?" I asked her.

"I'm not saying anything," Elaine claimed as she removed crab puffs from a catering box and arranged them on a platter. "What time is it? I expected those servers by now."

"Don't ignore the question," I insisted. "There is nothing going on between us."

"That's good, honey." Elaine fussed over packages of colored paper napkins she had pulled from a department store bag. "Which ones?" She held up a choice of dark green or metallic gold for my inspection, pretending she could not make up her own mind.

"We're just now becoming friends." I grabbed the dark green package of napkins and stuffed them back in the bag.

"That's good." She tore open the other package.

"Talk to me, 'Laine."

"It's just that..." she stopped talking to force a tumbler into the stack of napkins and twist them into a neat fan, "I don't think I have to say this."

"You think he's not good enough for me," I whispered in her ear.

"Stephen Croft asked me for your number," Elaine confessed. "He's a good man, Joule. He's an engineer. He's more your type."

"So that's what this is about." I began washing a basket of strawberries.

"Leave those for the servers," Elaine fussed. "What time is it? They're late. I'll never use them again. I can tell you that much. I'll never use them again."

"Okay, Elaine. Calm down. You can give Stephen my number."

The Kitchen Dance

* * * *

Allen

"I need to freshen up." Joule passed by me while I was talking to Philip. "I'll be back in a minute." She patted me on the shoulder like she wanted to make sure I was there.

I checked my watched. It was six and the guests were starting to show up. Philip left me and went to greet the other guests. Elaine joined Philip in the foyer. I was left there alone and wondering what the hell I was doing there. I thought that I could just blend in with the wall or the furniture, but everything was fancy and I'm sure I stuck out just like a brown paper sack.

Joule returned just a few minutes later with the same skirt on but different top, high-heeled shoes with thin straps that looked uncomfortable, and flashy jewelry: dangling earrings and a necklace that looked like real diamonds and probably were. Her hair was combed back and sprayed and her makeup was darker; blacker around her eyes, and dark red lips. She looked around the room and I looked right at her. She waved at a few people and for a second I thought she was going over to talk to them. Then she saw me and came to me instead.

"You look very nice," I told her.

"Thank you, Allen." She smiled and her teeth looked especially white behind her dark lips. "So do you."

"Well, I don't have the wardrobe. But it's amazing what you can find at Goodwill for such an occasion," I confessed. "Do you think I'll blend?"

"It's just one of those after work affairs. Most of the guys will be wearing suits because they just came from the office." I think she was blushing like she was embarrassed for me. She would not look me in the eye. "Allen, if I didn't think you could handle this, I would not have made you come."

"I wanted to come," I lied. "I wanted to see this side of you." At least I finished with the truth.

Joule gave me a curious smile, but at least she looked me in the eye.

The guests continued to come. When Mr. and Mrs. Prescott arrived, Joule took me over to meet him.

"Mr. and Mrs. Prescott, I want you to meet my friend, Allen Brooks."

"Allen, a pleasure." Mr. Prescott gave my hand a good shake.

"Allen, this is Elise and Taylor Prescott." Joule continued with her polite introductions while Elise Prescott looked suspiciously at my clothing.

"Excuse me. Joule, Mr. Monroe has someone he wants you to meet," Elaine interrupted.

"I will be back as soon as possible," Joule managed to say before Elaine pulled her away.

Elise Prescott saw someone more interesting to talk to and left Mr. Prescott with me. "Would you like a beer, Mr. Prescott?" I offered, "I know where they keep them."

"I would love one, and call me Taylor."

I walked with Prescott toward the bar. The bartender prepared a chilled glass for Mr. Prescott. Taylor. I just reached for the bottle. A couple of men in suits came along and started up a conversation with Taylor. I handed him his beer and started to walk away but Taylor stopped me and introduced me to the other men. They offered to shake hands but mine was wet from the cold glass of beer I held. I wiped my hand on my slacks and gave their hands good firm shakes, like I knew who I was and why I was there. I mostly stood around listening to the conversation. Joule looked over from where she was being detained. I think she was looking at me with pity. I knew I looked out of place. Prescott excused himself from the two gentlemen and pulled me away with him.

"I'm sorry, Mr. Prescott. I told Joule I'm not very good at these social functions. I don't have much to talk about with these guys."

"Allen, my father started a business with nothing but a few hundred dollars and a high school education. He worked nine to five and went fishing almost every weekend. I have an MBA. I took over my father's billion-dollar company when he retired. I work twelve hour days, six, sometimes seven days a week, and I never get to go fishing."

"Well, Mr. Prescott, I'm just going to have to take you fishing," I told him.

I glanced over at Joule who was looking at me and Taylor. She caught me making casting motions. Prescott was smiling and talking about lures.

Joule tried to pull me away from the party just after the fancy presentation her company did up for Taylor Prescott. For every two steps we made towards the door, someone stopped her and set us back three. She made sure everyone was happy first and made a special effort to introduce me to Mr. Monroe who told me about the contractor that did most of the construction for his company's designs. I saw what Joule did all day at work and I was impressed that all this talent could come from one person. She reminded me it was teamwork, but I saw her hand in every part of it.

When we finally got our break, I opened the door of the Jaguar for Joule to get in. She'd let me drive it from her loft because she'd taken a taxi to work and caught a ride with one of her assistants to West's cocktail party. Jaguar, lofts, taxis, assistants, and cocktail parties were words I rarely used in my forty plus years since I learned to talk, and now I could combine them all in a couple of sentences. It was after nine when we got back to the warehouse. We did not

The Kitchen Dance

stop for dinner because we'd filled up on all the finger foods, or *whore-derves*, another word I rarely used, that Elaine had at her party. Joule brought a box of food home from the party for Roosevelt. She knocked on his door and he stuck his head out of his room looking like he'd been sleeping.

"Did we wake you?" Joule asked him when she handed him the box.

"No, I was just watching the news channel. Did you kids have a nice time?" He seemed to perk up when he took the box.

Joule smiled back at me. "Yes, we had a very nice time. Allen spent most of the evening talking to Taylor Prescott, you know, the president of the company of the latest project I've been working on? They are big buddies now. Allen invited him up to the cabin for some fishing." Joule pointed to the box. "No mushrooms tonight.

Roosevelt opened the container. "Too bad. They're my favorites."

"You comin' up?" I asked Roosevelt as I started up the stairs carrying an overnight bag I found in Joule's parents' closet.

"No. I'm just going to finish watching the news," he answered.

"Do you mind if I join you?" I came back down the stairs. I didn't like the way Roosevelt looked. A little too ashy. "It'll give Joule some privacy."

Roosevelt sat in his dark blue leather recliner. His room looked like a fancy hotel room with a small kitchen, narrow refrigerator, miniature range and sink. The walls were painted tan and there was a large, colorful painting of a street scene over the bed. Across the room was a big window covered with heavy drapes that looked out over the front street. He had his own heat and air unit just like the kind you find in a hotel room. The other furniture, a dresser, a wardrobe that held the television, a nightstand, a little table and chair in the small kitchen were all good quality and looked like walnut with a dark stain. I sat at the end of the bed, made up with a dark blue and tan plaid cover with red stripes. The place was fixed up and Roosevelt kept it all nice.

I made it look like I was watching the news instead of being nosey, until Roosevelt turned around and said, "Joule seems real happy."

"I think she had a nice time." I was thinking about the party.

"I mean lately," Roosevelt pointed out. "Things are getting better for her. She seems happier these days."

"I'm sure things were pretty bad after Daniel died."

"That and the investigation," Roosevelt said.

"The investigation?"

"She never told you about the investigation?" Roosevelt asked.

"No. She hasn't."

"I shouldn't say anything." Roosevelt looked back at the news. "She should tell you."

Chapter Thirteen

Joule

I was in the bathroom. I just stepped out of the shower when I heard the gears rattle and creak as Allen took the elevator up. I could hear the gates sliding open to the loft and Allen walking around on the wood floors, hopefully making himself at home. He pulled the sofa bed out and retrieved the linens from the linen closet. He finished making up the bed and was drinking a glass of water in the kitchen when I came out dressed in my cozy robe. "It's all yours," I informed him about the bathroom.

He brushed past me at the kitchen's entrance. I fixed myself a glass of water and picked up the portable phone, carrying both to my bedroom. I called Elaine. It was a successful gathering and our presentation was intended to lure in another potential client. I wanted to see what transpired after I left.

Allen passed by my bed on the way from the bathroom. He was still steaming from his quick shower. His damp wavy hair was finger combed back and his widow's peak was more prominent than ever. His eyes never looked bluer when he glanced over at me lying on my bed. I was laughing at something Elaine was telling me over the phone.

"Allen, come here a minute," I called out before he cleared the doorway. "Elaine wanted to know if you had a nice time."

"I had a decent time." He stood at the end of my bed.

I motioned for him to sit down. He sat right beside me on my side of the bed. His hip fit like a puzzle piece inside the curve of my waist. He stretched his arm across me to brace himself. I was wearing a pair of silky short pajamas and I suddenly felt a bit underdressed.

I laughed at something Elaine said. "Elaine said Mr. Prescott liked you. He's sincere about the fishing trip." I sat up and smoothed down my shorts and

The Kitchen Dance

propped up the pillows behind my back. "She says Elise, Prescott's wife, isn't too thrilled about fishing. Elaine thinks we should make her scale the fish you catch, gut them or something. That'll bring her down a notch or two." I stretched out my legs inside the angle created by his arm and body and crossed my ankles modestly.

I tried to read his eyes while Elaine asked me about Roosevelt and if I gave him the container of food. "Yes I did. He was disappointed there were no mushrooms," I told her.

I absently licked my finger and wiped away a smudge of toothpaste from the corner of Allen's mouth. He smiled and I traced the lines framing his soft lips, sculpting their way to his perfectly proportioned nose.

Elaine had to go. The caterers were finishing up in the kitchen and she needed to settle the bill. She left a message for me to relay to Allen.

"Okay, I'll tell him." I spoke softer than I intended. "Goodnight," I practically whispered.

I turned off the phone and looked at Allen who was just sitting there smiling at me. We sat there silently for a moment. "I'm glad you had a 'decent' time." I took a deep breath. "So? Is this side of me as bad as you thought?"

"No. Your friends are okay. Not what I expected. I should thank you for making me go."

There was an uncomfortable pause.

"Elaine told me to tell you Philip said he wished he was able to visit with you more," I tried to get out in one breath and in the right sequence. "Some other time, maybe."

"Some other time."

We both sat on my bed, neither knowing what to do or expect next. "Let's just say good night, Allen." I decided to put an end to the tension.

"Good night." Allen stood up and started for the door. "Ah. Roosevelt said you seemed happier. Is that true?"

I smiled. "Yeah, I think so."

"He also said something about the investigation. Was he talking about Daniel's murder?"

I stopped smiling. "What did he say?"

"Nothing." Allen tapped on the door jamb nervously.

"It was nothing." I tried to talk it down. "It was just a typical homicide investigation. You know, the detectives have their jobs to do."

"I've seen a lot of cop shows," Allen said quietly.

"Something like that," I responded just as quietly. "Well, good night."

"Good night." He slapped on the door jamb with his palm and walked out.

Geri G. Taylor

* * * *

Allen

I had a hard time falling asleep. I could hear Joule tossing in her bed and thought about calling out to her to see if she wanted to talk. It was after two in the morning before I finally drifted off and I was already awake when Joule came out of her bedroom. She was bundled up in her robe. She tried to sneak into the kitchen in order not to wake me up. "I'm awake," I let her know.

"Oh, hey,"

"Hey," I answered back.

I got up and went to the bathroom. Joule fixed coffee. I came back to the kitchen to set up coffee cups and got the cream out of the refrigerator.

"I usually don't get to sleep this late. Roosevelt must be sleeping in, too."

Joule gave some thought to what she just said because she turned to me suddenly with a frightened look.

"I'll go check on him," I offered and ran down the stairs before she had a chance to answer me. I could tell Roosevelt's door was open as I ran down the steps. As I made it around the corner I could see Roosevelt lying on the floor in his doorway. "Joule! Call 911!" I called back to her.

But Joule was just a few steps behind me. "What's wrong with him?" She ran and grabbed the portable phone and pressed the numbers. "Is he breathing?"

I checked Roosevelt for signs of life. I could not feel his heart beat or feel him breathing.

When Joule reached us, I took the phone from her as she knelt down and cradled Roosevelt's head in her lap. She cried while she rocked him, stroked his head and held his hand. I didn't know what to say as I waited for the operator for what seemed like several minutes. When the man answered, "911. What is your emergency?" I told him about Roosevelt and listened to the instructions of the 911 operator. He told me to stay on the line.

"Is he dead?" Joule looked up at me desperately.

"I think so," I answered softly, trying to calm her down.

"He's still warm, Allen." She pleaded with me like it would make a difference.

"I know. It hasn't been long." I put my hand on her back. Her body shivered a little under my hand like a horse shaking off a fly. I pressed my hand harder against her skin. I was not going to let her brush me off that easily.

* * * *

The Kitchen Dance

Joule

It was just like when Daniel died. The warehouse even smelled the same. Clean. Daniel always liked the warehouse clean. I made the biggest mess cutting wood and trimming fabric. Daniel would fuss about the sawdust and scraps covering the warehouse floor. Everything was clean now. Just the way he liked it.

I cradled the head of my husband in my lap. "But he's still so warm." I denied it then, the way I was denying it now.

"I know, baby. But he's gone now. He's gone." Roosevelt's voice hummed in its low tone like an angel over my shoulder. Daniel was gone, and now, so was Roosevelt.

I cradled Roosevelt with what felt like a catatonic expression on my face. I could not feel any signs of grief creasing my forehead or pulling lines around my mouth. I continued to hold him and rocked him slowly. Allen sat on the lower step, his warm hand pressed against my shoulder with the phone in his other hand. We waited for the ambulance. It would be a long day.

* * * *

Joule

I was sitting on my bed when Allen brought me a cup of coffee. I took a sip. It was in the carafe for some time and tasted old and bitter. "Thank you, Allen. I'm glad you're here." I took another sip of my coffee then opened an address book. "I've already called Elaine. She's on her way over," I told him. "I've got a lot to do today. I don't want you to feel lost in the shuffle."

"Don't worry about me. I'm here for you."

That was something I needed to hear.

Within the hour the loft apartment was filled with mourners including Anna, who was Roosevelt's daughter, and the reverend Louis Giddings from their church. John and Gail brought some pies over from the diner and stayed a few minutes before getting back to work. A few of the homeless people Roosevelt and I met, including the man I recognized from that time I saw him urinating in the alley, were helping themselves to the buffet set up in my living room. They mingled with some of my friends from work who stopped in to offer their condolences. I was, at times, overwhelmed by the colors, smells, and the hum of voices filling my stark white intimate space.

I saw Elaine weaving through the group to find me sitting with Roosevelt's son, Benjamin, who had just arrived. She spoke to Allen, who was sitting on the back of the sofa behind me.

"Such a nice turn out," Elaine commented out of habit more than sincerity, "Roosevelt had many friends."

I introduced Elaine to Benjamin. "Joule, I want you to come to my house for a couple of days," Elaine offered after greeting Benjamin. "Let me get some of your things together."

I looked up at Allen who nodded his approval. "I'll be at the cabin," he assured me.

"Okay." Anna and Benjamin would be handling the funeral services and the wake would be in Anna's home. "Allen?" I looked back at him.

"What?" He rested his hand on my shoulder gently, almost tentatively.

"Take my cell phone in case I need to call you."

"Okay."

"And you should call your kids." He never asked to use my phone. I always had to offer. I wished he were comfortable enough to ask. He always seemed the slightest bit uncomfortable with me, and he could barely touch me. He barely could bring himself to comfort me.

* * * *

It was a week since Roosevelt Graham's death. Anna and Benjamin both came by to gather some of their father's personal belongings. I examined the remaining contents of Roosevelt's room. I filled boxes with his clothing, stopping to fondle the rough wool of his dark tweed overcoat. I already phoned Della. Owen and Randy would be by to pick up the clothes early in the morning. They would sort through the boxes and keep what they thought they could give out and send the rest downtown. I set the boxes outside the warehouse before I went to bed. I hoped to sleep in. Having spent the entire week with Elaine and Philip, I felt I had worn out more than my welcome. I was exhausted and knew Elaine was tired, having spent the time fussing over me every evening after work.

The next day I looked out of the window of my kitchen and noticed the contents of the boxes and Roosevelt's clothing strewn across the sidewalk. I went down the staircase and walked out of the side door. I picked up the remaining scattered clothing and items and stuffed them back in the boxes just as the van arrived. Owen and Randy helped close up the boxes and loaded them up in the van. It was the last traces of Roosevelt.

I made one last stop before leaving town.

Chapter Fourteen

Allen

I was working in the back bedroom of the cabin when I heard her pull up in the Jaguar. Joule entered the cabin with a bag of clothes over one shoulder, her laptop briefcase on the other, and a bag of groceries in each arm.

"Hey! It's just me." She sounded like herself.

Joule set the groceries on the counter, dropped the bag of clothes and her laptop, and then started putting away a few things. I quietly entered the kitchen and started helping with the groceries.

"You doin' alright?" I asked softly.

"I'm doing much better." She seemed sincere. "I brought some work with me and I told Philip I would be back next Monday."

I finished up the groceries and folded up the paper sacks. Joule picked up a loaf of French bread from the bakery and one of those cinnamon breads with the sugar icing.

"Do you mind if I stay here?" I could not believe she would ask to stay in her own place. "Is there anything I can do around here to help you out?" She acted like being at the cabin would cheer her up. She was looking in the refrigerator for what, I don't know. I hadn't been to the store lately and it was looking pretty bare. I hated to tell her things were not too cheerful for me lately, either.

She started making a list. "I can run back into town and pick up a few more things." I went to the sink and rinsed out my coffee cup from breakfast. "Allen?" She got my attention again. "You doin' alright?" She tried to sound like me.

"Tina had her baby," I told her.

"Oh." Joule stopped writing on her list. "So that's what's bothering you?"

I didn't answer. I did not know what to say. I'd not called Joule all week except for once to make sure she was okay. Elaine answered and told me Joule was not back from work. She hadn't called me back. I did not plan on telling Joule the news over the phone anyway. We continued to move around in the small kitchen with Joule looking for what we needed and me cleaning up the mess I left.

"Is everyone okay?" she asked.

"Yes. It's another boy."

"Did you go see her?"

"Yeah, I was there. I went for my parents' sake and the kids. They don't know."

"Was…?"

"He there?" I finished her question. "He was around." I thought about him. He was only there for a few minutes after I got there. Joe, he was young like Tina, skulked around the hospital like a ghost. "He was gone when the baby was born. It's not his first kid. He seemed more annoyed than excited."

"Who was with her when she had the baby?"

"Her mother." I could not have done it. Not for another man's child. "Tina thought it would be better that way. She'd not even told her mother about Joe. Tina was calling him on the phone when I went in to see her."

"What about your kids?"

"They're with my parents."

I thought about how much Jimmy and Tracy had grown. I choked on my words just saying hello. I carried Jimmy around in my arms for close to a half hour before I could set him down. I wanted to spend every minute with the kids, but my father had other plans for me. The first chance he got he pulled me aside for a long talk.

* * * *

"Son, if it's money you need, we can help you out." My Pop handed me a beer and sat with me at the kitchen table. My mother pretended to look busy around the kitchen so she could listen in.

"No thanks, Pop. I've got a job right now. I'm working on a house out at the lake." I drank a few long sips. "I don't have anything lined up after, but I may have some connections to a job in the city."

"Tina told us you lost all your tools. How're you getting work without your tools?"

"The woman I'm working for has the tools." I did not think it was a good time to mention any names.

The Kitchen Dance

"You workin' for a woman then?" he asked.

"Yes, Pop. It's her house on the lake."

"She a single woman?" Pop continued.

"Widow." I did not want to lie to my father.

"Tina told us she got a check from a woman." Apparently Tina invented a good story to tell my father.

"Yes. For the work I did on her lake house. Joule lives in the city."

"You haven't left your wife and kids to run off with some city woman have you?" Pop went straight to the point.

"What else did Tina tell you, Pop?" I asked. I could feel the anger building up but there was no point in lashing out at an old man. I downed my beer.

"Honey," my mother jumped in. "Tina's just been upset with you leaving her with the baby and all."

I wanted to scream at them it wasn't my baby. That I'd had a vasectomy three years ago and Tina'd been sleeping around. She is my children's mother, and although Tracy is wiser than her own grandmother, I didn't think her hearing her mother was a tramp coming out of her father's mouth was what any of them needed to hear right now.

"I didn't have a choice at the time." I crushed the beer can between my palms and threw it in a recycle bin in the laundry room off the kitchen. "I'm doing the best I can for everybody." I kissed my mother's forehead. "I want to read to the kids before they go to bed."

I fell asleep between my son and daughter. They would be going back to school in the morning and I would have to go visit Tina to keep up appearances. I already stopped by the hospital before coming to my parents' home. They would ask. I took some pictures with a cardboard camera Tina had in her room. When I developed the pictures, I'd pulled out the ones of Joe with his new son.

"Why are there no pictures of you with the baby, son?" My mother asked.

"I was taking the pictures, Mom." I tried to cover it up.

* * * *

"You should bring your kids out here sometime." Joule snapped me back to the present.

"I thought about going to see them in the morning. My parents were going to pick them up for the day."

"You should." She looked in the freezer to see what else she needed to add to her grocery list. "I brought chicken for tonight. Do you eat asparagus?"

"Never have, but I'll try it." I picked up Joule's bag. "I'll take this to your room," I offered.

"My room?" She followed me to the new bedroom. "Oh, Allen." She hugged me. "It looks perfect." She unwrapped her arms from around me and went straight to the bare windows and looked out over the lake.

I set the bag on the queen sized bed. "I didn't know what kind of bedding you wanted. I found all this in your parents' room but I couldn't find any drapes or curtains."

"It's great. It will all do for now. I just love it, Allen." Then she stopped smiling. "Does this mean you're finished?"

"I still need to work on the porch off your parents' room and I think I could get the hot tub running for you, again."

"Good." Joule smiled again. "When you get back."

"Yeah." I spoke optimistically. "When I get back."

* * * *

Joule

I turned on the stereo and selected a series of CDs with soft music. Allen was working in the garage and left the job of preparing dinner to me alone. I hoped for his company, but his not so subtle hints convinced me he would rather be alone. I thought a quiet meal and a relaxing evening might improve his mood. It was definitely something I needed.

The past week was overwhelming. Thoughts of Roosevelt hit me like the ocean crashing against a rocky shore and I still felt the suction of its undertow. I poured myself a sip of the wine which I'd chilled for dinner. It was still room temperature. The pungent fruity smell gave the wine an oddly sour taste.

I set the table with the thick white plates Daniel had selected. I hated these dishes. They were too heavy and I had dropped a few when washing them. I always wanted to select something else, a set with some color, like the Fulper pottery my Mother and Grammy collected, but perhaps easier to handle. I returned to the kitchen, the taste of the sour wine still in my mouth. I hoped the wine would go good with the chicken I prepared with rosemary and an orange maple glaze. The so-called wine expert at the Wine Seller told me this Pinot Grigio would be excellent with my meal and should kick up my sauce a notch. I was beginning to doubt it. Then again, my senses were a little off. I contributed this to a week spent crying every night, wreaking havoc on my sinuses.

I pulled out a couple of ice-cold beers from the refrigerator. I popped the top off one with an opener and took them both with me to the garage. Allen was tinkering with his truck. I tempted him with the cold beer. He wiped his hands on a shop rag and accepted it with a simple thanks.

"Dinner is just about ready. You should start cleaning up." I noticed he was dirtier than I expected to find him.

The Kitchen Dance

"Do I have time for a shower?" He twisted the top off the bottle.

"A quick one I suppose." I drank some of my beer. Even *it* tasted funny.

Allen took a long drink of his beer as if he was desperately in need of the refreshment, either that or avoiding conversation.

I returned to my kitchen duties as Allen cleaned up in the bathroom. I could hear the shower running as I checked the chicken. Any longer in the pan and the chicken would be dry. I could serve it up now but it would get cold.

Daniel always hated cold meals. I thought more about Daniel lately and always in the negative. Quick, I thought, think of something nice to say about the dead. The only nice things I could recall of the dearly departed pertained to Roosevelt, Grammy, or my parents.

Allen came from the shower smelling of a masculine soap or deodorant. Either way it was nice. I could not remember how Daniel smelled, and they say the sense of smell triggers the memory. I thought about how Roosevelt smelled of *Barbasol*. I felt my eyes sting and I tried to think of something else. The orange maple glaze smelled tangy and sweet. Everything had a strong smell today. Then I realized why.

Allen came in the dining room just as I was lighting the candles on the table. The wine was chilled. Everything seemed perfect except for a distinct distance between us. There was a certain sadness hanging like a dark fog over us and I could not find a way out of. I served up plates of chicken over pecan rice with bright green steamed asparagus. Allen brought our plates to the table and poured two glasses of wine that sparkled in the candlelight and the glow of the fire in the fireplace. We quietly prepared to eat our dinner, unfolding the napkins and adjusting them in our laps. The setting was romantic yet we could not interact.

We both seemed indifferent to our meals, picking and poking at our plates. I prepared this meal for guests a few times before and was graciously complimented. Now, with the meal half-eaten, we cleared the table. I blew out the candles which burned down significantly. We had spent a long period of time at the table without talking and apparently without eating.

Later, Allen walked into the kitchen where I was washing dishes. His hand brushed against mine when he set a wine glass in the sink. I pulled back my hand but he grabbed it and held it.

"I'm sorry, Joule. I know you wanted this to be special."

"It was just dinner." I watched his reflection in the kitchen window above the sink as I slipped my soapy hand from his. "Whatever all this is, Allen, we didn't do it to each other, did we? Did I hurt you somehow? Did I insult you by helping you?"

"No."

"Then what? Why can't we just be friends and help each other out? Talk to each other."

He stood beside me talking to my reflection. "Why am I still here?"

The question hit me hard. Did he mean literally, or was there some deeper reason he was searching for. Was there a deeper reason why I needed him here? "To fix things." Damn it, I hate my eyes! They were filling with tears again. I dried my soapy hands on the sides of my jeans and tried to wipe the tears away with my fingers. The soap residue on my hands stung worse than the tears.

Allen turned me around and took my face in his hands. They were still cool from the wine glasses and my wet soapy hand he held, and I felt them grow warmer against my skin. "I can't fix everything." He kissed me softly on the forehead and for an instant I believed that was all I needed in this world, just the one soft, careful, deliberate brush of his lips against my skin.

Then the dam broke. I was becoming an emotional wreck. I could no longer keep it bottled up or contained. The tears were not the foe I was fighting; it was much deeper, much lower and far too difficult to fight. I wanted to get away from him, to hide from him. He was too close and his hands were too warm.

Then he kissed my lips and I let him. I kissed him back, pulling his lips passionately into mine. His hands left my face and folded around me holding me close, moving me around slowly, turning me, and leaning me against the kitchen counter, then pressing me against the refrigerator. All the time I held him around his waist, my hands moving under his shirt to his back and shoulders and sliding down his spine beneath the waistband of his jeans.

His lips rarely leaving mine, he danced me around the kitchen and down the hall to my new bedroom where we began removing each other's clothing. The evening's sunset cast a dim light through the uncovered windows. Allen laid me down on the bed, kissing me as he pulled at my jeans. He stood up to take his jeans off. His body looked beautiful with the last of the day's light glancing off his skin and teasing his blue eyes. I was suddenly hesitant, as if the break in the flow, the disconnection of his body touching mine, was giving me cause to reconsider.

"Are you okay?" Allen asked me hoarsely as if my last kiss sucked the air from his lungs.

I smiled and shook my head.

Allen sat next to me. He was ready for me but I was not prepared for him. "I'm sorry Allen. I haven't been with anyone since…" I could not bring myself to say his name. "My husband." It sounded strange. "I'm not… you know…I don't have any birth control."

Allen stroked my hair and bent down to kiss my forehead. "It's okay. I had

The Kitchen Dance

a vasectomy."

Suddenly I wanted to shove him back and get far away from him. The words sounded all too familiar. I had a vasectomy. Daniel and I were married a couple of years when he had the procedure done while I was away at a convention without talking to me about it first. My stomach turned at the recollection of his deceit. Daniel told me he could have it reversed when we were ready for children one day. Even though we talked about it before he was murdered, I knew then one day would never come and it never did.

I wanted to shove Allen away as if somehow he shared in Daniel's ploy, but I stopped myself and I let him kiss my face, lips and neck. I pushed the thought of Daniel from my mind and absorbed Allen inside me. He started out slowly, patiently, as if to reassure me, and then continued almost awkwardly until eventually he was making slow, deliberate strokes inside me. I felt sore and tender. He was rubbing against places inside me I'd almost forgotten were there. Apparently he was feeling it too and the intensity finished him off. He braced himself on his elbows but my tender breasts absorbed most of his weight. He caught his breath then rolled us over to our sides where we could look in each other's eyes.

I thought of something funny that I was not sure was appropriate to share under such intimate circumstances. My smirk gave me away.

"What?" Allen smiled back. He was in the perfect position for the sunlight's last peek over the treetops to find its reflection in his eyes.

"I was just thinking. I'm almost too embarrassed to admit just what I was thinking." I blushed. "Okay. I was thinking. You're like my old Bronco."

Allen laughed as if he knew where my thought processes were taking me.

"It took some tinkering to get you started, but once you get going…you're a fun ride."

Chapter Fifteen

Allen

The next morning I joined Joule, who was sitting across the back porch swing wrapped in her favorite quilt. She was looking through envelopes of pictures she had processed. I handed her a cup. She sat up and I joined her on the swing careful not to spill our coffee. We sat quietly for a while looking out at the lake. Then we both took long sips. The chilly morning air was cooling it off quickly. She handed me the pictures she took of me working on the truck, some buildings, and the one I took of Joule with Roosevelt.

"That came out good. Could have used more contrast here." I pointed with my pinky to an area behind Roosevelt. "It'd make Roosevelt stand out better."

She smiled like she was thinking the same. Then she showed me a picture she'd taken of Roosevelt and me sitting in the chairs on the sidewalk by her loft.

"Damn," I said without thinking. I set down my coffee on the porch and held the picture in a way to get better lighting. "Look at my face, all those lines and wrinkles." I knew Roosevelt was a road map of lines but I hadn't realized how old I was getting. "Huh. I sound like an old woman, don't I?"

"On men they're called character lines. On women they're called wrinkles," she corrected me.

"I like this of Roosevelt though. That is all Roosevelt. Look how he's laughing. He did have quite a laugh. All deep inside him like it was just busting to get out." I studied the picture.

"It's just a split second in time. That is what I love about photography. Capturing the moment and knowing what they're worth to me." She was pleased with her work.

The Kitchen Dance

"You're going to be okay here by yourself?" I asked. What had I done?

"Yes. I'll measure for curtains, go see the Fuhrmans, and I brought my laptop. I can get some work done," she assured me.

Walking out of the cabin's front door was like walking out of a different life. I left Joule sitting alone on the back porch that overlooked the beautiful lake. Before I left, I kissed her warm lips. I wanted to stay with her. Sweet, generous, loving Joule. I wanted to fix everything she needed fixing and then stay around for maintenance. I wanted to live in the cabin. Drive a Jaguar. Have another home in the city. Start my own company.

I had walked away from my life before and started a new one. Cheryl saw to that. When I could not pay for the life she built up on credit cards, she had no use for me. I walked away from a life without my first son, my namesake, and created another life of a hardworking man who paid dearly for his choice in a partner. Cheryl remarried and rarely let me see my son while I worked hard to pay off the credit cards she left me with.

Resentment can shut a man down. I resented Cheryl and now I resented the hell out of Tina. Tina, who found another man to give her more children, had no more use for me either. I could walk away from her but not my children. Not again.

Joule was different. She had to be.

The truck wouldn't start.

I went back in the cabin to get the keys to the Jaguar. I called out to Joule but she didn't answer. I walked out to the back and saw Joule down on the pier. I took the stairs down. I still needed to replace some weathered boards. There was this one thing about Joule I noticed. She lived in a world of steep staircases.

* * * *

Joule

What had I done?

I was standing on the pier trying to envision my life a year from now. I tried to imagine myself as a very cosmopolitan woman who had a wild fling with her carpenter. I tried to laugh it off, picturing him as some stud in a pitiful porn video with no attempt at a plot. At the present it was not funny. I crossed a line I thought I was above. I'd had no desire to go there with Barry. I never felt drawn to him sexually. Why was I drawn to Allen? He had nothing, and was nothing I could have imagined I would ever have wanted. He came with baggage, kids and ex-wives, which were too heavy and too awkward for me to handle. I felt in my heart he was truly a kind, caring man. He would do anything for anyone. Maybe having sex with me could have just as easily been something he would do for anyone. Anyone who needed it.

To make matters more thought worthy, I felt the cramps when I woke up and, of course, it was, as I thought, my period. All the symptoms were present: irritable, anxious, a strangely acute sense of smell and taste, and the breast tenderness. I was still just as fertile as I was in my teens. Yet it was looking less hopeful I would ever have a child. I began to cry.

* * * *

Allen

"Joule." I called out to her.

She made quick swipes at her eyes. I realized she'd been crying.

"Hey." She kept her face turned out to the lake.

"The truck won't start. I thought I could use your car to jump it." I swapped the keys from one hand to my other.

"Sure. Do you need some help?" she offered without turning around.

"No. I've got it." I did not know what to do. I was never good with crying women and Joule probably knew it. The last time she cried I had sex with her and there wasn't time for that now. "I don't have to rush off. I could stay a little longer if you want me to."

"No. You'd better go." She would not turn around to face me.

I walked up behind her and wrapped her in my arms and kissed the top of her head. She smelled of a cool morning and I wanted to wrap myself up with her inside that quilt.

Pulling away from her and driving away from her cabin was harder for me than Joule would ever know.

* * * *

I stopped by the trailer to see Tina before I headed for my parents' house. I could hear the baby crying from the front deck. I knocked. I could hear footsteps and the sound of the baby's cries getting louder as Tina came to the door.

"What do you want?" She opened the door but did not ask me to come in. The stale smell of cigarettes, week-old garbage, dirty diapers, and dust wafted from the trailer.

"I just wanted to see how you were doing." I decided to try being nice. "How's the baby?" I asked over the baby's wailing.

"He's just fine." She bounced him in her arms.

"Let me take him." I held out my hands.

The Kitchen Dance

"Here. See if you can shut him up." She thrust him at me and I held him against me.

He was a cute baby, all red from crying, with a head full of dark black hair. He didn't look a thing like Tracy or Jimmy did as babies. They were bald.

"Maybe you should invite me in now," I suggested. "It is a little cold out here for the baby."

"His name is Joey," she hissed at me like a snake.

"Okay, Joey. A little obvious don't you think?"

Tina made a grab for the baby.

I stepped out of her reach. "Take it easy, Tina. See? I've quieted him down." I walked the baby around the living room away from Tina. "I need to ask you a question."

"What?" Tina plopped down in a chair and lit a cigarette.

"What the hell are you doing smoking?" I whispered loudly.

"Is that your question?" She puffed out a cloud of smoke.

"Jesus, Tina, what's gotten into you?" I could not believe what I was seeing.

"Or is that your question?" She tapped the ashes in an overflowing ashtray.

"I need to know if you still have our divorce papers." I patted the baby gently on the back. He was calming down now and gave a little shudder.

"What for?"

"Oh, come on now. You know what for. I would think you would want me to sign them so you and Joe could get married."

"Me and Joe?" she laughed. "Me and Joe. Right! It sounds to me like you're getting anxious to be with that rich bitch girlfriend of yours."

"What are you talking about?" I kept my voice low so I wouldn't upset the baby.

"I know what you're doing, Allen. I know about where you've been staying."

"I never lied to you. I told you, I was staying at her cabin while I worked on it."

Tina went to the kitchen. Dirty dishes from breakfast and dinner from the night before were piled up on the table and in the sink. She pulled a folder from a cabinet above the sink. "Here's your papers," she yelled causing the baby to start up again. "Sign 'em."

I exchanged the papers for the screaming baby. I opened the file and there was Tina's signature dated over six months ago. "I need to look these over first."

"Look them over. Hell, have your rich girlfriend get you a lawyer to look them over. I don't care." She jostled the baby around like a doll in her arm.

125

"But don't think you'll get those kids."

* * * *

I explained everything to my parents sitting at the dining room table while my kids watched a video in the family room. I showed them the divorce papers. Tina wasn't as greedy when she had the papers drawn up as she was acting now. She wanted custody but she arranged for me to take them every other weekend and split the other holidays and Christmas break. Summers; I could get them for six weeks.

"How are you going to pay all this child support?" Pop asked.

"I don't know. I'll do what I can. That's all I can do."

"Honey, I just wish you'd told us sooner," my mother whined.

"Why? What difference would it have made?"

My mother's cheeks looked a little redder.

"Well, Son, I can't say we were proud of your decisions. But at least we know why you left."

"I left to find better paying work, Pop. This town is dead and my family needed the money. I expected Tina to keep it together."

"Tina was just a young girl when you married her, honey." My mother was taking Tina's side.

"She's in her thirties, Mom. She should have grown up by now!" I realized I was getting too loud and I wasn't ready to have to explain things to the kids. "I can't do anything about all that now. What's done is done and I have no one to blame but myself. Now, if you'll excuse me, I want to spend some time with Tracy and Jimmy."

The next day I signed the papers and handed them to Tina's attorney along with the filing fees with some money my parents lent me.

Chapter Sixteen

Joule

I did not know what time Allen would get back on Monday and, when he arrived, I was surprised to see him in such a disoriented condition. He hugged me when I walked out to greet him but it was more out of desperation than the joy of seeing me.

"What happened to you?" I pushed him back to my arm's length and looked him over. He looked almost as bad as the photographs I saw in the police report. "I would say you've been in a scrape but I don't see a mark on you."

"I need to know how you feel about me, Joule."

"Come inside. I'll pour us a glass of wine, or maybe a beer."

"No. No alcohol. I need to know straight up. How forgiving a person are you?" He seemed startled and a little wild-eyed.

I sat on the steps of the front porch not knowing for sure if I wanted to let him in. "What happened?"

"I've lied to you. But, I have fixed it now." He sat on the step beside me but not close to me. "I lied to you about Tina. We weren't divorced. I'd not signed the papers. I've signed them now and her attorney will file them."

I put my face in my hands and braced my elbows on my knees. I could not cry. I was all cried out. I did not feel sad. I felt nothing.

"The other night, I just want you to know that I know you wouldn't do anything like that if you knew," he stammered. "Like with Travis. If you would have known I was still married, you would not have been with me. I should have told you. I'm truly sorry and I know it doesn't mean anything now," he rambled on.

Still nothing. I was speechless. No feelings. Not even the ability to talk. I got up and went inside.

Allen stood at the open door like he needed an invitation to come in.

"For God's sake, Allen, come in and close the door."

He timidly stepped over the threshold and gently closed the door like a thief sneaking in.

"Do you want something to drink?" I knew I could use something non-alcoholic. "How about coffee?" I just needed something in my hands.

"Coffee's fine." He came up to the bar dividing the kitchen from the dining area and sat on a bar stool. "Joule, if I had already signed the papers and I was already divorced and I told you I wanted to keep seeing you, what would you say?"

I let the coffee grinder run its course while I thought. "The same thing I would be saying now that I found out you weren't divorced." I poured the ground coffee in the filter. "I've thought a lot about this while you were gone. I like our relationship." I measured the water. "I'm glad we started out as friends." I poured the water into the coffee maker and turned it on. "We are friends aren't we?"

Allen nodded his head when I looked over at him.

"I like being around you. I really do." I leaned over the bar closer to his face. "Meeting you, especially the way I did, is good for me." I stood back up and looked around the kitchen for something to snack on. "I started thinking about all the things I wanted to do. Plans I never got around to when I was married to Daniel and dreams I've put on hold. After he died, I'd say overall, I've lived my life one day to the next. It was like being on autopilot." I checked all the cabinets. "Do we have any cookies?"

"No." Allen joined me in the kitchen and pulled something from the refrigerator. "But we have cinnamon bread."

I poured two cups of coffee and sliced off some of the cinnamon bread and toasted it. I set everything on a tray and took it out to the sunlit deck where Allen sat in one of the two Adirondack chairs he had moved there with a small table.

"I wanted to have children." I came right out and said it then let it just hang there.

"Well, I've got children I wanted, but can't have," Allen tossed back at me. "Except for every other weekend, split holidays and six weeks in the summer." He took a bite of the cinnamon bread. "And then there is James I don't get to see at all," he said over a cheek full of bread.

I picked at the sugar icing on the top of the loaf and tossed it over the side of the deck. "I'm getting too old anyway." I half laughed. "Other kids will think

I'm their grandmother."

"You know I can't help you there. I'm older than you. Aren't I? How old are you?"

"A lady never tells her age," I reminded him.

"I'm forty-five so you do the math."

"You win." I nodded. "You're older."

"Listen, Joule. I know this sounds pretty crude, but I'm not going to have any more kids. I can barely afford the ones I have. It's not just money. It's commitment. I don't want to be like Joe. He's got two other kids, Tina told me, and didn't marry either of their mothers. I tried to make a family. I must not have what it takes to keep a woman happy. I know it sounds like I can't provide for them. I tried, but it was never enough. I know you've got money and a good job, and could make a nice home for your children with or without the father around. I just didn't want it to be that way with my kids. I wanted to be around for them. Whatever it took. I gave up too easy on James, letting his mother take him away like she did. That's why I didn't want to sign those divorce papers. It was for Tracy and Jimmy."

"Wait a minute. Did I make it sound like I just wanted you around to father a child?"

"No. I guess you could have found just about any man who'd do that for you."

"Seriously, Allen. Do you think I'm one of those women who would go to a sperm bank or something? I don't want to raise a child all by myself. And I wouldn't expect a man to raise someone else's child." I gave quick consideration to my last statement. "But it's good when they do," I added before I stuck my foot any farther in my mouth.

"I just thought you might be one of those modern women who think men aren't necessary."

"Yes, I think I read that somewhere." I pulled my feet up into the Adirondack chair.

"It's getting cold out here. You want to go inside? I could build a fire," Allen offered.

"And then what?"

"We could warm up by it." He spoke each word slowly like he was explaining it to a child.

"And then what?"

"We could keep talking about this or something else."

"And then what?" I whispered as I stood. I gathered up the dishes on the tray and took them to the kitchen. Allen followed me grabbing an armload of wood from the rack before coming inside.

"Don't start something you don't plan to finish." He tossed the wood roughly in the fireplace and fussed over the lighter.

"Allen." I took the lighter and started the fire. "There's plenty of room in the cabin for both of us." I brushed back a strand of his soft brown hair traced with silver and kissed him on his forehead. "We can always go back to being friends and take it from there."

* * * *

I returned to the loft before the week's end to avoid any more of the tension building between Allen and me; physical tension. We were getting along splendidly. We spent the warmer part of the days fishing or walking. We shopped in town at the grocery or hardware store together and prepared our meals together. But the sex still haunted us. He never brought it up. I longed to be embraced in his warm arms. He warmed me instead with his stories about his children. I hoped I would get to meet them.

The loft was cold and empty. Roosevelt gave the place a heartbeat; Allen the breath. Now, when I returned home, there was nothing but the hollow sound of the stereo to fill the quiet. The weather was growing warmer, yet the loft felt colder. I wanted my life to be warm again. I called Allen.

"I miss you," I declared when he answered my cell phone.

"You just left." Allen laughed.

"It's not the same here without you and Roosevelt."

We talked for hours and then Allen said, "Remember those plans you put aside, Joule? Its time you got them going. I want to help you get started."

* * * *

The next day, Allen parked his old truck in the alley beside the garage door of the warehouse and was waiting for me when I got back from work. I pressed the remote opener and drove the car inside, almost forgetting to turn off the Jag's engine before I jumped out. I wrapped my arms around him and kissed his lips that were stretched tightly over his smile. He could barely stop grinning long enough to kiss me back. He backed me against the wall control and pressed the button closing the overhead door.

We closed up the garage and climbed in the elevator kissing and undressing the entire time. Allen fumbled with the gates while I unbuckled his belt and slid his pants down to his knees. He turned around and pulled off my blouse while trying to press the control button. After a couple of failed attempts I turned around and pushed the button while he tried to unhook my bra. He kissed my back and the back of my neck and cupped my breast, filling his open hand. As the elevator began its creaky assent, Allen slipped his hand up my

The Kitchen Dance

skirt and shimmied down my panties. He pushed himself at me from the rear and I bent my knees to let him inside. I wanted to scream it felt so wonderful, instead, I moaned and sucked in a deep breath through my teeth. I clung to the oak slats of the gate as the elevator reached the loft. It was like something from a scene in a nasty movie except we were experiencing it and it was fabulous. The elevator reached its destination but we had not.

Allen pulled away from me and attempted to open the gate but I stopped him. It started here and I wanted it to finish here. I slid my panties completely off. He pressed my naked back against the elevator's cold metal wall but the heat of his body against mine quickly compensated for it. He entered me again and his body fit smoothly against mine. He had minimal chest hair. His back felt smooth and firm beneath my fingertips. He teased me, and then kissed me passionately until his concentration strayed and he braced us against the wall. I felt him pulsing inside me and a strange feeling, as if ants were scurrying under my skin, caused me to giggle.

Allen and I gasped for air as if we ran the steps to the loft instead of taking the elevator. We did not consider our next move. Even though I wanted to just fall in a heap on the elevator floor, the cold hard metal surface was none too welcoming. We gathered our clothes and headed for the shower.

We spent the next couple of hours exploring every inch of each other's bodies, and telling stories of scars, like two curious kids playing doctor or a game of show and tell.

Hunger finally tempted us out of bed and we cooked dinner in the nude, rubbing and caressing each other each time we passed. I found a few frozen entrees in the freezer and heated them in the microwave. I selected a chicken breast with pasta, chicken piccatta, and a pot roast with whipped potatoes. We worked up such an appetite. I had a Zinfandel from Australia chilling in the fridge that would have to do.

Allen turned on some music while I placed the heated meals on a tray and set our dinner on the ottoman. We sat together on the sofa and ate with our fingers. It was the most sensual meal I ever experienced and even the frozen dishes, usually more filling than they were flavorful, had a wonderful taste.

"Did you get enough to eat?" I ran my finger around the edge of the microwaveable container and tempted Allen to suck off the creamy gravy.

"Mmmm." His lips closed around my finger and pulled away the sauce. "We could always go to the diner for some pie."

"Like this?" I laughed gesturing to our naked bodies. "That would certainly get John out of his kitchen."

"Do they deliver?" Allen asked.

"I don't know. Maybe." I laughed. "Can you imagine Gail's face if you answered the door like that?"

"I bet she'd give me a lot better service from now on." He smiled proudly.

"Only if you gave her a big tip." I cocked my brow and jumped from the sofa before he could grab me.

"Where are you going?" he protested.

"To look up the number." I pulled the phonebook from the kitchen drawer and thumbed through the white pages.

"You're kidding, aren't you?" Allen asked seriously.

"I'll answer the door," I answered seriously.

"I don't think so."

"I'll put on a robe!" I placed the call. "Is this Gail? Carrie, hi, this is Joule Dalton. Do you deliver?" I placed my hand over the handset. "They don't," I told Allen. "Do you still want pie?"

He nodded.

"What kind of pie do you have left?" I asked Carrie, Gail's teenaged daughter who helped her out a few nights a week. "They have chocolate cream," I drawled and nodded my head yes encouraging Allen to agree.

He did.

"Save me a couple of pieces. We'll be right over." I hung up the phone and went to the sofa where Allen was sitting back with his head sunk back in the soft sofa cushion. "Come on." I offered my hand to help him up. "Gail's chocolate cream pie is worth getting dressed for."

"It better be." Allen stood up and wrapped his arms around me. His face smelled of roast and grilled chicken. I kissed him, tasting the salty gravy. He pawed at my naked body and I slithered away.

"I want pie," I whined teasingly.

"Oh, I'll give you your dessert." He pushed me playfully into the bedroom and blocked the bedroom door.

"Never stand between a woman and her chocolate!" I picked up his jeans from the floor and tossed them at him. "But when we get back…"

* * * *

Allen

The day drug on when Joule was at work. I had a strange idea of what Tina went through when I was away for so long. I missed Roosevelt now more than ever. I found his chairs in the warehouse and set them up on the sidewalk along the busy street. I sat in one and watched the people go by. An older woman with a scruffy dog walked by pulling a thin cart with what at first I thought was all her worldly possessions. As she passed I noticed she was just carrying her

The Kitchen Dance

shopping and some bread from a bakery thrift store about a block from Joule's warehouse.

A tall, heavyset black man, who wheezed when he walked, crossed the street and stood over me, blocking the sun like a building. "D 'you know Roosevelt Graham?"

"Yeah." I looked up at him and he stepped aside, causing me to squint as the sun shone in my eyes. "Have a seat." I offered him the other folded chair.

The folding chair creaked as the big man settled in. How it did not collapse under him, I don't know. We introduced ourselves and started talking about Roosevelt but the topic quickly changed to overpaid sports stars, politics, his health, the history of all the surrounding buildings, and ended up about our families. I could see why Roosevelt spent his days here. It was already past lunch. I would have offered the old man a meal at John's but I was still short on cash. I told him I needed to go but I could leave the chairs. He declined and I helped him stand and watched him as he struggled with each step and breath to cross the road. I gathered up the chairs and returned to the loft.

I found some cheese and thinly sliced deli style roast beef in Joule's refrigerator and made myself a sandwich. I would not be able to hang out here all week. I had work to do back at the cabin and there wasn't much to do around the loft. I found the key to Roosevelt's apartment in the thin table by the entry door and I took my sandwich down to his apartment. Joule did not have a television in her loft and I thought it would help pass the time.

When Joule finally got home, I told her I would be heading back to the cabin. I knew she would be disappointed.

She had stopped by a restaurant on her way home for takeout and had bags to hand me when I took the elevator down to greet her. I took both of the bags and she wrapped her arms around my waist and kissed me. "This is nice to come home to," she added making my decision to leave even more difficult.

"Shall I get naked or are we eating at the table?" I called back to the bathroom as I stood in the kitchen removing the containers of food from their bags.

"The table!" Joule laughed.

I dumped the salads into two white bowls arranging the lettuce and fixings to look a little less dumped.

Joule came into the kitchen. She had changed from her suit into a pair of silky pajama pants and a matching loose-fitting top that clearly showed she was not wearing a bra. She spooned out fettuccini noodles with a thick creamy Alfredo sauce and arranged sliced fried veal with a marinara sauce on one of the white plates. "I hope you like veal." She reheated the plate in the microwave. "I called home to ask but you didn't answer."

"I was out most of the morning," I answered as I poured two glasses of water.

"What were you doing?" She prepared another plate.

"Being Roosevelt."

"What does that entail?" she said with a laugh.

"I hung out on the sidewalk and talked to this big black guy who was fond of Roosevelt," I told her.

"Was it Lou?" She sucked some of the white sauce from finger.

"Yeah." I took her hand and licked a smear of white sauce from her thumb. "It was Lou."

The microwave beeped and she pulled back her hand to take out the dish and replace it with the other. "You were bored weren't you?" She took the heated plate to the table. She found the lighter in a drawer and lit the candles on the table.

I brought the salads to the table. "I have work I could finish at the cabin."

"Hey. I know how quiet it gets around here." She brought the other plate to the table. "But I have an idea. Could you get the silverware?"

I went back to the kitchen and found some silverware in the dishwasher and brought it back to the table. "What was your idea?" I asked as I sat down.

"I forgot the bread!" Joule jumped up and found the bread wrapped in foil in one of the bags. She held the foil package against her cheek. "Still warm." She came back to her seat. "You need a project." She opened the foil and offered me a roll soaked with a garlic butter and parsley spread.

"What did you have in mind?" I took a bite of the roll. It was soft and chewy.

"Why don't you fix up your camper? You can have any of the fabric in the warehouse and there is foam piled up in the back. See if any of it will work. I can help you with the sewing when I get home."

I liked the idea and it would keep me busy during the week. "Sure." I tried to swirl a pile of noodles around the fork.

"You don't sound too thrilled." Joule cut off a piece of veal.

"I just haven't worked with fabric before." I stuffed the dripping noodles in my mouth. "This is good," I managed to muffle as I pointed at the plate. "Da Vinci's?"

"No. The Italian House. It's a little place just a few blocks from here."

"I'm sure you know everyone who works there's name."

"I try to. It's just common courtesy."

"I agree." I ate another bite of the veal.

* * * *

The Kitchen Dance

The next part of the evening was spent rolling out bolts of fabric, instead of rolling around in bed as I'd hoped. We found a pattern I thought would work but Joule was looking for something more durable. She found a wild pattern, originally meant for a slipcover for a sofa she designed for a client. "I'm sure she's changed her mind by now." Joule rolled out the bolt of fabric across her work table. "It's perfect."
"The kids will love it!" I agreed once I saw it all opened up.
"Yes." Joule suddenly seemed a little sad. "I'm sure they will."
I thought I knew why. "Joule. I can't wait for you to meet my kids."
She smiled and rolled up the fabric.
We sorted through the foam next and found some pieces that would work.

* * * *

Joule sat on her bed with her knees pulled up to support her laptop and in a matter of minutes designed a pattern for me to go by. I snuggled up to her neck and she pushed me away, laughing, and took her laptop to her printer where she printed out the scaled down version of the patterns. Tomorrow would not be dull, spent cutting out the fabric and foam to Joule's specifications. She would show me how to use her fancy sewing machine after work. For now, I wanted to show her my gratitude.

Joule handed me the patterns and I took them from her and set them on the kitchen counter. She went to the kitchen to pour herself a glass of water. I slid my hands around her waist and looked at our reflections in the kitchen window. She tipped her glass and looked into the reflection of my eyes over her glass. I slid my hands up her silky shirt and she laughed, almost choking on the water. She set down the glass, turned around and wiped the water from her mouth on the hem of my shirt then rubbed her cool hands against my bare stomach.

I ran my hands through her hair and kissed her cool wet mouth. I kissed her lips and sucked on her tongue until it was warm again. Her skin was as silky as her pajamas and her breasts fit perfectly in my hands. I pulled her from the kitchen and led her to the bedroom. She turned off the lamp by her bed but her room still glowed softly from the small lights in the ceiling.

She stepped out of her pajama bottoms while I stripped down to nothing. She climbed beneath the covers and waited for me to join her.

"Take off your shirt." I slid in beside her.
"No," she teased.
"Come on." I tugged at the shirt but she held it down.
"No," she still teased.
I gave her a curious look. "Okay. Am I going to have to work for this or something?"

"No. It's just a little more erotic when there is something you can't have." She straddled my legs and slipped me into her wet, warm box. She moved up and down, slowly pulling at me, creating suction, urging my climax. I felt the rim of my penis bumping against I don't know what, but I was willing to do some investigating. Her body moved like a belly dancer's, and I reached for her shirt, but she pushed my hands away.

I couldn't bear it any longer. I did not know if I wanted to stop her or make her go faster. Hanging on the edge was a struggle and her shirt just had to come off. I made another attempt to at least slide my hands up and grasp her breast but she would have none of that. She knew how to play and I was having a blast. I would never have thought Joule, who seemed so businesslike when need be and laid back at the cabin, had a bit of a wild side. It was time for the tables to turn. I was going to get her out of that shirt. I pulled up on my arms and flipped her over and fought to get her shirt off like a drowning man fighting to swim. She was just as interested in getting me back inside her and wrapped her legs around me and squeezed her thighs together pulling me closer to her. Damn, she was strong. She wasn't going to get me inside her until she gave up that shirt. Two could play at that game.

We tussled across her big bed, throwing the white sheets and comforter on the floor. "I'm getting too old for this." I laid my head against her chest and panted like a dog after failing to pull her shirt off.

"Poor, sweet baby." She ran her fingernails lightly over my scalp. "Are you too tired to finish?"

"Maybe if you take off your shirt." I kept my cheek against her breast. It was the closest she let me get to them since we started this.

"No," she kept teasing.

"Okay. Let's compromise." I propped up on my elbows. "Let me just stick one hand up your shirt for one minute."

"See? I knew you would get obsessed." She laughed at me.

"One minute," I pleaded and kissed her playfully.

She was stubborn and calmly combed her fingers through my hair, gently scratching her nails against my scalp until I no longer felt like playing. Instead, I just wanted to consume her. I felt my heartbeat pounding against my chest and I knew she could feel it against her stomach. I kissed her again as she twisted my hair in her fingers and pulled my face into hers. My mouth covered hers and my fingers searched for her wet heat. I slid back inside her and pulled her leg up to thrust in deeper. She cried out in gasps, sucking at my lips, pleading for me to kiss her. I played her game and kept my lips just inches from hers.

I watched as her green eyes glinted in the soft lighting. Joule knew her stuff. The little bit of lighting in her bedroom made her skin glow against the white bedding that now looked pale pink. Her face was flushed with passion and I wanted to help her let go. I felt my cum building up and I buried my face against her neck and felt her body rise up to meet me and we both let go together.

She raked her fingers through my hair again as I breathed against her neck. "If I'd asked you to go to bed with me the night we met, what would you have done?" she asked.

I laughed and propped myself back up on my elbows to look at her. She looked serious. "You really wanted to sleep with me the night we met?"

"If I had?"

"Joule. Honestly, I doubt I had the strength. But thank you anyway."

"Just to let you know, I did not have a secret agenda to sleep with you that night. Far from it." I felt her body jerking under me with a laugh. "But the day I saw you on the pier all cleaned up. That did something for me then and I'm glad we're here now. Regardless of where this goes, I'm just glad to be right here, right now."

"I remember when you came back to the cabin that day." I caught my breath, "Thinking something like I wished I knew you longer like a month, or year and we were ready for something like this."

* * * *

By Saturday morning, we were ready to take the camper on the road. I ordered a new table from the internet but did not expect it for another week. I patched a hole in the floor and found a remnant of linoleum at a building supply store and installed it while Joule was at work. I stopped by the market and picked up some basic supplies and standard camping food. I packed the camper and was ready to go by the time Joule finished her coffee.

We took the camper and headed south in search of warmer weather and drove as long as the day would allow. I set up the camper before dark and built a fire inside the metal ring provided by the campground. Joule covered the old wooden picnic table with a cloth and set out candles to dine by. It was a bit fancy for chili dogs and chips but Joule knew how to make any meal special. We sat in a pair of fabric chairs Joule had picked up on her way home and drank beer around the fire pit until the flames died down.

Inside the camper was pretty small for two adults. I forgot what it felt like having someone else in there with me. I squeezed past her to wash my face and hands in the little kitchen sink.

"I smell like smoke." She pulled a handful of her hair to her nose and sniffed. "I could use a shower."

I sniffed the back of her exposed neck and smelled the woody smell of a campfire and it excited me. I pressed my hardness against her soft round butt and took a hold of her handful of hair. Pulling her head back I kissed neck and jaw line then turned her face to mine and found her mouth with my lips and tongue. She twisted her body to face me and tried to brace herself against the narrow counter. She tossed back her head and banged it against the upper cabinet.

"Oh, poor baby." I cooed and rubbed the back of her head. I kissed her again, harder this time, and tugged at her jeans. She pushed me away to get at my snap and zipper and I stumbled back into one of the dinette bench seats. With only a couple feet of floor between the seats, I managed to struggle out of my pants while Joule attempted to undress in what little space was left in the camper. I pulled her down straddling my lap but her head brushed against the bottom of an overhead storage cabinet. I slid down on the bench until my knees banged against the opposite bench as Joule tried not to hit the top of her head on her up down motions. It was like making love in the back of a Volkswagen but somehow we managed laughing, kissing, and rocking the camper against the uneven ground. She slowed the swaying of her hips, pulling at my member in slow steady tugs, the tight muscles inside her gripping me and coaxing me to come. I could not wait for her. It was all too much. Being in my own place, even though it was just a camper, sitting by a fire and talking, touching, being close, or maybe it was the beer, but I quickly erupted in a satisfying release.

"Well the good thing about small places," Joule struggled to keep me inside her as she reached across the camper for a roll of paper towels on the small countertop, "is that everything is handy." She tore off a couple of towels and attempted to gracefully dismount me without making a mess. "I need a shower." She untangled herself from our cramped space and confronted the tiny bathroom.

"Let me help you with that." I slid the portable toilet from the bathroom and attached a hose with a shower head to the bathroom sink. The small water heater did not offer much of a warm shower so we washed off together, twisting and turning like eels in a milk carton, until the water turned cold. I kissed her cool clean lips, neck, and tried to bend down to her breast, but the narrow walls closed in on us and she playfully pushed me out the door. There was even less space with the toilet in the middle of the camper living area so I sat on it while I dried off and let Joule have the shower. We climbed up in the newly upholstered mattress above the cab and Joule looked up at the ceiling just a few inches from her nose and announced she was claustrophobic. Without the table I could not make up another bed but she managed to curl up on the dinette cushions spread out on the floor.

The Kitchen Dance

"You're not a camper are you?" I asked her from my bed.

"I'm more of a cabin by the lake kind of girl," she admitted. "I have enjoyed it up to this point."

"But you did such a good job with the cushions and drapes," I tried to encourage her.

"My job is to imagine what it is like to live in the space, not necessarily to live in the space."

"I was looking forward to cuddling up with you and sleeping together." I rolled over on my side. "Tina never went camping with me either. I used to take the kids. Tracy would sleep down there and I would keep Jimmy penned in up here."

"It's a good space for kids. Most kids like little spaces," Joule added.

* * * *

The wind picked up and a storm blew in around three thirty, waking us both up to the rocking and the pounding of raindrops, which sounded like rocks hitting the aluminum roof of the camper.

Joule got up to go to the bathroom and found it just as cramped as being in the bed. The rain and the beer made me have to go too. I climbed down from the loft bed and waited for Joule. She jumped when she walked out of the bathroom, startled to find me standing there. When I came out of the bathroom she was sitting at the dinette watching the rain coming down outside the tiny window.

"Do you think you'll be able to get back to sleep?" I sat down beside her.

"I'm sorry." She leaned forward and wrapped her arms around me. "I didn't want to let you down."

"You're not letting me down. I don't expect you to like everything I like. I hope you don't expect the same from me." The lightning flashed and I felt her flinch. I pulled her closer to me. "I camp because I don't have a lake house and this was a way for my kids and me to get away." The thunder boomed and shook the little camper.

"How did you live in here?" Joule asked.

"It was better than living on the street."

Chapter Seventeen

Joule

    Allen kept me warm the last of the winter days. Then it was spring and the change of the season brought changes in our relationship.
    The cabin was different. The front two bedrooms were freshly painted and there was colorful new bedding. Allen would stay in the new master bedroom to be closer to his children when they came to visit. I moved to my parents' room. I sat at my father's roll top desk, shutting down my laptop. On top of the desk was the framed photo of Roosevelt and Allen I took in front of the warehouse. I heard Allen's truck bumping up the driveway. My heart started pounding with excitement. I met them at the door.
    Tracy rolled out of the truck first, and looked up at the cabin as if her father crossed a drawbridge into a castle. Her face lit up with excitement and held the glow when her eyes met mine. Not yet in her teens Tracy was still wise for her years. She sized me up quickly and smiled at me. I smiled back.
    Jimmy jumped out of the truck on his father's side and immediately took to the ground running. Allen put off telling them about us until his divorce was final. He simply told his children we were good friends and shared my cabin on the lake on weekends. Allen and I refrained from any affection towards each other even though the thought of Allen with his children made me want him more. He smiled in a completely different and wonderful way when he talked about Tracy and Jimmy and I adored him for it.
    "Hold up, Jimmy," Allen called out to the blur dashing past me. Jimmy was bursting with excitement to be here. Allen jogged by, trying to catch him before he darted around the cabin to the lake.
    "We can meet them in the back. I'm Joule," I told Tracy.
    "Yes Ma'am. Daddy told me. Like a unit of energy."

The Kitchen Dance

I guided her in and showed her straight to the room we prepared for her.

"It's a lot bigger than my other room." She dropped her overnight bag on the bed and ran her hands over the fuchsia, gray, bright yellow and green floral bedspread.

"This was my room," I told her. "Your Daddy picked out the bedding. What do you think?"

"He did? It's perfect." She seemed genuinely pleased.

"The room across the hall from the bathroom my family used for guests but your Daddy and I dressed it up special for Jimmy." I stepped back in the hall to allow her to go first.

She looked in the room with the brightly colored race cars and checkered flag design on the bedspread. "He'll love this."

I took her back to the master bedroom across the hall from hers. "My Grammy stayed in this room when I was growing up. Your father helped remodel it." I showed her Allen's room. The queen bed was replaced with a king sized bed. Rich gold raw silk fabric with rusty reds and deep gray accents draped the window with a matching duvet cover and decorative pillows.

Tracy looked around with amazement. "This looks just like a magazine cover." She ran her hand along the bumpy silk bedding. "I can't see Daddy sleeping in a bed like this. It's fancy. You must be very rich."

"To tell you the truth, Tracy, I bought the fabric on clearance and I sewed everything myself." We looked through one of the ceiling to floor windows facing the open lake where Jimmy already made it down the staircase and was standing on the pier with Allen.

"We're up so high, just like a tower or something." Tracy was almost as tall as me with long thin legs and arms. Her brown hair was wavy like her father's and cut just below her shoulders. Her heart shaped face and widow's peak were also like her father's and she had a scattering of freckles across her nose and cheeks. Her eyes were more almond-shaped than Allen's and a warm green instead of his light blue. She had her father's smile except with slightly crooked teeth.

"Do you want to go down to the lake with your Daddy?" I asked her.

"No. I want to look around here first if that's okay."

"Do you want the guided tour, or do you want to explore on your own?" I asked her.

"Can I? Would it be all right?"

"Sure. Take your time. I will be down by the lake with Jimmy and your Daddy."

Jimmy was throwing rocks in the lake from the edge of the water when I came down to meet him.

"Hey, Jimmy." Allen tapped him on the shoulder. "This is Joule."

Jimmy turned and ran to me throwing his arms around my waist in a big wet-handed hug. I was surprised at first, but instinctively hugged him back, placing my one hand on his back and the other on his dark blonde tangle of hair. He looked up at me with his round face, big dark chambray blue eyes fringed with long dark lashes and a smile missing several teeth. "Are you throwing all my rocks in the water?" I teased.

"Can we go fishing? Daddy said we could go out in a boat," Jimmy started rattling on.

"Mr. Fuhrman told me we could use his boat," Allen told me.

"That sounds great. Would you like to eat some lunch first?"

"Could you just pack up something?" Jimmy squinted up at me. "We could take it on the boat. I like peanut butter and honey sandwiches. Can you make me one of those?"

"Oh, sure I can. Looks like you've got yourself a fisherman." I nodded to Allen.

Tracy was coming out of my room when we came back in the cabin.

"Now, Tracy. That's Joule's end of the house. Let her have her privacy." Allen warned her.

"It's okay, Allen, I told her she could look around." I looked over at Tracy who was discovering the magic of the pit group. "What would you like for lunch?"

"I'll have whatever you're having." She looked back at me over from her sunken position in the sofa.

"She's a lot better about all this than I thought she would be," I told Allen as we walked the kids down to the Fuhrman's house. "Either that, or she's playing me."

"Tracy's always been a sweet girl. It's just lately she's growing up too fast. I get sick with worry about her."

"You're her father. You're supposed to worry."

We took out the Fuhrman's boat for a few hours where we ate a picnic lunch and fished. Tracy brought a book to read, but spent most of the time talking to me, telling me about her friends, and a boy she had a crush on.

Jimmy had plenty to say, and monopolized most of the conversation with a variety of topics, from animated characters on video games to zoo animals. He was a handful for two adults and big sister. I could not imagine what he must be like at home with Tina.

Mrs. Fuhrman baked a chocolate cake with peanut butter icing for us when we returned the boat. After the refreshments, Mr. Fuhrman took Jimmy down to his den but, after ten minutes of asking him not to touch anything, the visit was

The Kitchen Dance

cut short.

Jimmy was determined to go swimming off the pier even though the water was freezing. Allen finally gave in and let him jump in. It lasted a little longer than his visit to Mr. Fuhrman's den but still was not enough to wear him down.

Our last attempt to calm him down before bedtime involved lighting a fire in the fireplace even though the spring nights were getting a bit too warm for it. I turned up the air conditioner to compensate for the excess warmth. We all piled up in the pit group and, although it took almost an hour of talking and story reading, he was finally out.

Tracy wanted to stay up and watch the fire die down the same way I always did. I found her the next morning asleep in the pit group. I let her sleep while I started the coffee. After a big breakfast of eggs, bacon, and cinnamon bread, Allen drove the kids back to his parents' house for the time being. It was easier for Allen having established a meeting place versus seeing Tina. He would take his children to church with his parents and stay for lunch before coming back to the cabin.

It was the same routine every other weekend until school was out. We were looking forward to having them around for the summer. We made so many plans.

* * * *

I sat in the dining room to finish going through a box of recently collected photographs and mementos. I sorted through various photographs of the before and after of the renovations. I set aside a photo of Allen posting a "For Sale" sign on the warehouse and pulled out several photos of Allen taking Jimmy for a tractor ride while clearing land at the cabin for the workshop expansion.

I turned on some music and spread more photos out to fill the pages of an unfinished scrapbook. I looked through the pages I had completed. One page was a group of photos of me with the kids, dragging limbs to a debris pile and working in a flower bed. Jimmy's crayon rubbings of leaves and Tracy's drawings of flowers decorated the page. Another page featured the Fuhrmans, who'd already become honorary grandparents to Allen's kids, with everyone fishing off their boat. Elaine, Philip, even the Prescotts made it in the scrapbook when they came up with their families for a fish fry one weekend while Allen's kids were here. A favorite page of mine included a picture of Allen, his children, and even I got to be in the picture when Mr. Davidson offered to take a picture of us with his stock boy dressed as the Easter Bunny. I added the hand drawn Easter card Jimmy made for me at Sunday school. Another page showed Jimmy getting a haircut by one of the local barbers and a beautiful picture I took of Tracy by the lake. I sent her home with several copies to give to her mother, her grandparents, her friends, and perhaps even the boy she liked.

I was about to toss some of the culled photographs in a box. I stopped to look at the assortment of photographs from publicity pictures taken at a party hosted by my firm for the newspaper's society page. Allen was wearing a tailored suit. I refused to tell him how much it cost. Deeper in the stack I came across Allen in a sweat stained t-shirt and jeans beginning construction on the new workshop. The phone rang, dissolving my memories. I answered it and my blissful moment was soon ended. With great disappointment I listened to the caller. I walked out of the cabin towards the workshop and flagged down Allen, who was using a sander against some unfinished furniture pieces.

"It's for you." I pointed to the phone in my other hand. "It's Tina."

* * * *

Allen

Joule reluctantly handed me the phone. She walked away and started pulling weeds from the flower beds while I took the call.

"Tina?" She never called me. If she left a message for me it was always left with my mother to pass it on. I knew this could not be good.

"Joe's left me." Tina sobbed on the phone like I was her old friend instead of her ex-husband.

"I'm sorry to hear that." But I wasn't.

"I can't do this. I can't handle these kids," she wailed.

"Do you want me to come get Jimmy and Tracy?" I knew she could use a break from Jimmy, but I doubted she would let Tracy go. Tracy could help her with the baby.

"NO! They still have school for two more weeks. I need you here, Allen. I need to talk to you. Please, come help me. I need you. Your kids need you." Joule looked back at me and I knew she could tell by my face the conversation was not going well.

"And what happens when Joe decides to come back?"

"He's not coming back! He—I told him to get out." Her crying turned to sobs and she coughed and tried to catch her breath. I could hear a funny sound over the line. Then she blew out another breath.

"Tina? Are you still smoking?" I asked.

"I'm trying to quit." I could hear her inhale again. "I only smoke outside." I could hear her exhale.

"I can't have you smoking around my kids, Tina. You know I don't like it."

"I know. I know." Tina's mood changed from sadness to anger. "Look,

The Kitchen Dance

Allen. I need you here to help me with your kids. What I don't need is you here to tell me what to do."

"Tina. I know it's hard for you to manage three kids. Why don't I call my mother to see if she and Pop could take Jimmy? They can get him to school in the mornings."

"Nobody's taking my babies from me." I could tell her hysterics were coming back.

"I'm not talking about her taking him forever, just until you feel better," I suggested.

"I feel just fine! Do you hear me?" she yelled. She was probably sitting on the front deck and most of the people in the trailer park could hear her. "I just can't be doing everything for these kids! Your kids need you, Allen. What kind of father are you? You'd rather lay up with your rich bitch than take care of your own kids."

"Tina, I'm not going to argue with you over the phone about priorities." I could see for my kids' sake I needed to go there and calm her down. "I need to take care of a few things here. I should be there by this evening." I hung up without saying good-bye.

I walked over to the cabin's front porch and stood by the steps where Joule was weeding.

"Tina's boyfriend has left her." I sat down on the steps. "I guess you know she's pretty upset."

Joule did not reply, instead, she looked up at me squinting in the sun as she studied my face.

"She wants me to come." I avoided eye contact. "She needs some help with the kids."

Joule returned to weeding. "Are you going to bring the kids here?"

"Not until next weekend. They're still in school."

"Maybe this summer they can stay here with us most of the time."

"Maybe." I stood up feeling things would not be that simple. "I'll go put the tools away and close up the workshop."

Joule came into the shop a few minutes after me and helped me clean up. "I'll be back next weekend."

She wrapped up a bolt of fabric. "I think I'll stay at the loft," she said. We hadn't been back to the loft in over a week. She hadn't been there alone in over a month. The place was for sale but there hadn't been any offers.

"I'll call you there, then." I swept up the sawdust and she helped me close the large doors of the workshop.

Chapter Eighteen

Joule

I heard the sound of a buzzer downstairs. No one had used the buzzer in years. I was not even sure it still worked. It was a rusty old push button with a stamped sign over it that read, "For Deliveries Only." I rarely had visitors and those I did expect came straight up to the loft. It suddenly dawned on me as I looked out of my kitchen window that Roosevelt always manned the door before and now I always kept the place locked up.

I attempted to ride the elevator down but apparently the door jammed again and was not working properly. I took the stairs. I opened the smaller door of the warehouse to reveal Allen silhouetted by sunlight. His old truck, not visible from the kitchen window, was parked by the curb. The camper was gone.

"I thought we were meeting at the cabin this weekend?" I greeted him with a hug. He felt stiff inside my embrace.

"That's what I came to talk to you about," he stated flatly.

"Come on in." I invited him up apprehensively.

Allen walked past me towards the elevator.

I stopped at the base of the staircase. "It stopped working again."

Allen examined the doors and began to fiddle with the controls.

"Don't worry about it now," I called out to him.

Allen followed me up the steep staircase.

"Can I fix you something to drink?" I offered as I walked into the kitchen. Allen remained around the counter as if using it as a buffer.

"I'm fine." He hesitated while I poured a glass of water. "I don't know how to say this."

"Are you going back to Tina?" I said it for him.

The Kitchen Dance

"I need to for the kids." Allen moved the barstool but did not sit down.

"What about us?" I took a drink of the cold water to cool down the frustration I was beginning to feel.

"I'm just not part of your crowd." Allen ran his hand over the smooth curved wood on the back of the barstool.

"What do you mean? We don't have to hang around Elaine and Philip or the Prescotts. We'll find new friends." I could not believe he was using this as an excuse.

"It's not that. They're great people. They're smart, successful, and rich. Like you. I'm not any of those things." He was either trying to convince me he was not good enough for me and I should have pity on him, or Tina drilled that into his head.

I shook my head with confusion. I found it hard to breathe. I wanted to scream at him, but then again I felt this was going to happen all along. Allen finally took a seat on the barstool, propped his elbows on the bar and buried his face in his hands. I watched him as he rubbed his face and combed his fingers through his hair. I just hoped he would stand up to Tina.

"I don't know how to make this easier." His blue eyes met mine and suddenly I felt ill. I would miss those eyes and the beautiful eyes of his children.

I moved to the kitchen sink.

"She needs me. You don't. You'll be okay. You have a lot of friends, a great job, and two homes. You have everything. She can't make it without me." He tried to convince me as if all this could compensate for my losing him.

"But I love you. I *love* you," I repeated as if emphasizing the word "love" would set it apart from the word "need". "We were going to start our furniture business. What are you going to do now?"

"I'll look for work."

"Allen! Why can't your kids just come live with us? Tina can manage with just the baby. Don't your kids like me?"

"They love you." He sounded as if he were getting angry with me. "But they're her children too! She won't let me take them. She wants me to come home. It's the only way she'll let me see the kids now. She's threatening me with all sorts of legal shit."

"What about what you want? What about what I want? And what legal *shit* is she talking about?" I was getting equally as angry.

Allen did not answer.

I tried to calm down. "Allen, what do you want?"

"I want to be with you. I want to start our furniture company. But..."

I banged my glass in the sink. Allen ran around the counter to me by the kitchen sink. He grabbed me and tried to embrace me but I resisted.

"I'm sorry." He continued to attempt his embrace.

I continued to resist but he would not release me. "I have a responsibility to my kids."

He was right. I relaxed in his arms and he pulled me in closer while my arms hung loosely by my sides. I could not hold him in return. I feared if I did, I would not be able to let him go.

"I don't want to leave you." He took my face in his hands. "I love you. I do love you."

We never spoke the words before. I knew I adored him. Maybe I confused that with actual love. "You love her, too?"

He embraced me again. "I love my kids. I need to make things better for them. I didn't get to do that for my first son. I don't want to lose them, too."

I finally put my arms around him and we held each other tightly. I hugged him because he was my friend and I felt sorry for him and I felt sorry for myself because I was losing him, losing his children, and losing the special family we had created.

* * * *

Allen

The baby was crying in his crib next to the bed where Tina and I slept. Tina, whose sheets were twisted around her naked body, made no attempt to stir. I was lying beside her, awake, staring thoughtfully at the ceiling. I was thinking about waking up at the cabin all peaceful. I was thinking about making a pot of coffee in the kitchen with the window looking out over the lake. I was thinking about taking a cup to Joule who would have gotten up and brushed off the dust on the Adirondack chairs on the deck overlooking the main lake. We would sit there and talk about our plans for the day.

Instead, I got up, put on my pants and changed Joey's soaked diaper, then carried him to Tina who turned over in the bed away from us. I took the baby in the kitchen where Jimmy was already up sitting at the table watching the television in the family room.

I removed a large butcher knife from the table Jimmy just used to cut open the bag of dry cereal. Another sign of Jimmy's trying to fix breakfast himself spread across the table and dripped on the kitchen floor. I balanced the crying Joey in one arm and I tried to rinse out a dirty saucepan from the night before. I checked the cabinets for a clean bottle. There weren't any. I looked for formula in the pantry and found half a can. I searched the kitchen for a jug of water while Joey's cries got louder.

The Kitchen Dance

I could hear Tracy in her room. Thank goodness she was up. "Tracy?"

"Yes, sir," she answered through her closed door.

"Could you lend me a hand in here?"

Tracy came to the kitchen sink and began preparing a powdered baby formula with tap water in a bottle she pulled out of the dish rack buried under a pile of dishes. She shook up the mixture and stuck the bottle in the microwave. Joey kept wailing. Jimmy, frustrated, left the table and slopped cereal and milk across the floor as he made his way to the T.V. He cranked up the volume louder than Joey's crying.

A cranky, sleepy Tina finally came into the kitchen. She took the bottle from the microwave and the baby from me then went back to her bedroom.

I cleaned up the messy kitchen and washed the large butcher knife and set it on a cutting block on top of the refrigerator and gave my son a disapproving look. "That knife is not a toy, son. If you need to cut something open, I suggest you ask for help."

* * * *

Joule

I was in my office sitting at my long desk looking over some sketches. My new office Philip surprised me with, or perhaps bribed me with, had a larger desk which consisted of three components. The center section attached to the wall was about eight feet long and housed my computer and a cabinet for storing drawing tools, along with too many drawers for me to ever fill.

Another long table faced the window with a view of adjacent buildings and a busy street below. It was not an inspiring view, but it was a window permitting access to some actual sunlight for a few hours a day. The eight foot long table made it possible to spread out several samples at once making it more convenient for me in my process of creating human environments.

A shorter table, about five feet long, more accommodating for meeting clients, was attached to the opposite side of the computer cabinet. This space must remain clear for meetings with project managers, assistants, and real estate developers, in addition to presidents of companies. Everyone using the space provided input essential in the decisions I would make in designing the space. My current project was the reception area, management offices, and common areas of a new condominium complex where Philip and Elaine were trying to lure me into purchasing a unit.

"Joule?" My assistant, Margaret, tapped on the open door.

"Yes?" I turned from the floor plans I was working on.

"I'm going to lunch now." She popped just her head in the open doorway.

"Are you heading out?"

I shook my head and went back to studying the plans.

"Do you want me to put your calls through?" Margaret asked.

"Sure."

Within minutes of Margaret's departure, my phone rang. Normally I only got interoffice calls and it's usually quiet around lunch time.

"Joule Dalton," I answered distractedly.

"Joule?" I recognized Allen's voice immediately.

"Hello, Allen," I answered with obvious distance.

"I need to talk to you. Are you busy?"

"Yes." I was indeed busy. I had an afternoon meeting and there were sketches to complete. "Right now I am."

"I just need to talk to you about, well; Philip offered me a job. I would not actually be working for him, but he set me up an interview with a contractor who works with your firm. I talked it over with Tina and she didn't think it was a good idea me working with you and all."

"You wouldn't be working with me, Allen. You would be working for the construction company Philip contracts on some of our firm's projects." I was getting peeved. "How does this have anything to do with me?"

"In her mind it does. Still, it's just not a good idea, but I wanted to thank you. I'm sure you put Philip up to it."

"No, Philip never mentioned this to me. You need to speak to Philip. Hold on and I'll put you through."

"Joule, wait!"

"Yes?"

"Please don't be cold. I know this is asking a lot from you but I just can't end it like this. I want you to understand. I wish you could respect my decision."

"I'm sorry. I just can't do this right now. We made plans for our future. In the back of my mind I knew this was coming. I just didn't want to see it. But now you have other plans and I need to make other plans for me."

"What are you going to do?"

"Look, I'm very busy right now. Let me transfer you to Philip's office."

I pushed the hold button before he could respond and transferred the call. I watched as the flashing light on my phone glowed and then went out.

Distracted, I checked my purse for some cash, set the phone to voicemail, and took the elevator down to the commissary. I selected a chicken salad sandwich and a bottle of grapefruit juice from the refrigerator and, because the lunch special included them, I chose some processed wavy multigrain chips.

"Hello, beautiful." Barry sidled up to me in the checkout line. "How have

The Kitchen Dance

you been doing?"

"I doubt you'd be interested." I set my tray on the tubular rails and guided it toward the register.

"Of course I'm interested. Maybe we could get together for a drink after work." Barry stood over me and spoke softly in my ear.

I looked up at Barry's artificial smile and realized how hopeless this all was. If Barry was any indication of the type of man who comprised part of my crowd, I did not care to be a part of my crowd either.

Lena, the elderly woman who had worked at the commissary as long as I was with the firm, rang up my meal.

"Let's at least have lunch." Barry pulled out his cash to pay the clerk for my lunch.

"No, thank you." I blocked his hand. "I will be taking it back to my office. I have some work to finish up."

Lena bagged my lunch and I left Barry to hit on a young female intern who was sitting alone at a table close to the register.

When I returned to my office, Philip was waiting by my door about to jot down a message in a notepad on my assistant's desk.

"What's up?" I asked as I unlocked my office door. I set my bagged lunch on my short desk facing the door. "Have you eaten lunch?" I acted as if I had no idea why he stopped in for a visit.

"I talked to Allen. He's turning down the job I recommended him for. He's making a big mistake, Joule, and I thought since he was your friend—"

"Philip," I interrupted him. "I'm sure even though I asked Elaine not to tell you, she told you Allen and I are no longer seeing each other."

Philip pulled up a chair and sat across my desk from me. "I'm sorry to hear that."

"Don't look so surprised." I passed the chips across the table. "Have some chips." I took a bite of the sloppy sandwich I would not have bought if I'd known I was having company for lunch. The commissary's chicken salad is wonderful but best consumed in privacy. I wiped the mayonnaise from my mouth. "Was there anything else you wanted to tell me?" I managed to mumble.

"I'm glad you have decided to return on a full-time basis." He told me, "I was concerned we might be losing you."

"Philip." I took a sip of the sour grapefruit juice and winced. "Have I been slack with my work? You told me yourself my ideas and new designs are better than ever."

"Your coming in less and less does not appeal to the clients, not to mention some of your other design team members."

"I have never missed a meeting, much less been late or unprepared." I looked down at my sandwich which suddenly lost its appeal. It was soggy and sloppy and my stomach turned at the sight of it. "I thought we agreed I could work from home occasionally."

"I know you have some things to work out and working from your home was sufficient for a while. Now that Allen is out of the picture, you need to be here. I will gladly give you your pick of your own design team."

"I don't want to lead a team. I certainly do not want to tell some arrogant architect right out of graduate school what to do. It has nothing to do with my job, Philip. This job has been my entire life, and the truth is, I need something else. If I gleaned nothing else from my relationship with Allen, I learned I could have more."

"You are my top designer. You're probably one of the best and one of the highest paid female designers in this city."

"I'm not talking about success. I mean more of the things that bring me happiness, joy, and real laughter, not this phony cocktail party schmooze. You and Elaine have children. I know they are grown now but they are still your family. Your life consists of more than just work." I wrapped up my sandwich and stuffed it back in the bag. "You have it all. How can you sit there and tell me what I need."

"I don't know what I would have done without Elaine," Philip confessed. "I could never have had it all without her."

"Neither could I." I took back my bag of chips and munched on one.

"You and Elaine are my package deal. I have two partners, one for home and one for work. Losing you would be like losing Elaine and God knows she is not the same when you are not around."

"I'm here now, but I can't make you any guarantees. My heart just is not into it."

"Broken hearts are like that, I hear." Philip stood up and went to my long table by the window. "You will get back in the swing of things," he assured me. "You are a professional." He tapped the sketches for the latest project on the table in front of him.

"Of course I am."

"And Joule," Philip added as he crossed my office to the doorway, "Elaine wanted me to remind you Stephen Croft is still available."

I tossed a balled up napkin at him as he walked through the door.

Chapter Nineteen

Allen

I walked into the trailer wearing the nice suit Joule bought me that now looked rumpled from the summer heat. I felt defeated. "Where is your mother?" I asked the kids.

"She left this morning after you did," Tracy told me.

"Where's the baby?" I looked in the refrigerator for a cold drink. There was very little on the shelves and nothing to drink.

"She took him with her," Jimmy answered when Tracy didn't.

I looked at the mess the kids made. An empty box of dry cereal was the last remaining evidence of food in the house. I saw the large butcher knife on the coffee table. I looked at Jimmy with one of those *didn't-we-just-talk-about-this looks* then took it back to the kitchen. "Have you eaten?"

Jimmy and Tracy looked up at me pitifully shaking their heads.

"Get dressed," I told them as I checked my wallet for money but only had found a couple of dollars. I searched a variety of containers and drawers where Tina may have kept spare change. Tracy walked in. "Do you have any money?" I asked.

"Duh! No!" She had changed clothes but looked a little ratty. Her clothes were wrinkled and looked like she pulled them from the dirty clothes pile she kept stuffed in a corner of her bedroom.

Jimmy walked in wearing a clashing ensemble and his shirt inside out.

"What about you? Do you have any money?" I slipped his shirt over his head and put it back on the right way. Jimmy shook his head with disappointment.

"He never gets money," Tracy let me know.

"Get some shoes on and comb your hair," I told them.

The kids followed my directions while I left a note for Tina. We got in the truck and drove away.

* * * *

I searched my parents' refrigerator for something to feed the kids.

"Why didn't you tell me these babies haven't eaten a decent meal?" My mother ducked under my arm to fetch a casserole dish from the lower shelf. "Pour them a glass of milk."

"I'm out looking for work thinking Tina is taking care of the house and feeding the kids. Hell, I don't know what she's done with all our savings." I pulled the jug of milk out and set it on the counter. "I hate to say I told you so Mother, but I did. I just can't do this."

"Son, I still think you did what was best for your children." She spooned out the casserole on dinner plates.

"No. I did what you thought was best for my children, not what I thought was best." I picked up a plate of casserole and stuck it in the microwave and set it to reheat. "Tina insisted I turn down the job Joule's boss offered me. Now I'm thinking I should call him back to see if the offer is still available. I'll take the kids to the city. We'd have to move to an apartment for a time but I think we can manage."

"Do you think it's going to be easy, son?" My Pop joined us in the kitchen. "You know Tina is going to fight for those kids. Everything you'd make would go straight to the attorneys."

"Thanks for your little pep talk, Pop." I removed the heated dish. "Jimmy, come eat."

"You should call Tina and let her know you and the kids will be staying with us tonight. You two can work things out in the morning."

"I'll call her, but we won't be staying here tonight."

* * * *

Joule

I was sitting on my bed at the loft, my laptop settled on a pillow in my lap. The screen cast a soft glow in the dark room. I rubbed my tired eyes and raked my hands through my hair, hoping the stimulation might dredge up some ideas sunk in the sludge of my brain. My latest designs lacked originality, Philip told me, and he was right. I was digging through old projects trying to resurrect and repurpose old ideas. It was not working. Now, the only thing to define my life, and my career, was in a slump.

The Kitchen Dance

The night before was miserable and I started the day suffering from little, if any, sleep. The prescription sleeping pills offered no influence. I could not get Allen off my mind. I called in sick and turned off my phones and, after another dose of the medication, crawled back in bed and fell in and out of a sedated stupor. Sleep only offered fragmented dreams and I woke with heart palpitations and a profound sense of dread. I forfeited any hope of rest and spent the morning consuming half of a pot of coffee. I hoped to get some work done at home once the chemicals I ingested stabilized, but everything went south when I heard the buzzer from the warehouse door. Only Allen used the buzzer. I untangled myself from the bedding and peeked through the blinds on the window overlooking the bay door.

Allen stood below dressed in his suit. His jacket was open and his tie fluttered in the breeze. As if he could feel my eyes on him, he looked up at the window. I stepped back quickly but he called out to me and begged me to let him in. He pressed the button incessantly and banged on the bay doors. I climbed back into my bed and covered my ears with a pillow. After several minutes the noises stopped. I returned to the window but did not see him. I ran to the other windows, each providing a different view of the street, but when I searched for him, he was gone and there was no sign of his truck.

I screamed, I cried and I slept. I awoke mid-afternoon to the remaining pot of stale coffee and tried to bury myself in my work. I set the laptop aside and stretched. I looked at my watch. It was getting dark out and I had not eaten all day. I stepped out of my rumpled pajamas and slipped on a bra from the hamper and a hoodie. I found some cash in my purse and tucked a few dollar bills in one pocket of my jeans, grabbed my warehouse keys, and slipped on some athletic shoes. When I left, I locked the warehouse door and stuffed the keys inside another pocket of my jeans. I walked down the dimly lit street towards the diner. Suddenly a man stumbled in front of me from a recessed doorway.

"Excuse me." I tried to pass him. I recognized the coat he was wearing and made an absent gesture to touch the coat but withdrew my hand suspiciously. I also recognized the man. He was of average height with a thick barrel chest that the coat strained to cover. He was balding but kept his remaining light brown hair long and pulled back in a tight band. His skin was pale and oily. His narrow eyes were a yellow green. He was the same man I saw hanging around the warehouse district urinating in the alley, eating from the buffet at the loft when Roosevelt died, and now he was wearing Roosevelt's coat.

The man grabbed me and, putting a knife to my throat, pulled me towards the alley. I struggled to get away but he pinned me against the wall with his forearm at my throat. "Give me your money, bitch!" He hissed his sour breath into my face.

With my heart leaping into my throat, I reached in my jeans' pocket.

The mugger slapped my hand away and dug for the money himself while bracing me against the wall. He fanned the money between his fingers. "Nine bucks! What the fuck!" He pressed me tightly against the wall, his face in mine. "I know you got more than that! You're that rich lady who lives over the warehouse. Drives a fancy car. I bet you got a lot more money back there."

Suddenly my fear turned to rage. I kept my eyes locked on his. "And if I don't?"

"I'm sure I can find something of value." He reached under my sweatshirt and pressed me back harder against the wall pinning me with the knife at my throat.

"Go ahead. Rape me! Kill me!" I screamed instead of yelling for help. "I really don't care." I managed to push him away. Then I advanced on him as I unzipped my jacket baring my bra. "Rape me! Isn't that what you want?" I grabbed at his hand that held the knife. "Kill me, you mother fucker!" He backed away. "Just kill me!" I continued to yell as I reached in the other pocket of my jeans, retrieving my keys. I threatened him with the keys protruding between my fingers as if they were blades. "Take the keys." I hurled them at my attacker. "Take whatever you want!"

The mugger cowered from the flying keys as I continued to advance.

"Take the keys." I pointed at the keys that landed precariously on a grate. "Go on. Take everything you want. You can have it all! You can take my whole fucking life!"

The mugger stumbled over some debris.

"Get up!" I screamed. I bent over and picked up the keys then reached for his arm and tried to yank him up. "Well?" I extended my hand bearing the keys. "What the hell are you waiting for?"

"You're crazy, bitch!" The mugger tried to get away. He pulled from my grip on Roosevelt's coat sleeve and stepped away from me. "You're fucking crazy!" He ranted as he ran out of the alley.

I was breathing hard. I leaned against the alley wall. I was angrier than scared. Then rage converted to panic, and panic to despair. I began to sob and then cry hysterically. I fell to my knees among the garbage and debris asking God why? Why was all this crap happening to me?

The old woman, whom I'd seen many times before, with her cherished belongings bursting from shopping bags overwhelming an old baby stroller, walked towards me but maintained a cautious distance of just a few feet from where I knelt. I gathered my wits and looked into her haggard face and her dull gray eyes softly illumined by the streetlights. She was neither frightened nor concerned, and locked eyes with me in an unresponsive stare. In that bleary

The Kitchen Dance

moment transfixed in her gaze, I saw everything so clearly.

At first, I walked quickly and then I ran back to my warehouse.

I continued running up the staircase. I grabbed a bag and started stuffing it with clothes. I tossed the bag of clothes down the staircase. It tumbled down until it hit the lower landing. I picked up my handbag and secured it on my shoulder then tucked my laptop inside my briefcase. I locked up the loft and ran down the stairs, grabbing the bag on the lower landing. I tossed everything I carried into the passenger seat of the Jaguar, pulled out of the warehouse's garage area and sped away.

* * * *

Allen

I parked in front of the trailer. My kids were seated beside me in the truck. I came back to pick up some clothes for the kids and me. Another vehicle was blocking the driveway in front of the trailer. According to Tracy, it belonged to Joe. Through the trailer window, the children and I watched what was taking place inside. Tina and Joe were making out in the kitchen.

I turned to Tracy, who was seated by the passenger door. She gave me a knowing look. She'd seen too much for her young years, I thought. I gave her the same knowing look and a wide smile spread across our faces. We both looked at the six-year-old Jimmy between us who didn't know what was going on because he could barely see over the dash. I put the car in reverse, backed out of the driveway, and pulled away.

I drove for a couple of hours when I pulled up to the warehouse. It was my second trip to the city that day and somehow I ended up at the same place I just left. The kids waited in the truck while I pressed the button by the warehouse door. I could hear the buzzing sound inside. No answer. I stepped back and could see the light over the kitchen sink was on. I pounded on the door. There was still no answer. I put my head against the metal door to listen. I heard my children scream.

I turned around to find a big man by my truck. He was wearing a heavy coat even though the weather was way too warm for it.

"Get away from there." I yelled and ran back to my children on the passenger side of the truck. Tracy locked her door. I ran around to get to the driver's side. Tracy grabbed her brother just as Jimmy unlocked the driver's side door for me. The strange man beat me to the door. Tracy screamed and reached across her brother trying to lock the door.

"Are you looking for the lady who lives here?" The big man snarled at me.

"Yes." I stood up to him. "I am. Do you know where she is?"

"That bitch is crazy." He laughed. "She just tore out of here in her fancy car."

I was still not sure whether this guy was going to mug me or not. "Thanks," I said softly.

"No problem." The homeless man shrugged and walked away.

I watched him for a moment before getting in the truck. Something about his coat looked familiar. I got in the truck and locked the driver's side. "You two alright?" I looked over at Tracy who still had her arms around Jimmy. I pulled them both into my arms and held them for a moment.

"What are we going to do, Daddy?" Jimmy asked.

I checked the gas gauge on my truck. A quarter of a tank, that and two dollars would not get us very far. The kids had no change of clothes. I should have stayed at my parents. Joule may be at the West's, I thought, or hopefully the cabin. I could get into the cabin. There was a key under the back deck.

* * * *

The Jaguar was parked in front of the cabin. I told the kids to wait in the truck. I went to the front door but it was locked. I walked around the cabin. The back door was open but I did not see Joule inside. I took the steps from the top of the hill down to the lake.

Joule was sitting on the dock looking out over the dark lake lit only by the lights from the other lake homes. She heard me on the steps. She turned around and looked back up the hill. I stopped on one of the landings under a mercury security light. Joule got up slowly and walked up the long dock increasing her speed as I came down the staircase to meet her. When she reached the stairs, she began to run towards me and stumbled on a rotten step. I ran down to help but she gathered herself up and shook off the fall and we met each other on a lower landing where we hugged each other tightly.

"I've got to fix those stairs." I laughed through tears. "I'm glad you're here." I held her and kissed the top of her head. She smelled different, musty and of stale coffee.

"Why are you here?" She pushed back and looked up at me.

"I've brought the kids. They're still in the truck."

Joule ran past me up the stairs and around the cabin. As soon as Jimmy and Tracy saw Joule they climbed out of the truck and ran to her. I caught up with them and we all hugged and clung to one another as we walked in the front door.

"So we get back home and Mom's boyfriend is back." Tracy couldn't wait

The Kitchen Dance

to fill Joule in.

Joule cut me a look with a cocked eyebrow. I tried to give her a reassuring smile. She looked tired; her eyes swollen and red and her tangled hair pulled back in a ponytail. She wore jeans with scuffed and dirty knees and a hooded jacket only halfway zipped. I stood between her and the children and softly slid the zipper above her bra. She gave me a resigned look and it was as if I knew what she'd been through was not to be shared with the children.

"Do you have any cinnamon bread?" Jimmy broke in. He expected every day to be like a weekend visit.

"No, Sweetie. The bakery closed by the time I got here," Joule answered calmly. "Why? Are you hungry?"

"Yes," Jimmy answered. He didn't care for the casserole his grandmother cooked and had only picked at it.

Joule looked in the kitchen pantry while Jimmy stood beside her, his head barely reaching her elbow. "Do you want some peanut butter?"

Jimmy reached for the peanut butter. "Do you have any bread?"

"I don't think so. I haven't been up here since…" She stopped talking when she looked over at me going over the photos and scrapbook pages still spread across the table. "I think I have some crackers."

Joule found the crackers. Tracy found a dinner knife in the utensil drawer and the two kids stood together at the kitchen counter making peanut butter crackers. Joule and I moved to the living room and sat in the pit group.

I was tired. I leaned back and raked my hands through my hair. "Why didn't you let me in today?"

She gave me a hard look that spoke volumes.

"I went by the office. I wanted to see you and to talk to Philip. They told me you'd called in sick and Philip was in appointments all day. I knew I shouldn't just drop in but I'd hoped that job was still available and I wanted to ask Philip about it in person. After I blew it with Philip, and you wouldn't let me in, I just drove back home. I was home by the time the kids got home from school. Tina was gone again. I hoped this time for good. I took the kids by my parents for something to eat then back to the trailer to get some clothes. Joe was there so we left. I brought the kids by your loft. I didn't come just to ask you for help. I don't want you to think that." I looked over at Joule who was waiting for me to continue. "I'll take the job Philip told me about if I still can. I don't want to ask you for money or anything. But I was wondering if we could stay here. Just for the weekend. I could stay with my parents but the kids love it here. I will work in the workshop; fix those steps to the pier, or anything else you need."

Geri G. Taylor

* * * *

Joule

Reality hit. I didn't know if I could trust him. I looked into Allen's clear blue eyes. He realized what I was thinking.

"I'm going to get custody of my kids," he tried to convince me. "After I came by to talk to you and Philip today, I stopped by this place that gives free legal advice, you know, to see if I needed to get a lawyer. Of course, I explained to the lady lawyer why I couldn't afford her and I'd not been able to support the kids for a while but I told her I could get a good job. I was interviewing around town. I wore this nice suit you bought me." He indicated his rumpled suit.

I held a pillow in my lap. Allen reached for my hand but I pulled back. "Tina's boyfriend is back in her life now? Is that why you came back to me? What happens if he leaves again? Are you going to leave me again?"

"Oh, God, no! I'll never go back to her, Joule."

He slid over closer to me. "I know it looks like that now. I didn't know he was back until tonight. When we got back from my parents, he was there at the trailer making out with Tina in my kitchen." He dragged his hands down his face. "Damn. I need to call my parents and tell them where we are and I should tell them about Joe."

"I'll get my cell phone." I stood up as Allen sat back and raked his hands through his hair again.

"You don't know what a huge weight was lifted off my back. When I saw Tina with Joe I felt I was finally going to get my life back in order. I could have run in there and hugged the loser."

"Are you sure he's back with her?" I handed him my phone.

"Who cares? The point is he was making out with her. Tracy saw it. I'll just tell that to the attorney and maybe it will help my case. Oh, that reminds me, I should call Tina so she won't accuse me of kidnapping."

Allen stepped out to the deck to talk to his parents and I watched him through the kitchen window as he descended the steps towards the lake for better reception. I helped Tracy clean up their snack then I took Jimmy to the bathroom to start the water for his bath. I was going back to my bedroom to look for something for Tracy to wear to bed when I discovered Allen returned to the deck with the phone. He was pacing as he talked and I overheard the muffled side of his conversation.

"Tina. When I brought the kids home, I noticed you were busy so I brought them with me to a friend's house," he told her calmly.

The Kitchen Dance

Allen saw me and came inside. I could hear indistinguishable remarks she yelled all the way across the living room. I went into my parents' old bedroom and shuffled through a drawer.

"Look, they're fine. There wasn't any food in the house and I didn't have enough money for groceries. I'm not going to discuss this with you now. No, I won't be coming back. No, you don't need me. You've got Joe. I can't help you with that, Tina. I can't help you anymore." I could hear Allen from my bedroom.

I walked back through the cabin towards Tracy who was standing in the kitchen. I could still hear Tina through the phone. Tracy, who was standing in the kitchen with her father, was able to make out what her mother was saying, turned with a concerned look from her father to me.

"Yes. I'll talk to you tomorrow when I bring the kids back to get some of their clothes."

We all could hear Tina's screaming over the handset until Allen pushed the button canceling the call. "She didn't take it too well."

I handed Tracy a short sleeved night gown. "Just take a shower in Daddy's room." I joined Allen who returned to the pit group.

"I don't expect you to take me back but I wish you would," he said when I sat down. "I wish we could be like we were."

I still could not respond. I thought about Daniel and how he used to get so mad at me he could not speak. Now I knew how he felt.

"Have you made other plans?" Allen asked.

"What?" I did not know what he was talking about.

"When I talked to you on the phone the other day, you told me you needed to make other plans. Did you?"

"No."

"And Joe's not staying. Tina tried to get him to stay but he's not going to." Allen thought I would like to know.

I picked up my favorite pillow, hugged it, and closed my eyes.

"I owe her nothing. I tried to help her but I just can't." He shook me gently as if to wake me up. "Joule?" I opened my eyes but could not look at him.

"I wanted to make sure I could get the kids. Pissing off Tina did not seem the right way to go about it. If I got a job with you, or a job Tina thought had anything to do with you, she would find a way to use it against me... I thought about calling you but I couldn't, not until I'd worked out everything. I tried to talk to you earlier today to tell you everything. Joule, I could not be with you if it meant losing my kids. Do you understand?"

I finally looked at him and thought about his love for his children. "Yes, Allen. Of course I do."

"Then, tonight, when I went by your loft again, your kitchen light was on and I was glad. I knew if you saw the kids you'd let us in and we could talk. But this guy was standing out there. He told me you left."

"What guy?"

"I don't know. Some homeless guy. He was kind of… Well, he scared the kids."

"Oh great, I know the guy. Wearing Roosevelt's overcoat?"

"Yes, he was."

"He's probably robbing my loft as we speak!" I tossed the pillow from my lap.

Allen took the opportunity to get closer to me. He took my face in his hand.

"Listen to me. Every day, since the day I left here, I have tried to find my way back to you. I wanted to make Tina think I was going to help her. I was helping her and I guess I'll always be helping her. But I can't be with her. I don't love her. I love you. I want to be with you and I know the kids love you and want to be with you, too."

I reached over, touched his face with the back of my fingers, and gave him a relieved smile. Allen pulled me into his arms. Jimmy bounded in and climbed over the back of the pit group. His hair was still damp from his bath. He piled in between us. Tracy joined us wearing the gown I loaned her and her hair still wrapped in a towel. She slipped in beside her father and we all hugged and snuggled. The phone rang. I pulled free from the entanglement of arms and legs to answer the phone Allen left in the kitchen.

"Hello." I could hear a baby's cry through the handset.

"Who is this?" I recognized Tina's voice but she apparently did not mine.

"This is Joule, Tina." The baby continued to cry.

"Is my…is Allen there?"

I extended the phone in front of me as I walked towards Allen. The baby's cry could be heard through the handset all the way to the living room.

"Yeah, Okay." He reached for the phone.

I motioned for the kids to join me in the back of the house and got them ready for bed.

* * * *

Allen

"I need you to come home," Tina pleaded with me.

"Look Tina," I told her, "that's not my home anymore."

"I want my kids back right now!" Tina screamed over the handset. "I need

The Kitchen Dance

Tracy to help me with this baby!"

"Not tonight, Tina." I tried to speak calmly. "I'll be by tomorrow."

The baby continued to cry. Tina must have been balancing the phone on her shoulder with the baby in one hand and lighting a cigarette with the other. I could hear the click of the lighter. She inhaled then let out a long exhale.

"Look, Allen." Tina seemed calmer now. "If you think you are going to get those kids—" I could hear her drag on the cigarette. "You're wrong." Over the baby's cry I could hear her shaking something liquid. Probably one of the baby's bottles of formula. "And if you think that rich bitch you're fucking is gonna fix this for you..." She sounded as if something, like the cigarette, was clenched between her teeth. "It ain't gonna happen either." I heard her take another drag. "When I get through with you, Social Services won't let you within five hundred feet of your kids!"

"Tina, why don't you just call your boyfriend? He's the one that should be helping you with your baby, not me. Just let me keep Jimmy and Tracy for a few days so you two can work things out."

Tina finally pacified the baby with the bottle.

"Allen. I don't want him. I want you." She tried a new tactic and was pretending to cry. "Can't we be a family?"

"I'll talk to you tomorrow. And Tina, I don't want you calling back here." I made one last attempt to calm her down. "Please—"

The phone went dead.

Joule got the children ready for bed. She was reading Jimmy a story and I didn't want to disturb them. I waited outside his bedroom door until she tucked Jimmy into his stuffed toy covered bed.

I could feel my heart pounding in my chest. I pulled her into the larger bedroom. I wanted to kiss her. I wanted to feel her body against mine. I wanted to be inside her but I knew she would want to talk first.

"I didn't sleep with her. I mean I didn't have sex with Tina." I whispered so the kids couldn't hear. "I mean I slept in the bed some nights but that was because the sofa is too short and Jimmy kicks like a mule. That's all it was though; sleeping."

"I didn't ask," Joule said.

"You wanted to know."

"Yes. I wanted to know how someone could be with anyone who had an affair, got pregnant with the man's child and expected you to come back and help her raise it." She ticked them off on her fingers as she spoke in a hoarse whisper not wanting to disturb the kids. "Then I realized it was because you loved her and you wanted to take care of her just as much as you wanted to take care of your children. And the funny thing is I don't blame you. But I do have a question for you. If it was Tina living here, in this cabin, with a high paying career and enough money so you could live happily ever after and it was me living in the trailer park, screaming at you, and sleeping around on you, who would you pick? Would you still love me?"

I didn't know what to say. I let her walk out. I sat down on the bed. Nothing had stirred in the room since I left a few weeks ago and a thin layer of dust coated everything, yet it was still cleaner than the trailer.

"That's not fair!" I yelled and ran down the hall after her, not caring if it woke up the kids. "Think about what you just said." I found her in the kitchen. "You're making it sound like I just love you for your money. Yes. I enjoy being here, and I know my kids are happy here, but it's more than that. We are all here together. That's what makes me happy."

"And if Tina were here instead of me, you'd still be happy."

"God damn it, Joule, stop messing with my head. I know you're smarter than me with your college degrees and your fancy career but stop making me look like a damn fool. Tina cheated on me because I wasn't good enough. Cheryl left me because I wasn't good enough. You picked me up off the street when I was at the lowest point in my life and you loved me. You loved me."

"But it doesn't mean you have to love me back." Tears filled up her eyes.

"But I do." I felt my eyes sting. "You're my best friend, I care about you, I miss you, and I'm proud of you."

Joule stood there with her hand covering her mouth and tears in her eyes.

"I could have gone back to my parents but I came here." I remembered seeing her running up the steps. "And you hugged me out there." I found myself pointed at the steps leading down to lake. "You were glad I came back, weren't you? Hug me again." I held my arms out to her. "Forget all this other stuff for a minute and just hold me like you did out there."

Joule hugged me. I kissed the top of her head. I kissed her forehead and her cheeks that tasted salty from her tears. I wanted to find her mouth but she would not let me. She wasn't ready to trust me again.

* * * *

The next morning I woke up first and started the coffee. Thank goodness there was still coffee in the place. I liked mine black but Joule liked cream and sugar. The cream in the fridge smelled sour. I called the Fuhrmans and took the truck down the road to borrow some cream. When I got back, I found Joule in Tracy's room brushing my daughter's hair. Jimmy was in a bundle under her covers.

"Hey, man." I dug through the covers to find him. "Let's get some clothes on you so we can go scare up some breakfast."

The Kitchen Dance

Jimmy's head popped out of the covers. "Who are we going to scare?"

"It's just an expression, son." I pulled him out of the pile of blankets.

"Can we go fishing?" he asked as I carried him out of the room.

"Not today."

Since there was nothing to eat in the cabin, Joule offered to take us to eat breakfast in the lakeside town. Getting out of the cabin was like spinning plates. "Did you leave them in the living room?" I came out of Jimmy's room looking for his shoes.

"No, I think they're in the bathroom," Jimmy called out from the living room.

"They're not in here!" Tracy yelled from the bathroom.

"Look under the bed," Joule suggested.

"I did," I told her.

"Look under the other bed," Joule yelled.

I looked under Tracy's bed. "Found 'em!"

We piled in Joule's car. I drove. The kids were excited about the Jag and going out for breakfast and talked the entire way. We pulled up to a fast food restaurant. The kids wanted to eat in the car. I insisted we go in.

When Joule, the kids, and I got back to the cabin, we got out of the car and Joule walked around to the driver's side. I told the kids to get in the truck and held the car door open for Joule.

"Don't go by the loft alone." I closed the door and leaned on the door. "I'm afraid that bum may still be hanging around. Wait for me at your office and I will come with you."

"I'll be fine. If I see anything suspicious when I get there I will call the police from my cell phone and go to the diner."

I reached for her inside the car and kissed her forehead then softly kissed her lips. "I'll call you later then."

She handed me sixty dollars. "For gas or whatever."

"No." I stepped away from the car. "I've got enough gas to get home. I'll borrow some from my parents. You know, hat in hand and all that. They're used to it. And they know I'm good for it."

Chapter Twenty

Allen

    I stopped by my parents and ended up spending most of the day with them. It was after five by the time I arrived at the trailer. I felt disappointed to see Tina's car was gone again. "Okay, kids, let's grab some of your things. We'll meet Joule at the loft and all head back to the cabin. I'll just leave your mother a note."

    The kids entered the trailer and headed for their bedrooms. I went to the kitchen looking for something to leave a note with. I saw a thick phonebook on the counter, opened. I picked up the phone and hit the redial button. An automated voicemail answered. I heard Joule's recorded message. I lifted the phonebook to find it was sitting on top of the cutting board. I looked around to see if I could find the butcher knife. I looked up and noticed Tracy walking down the hallway towards Tina's bedroom. I watched her as she stopped to look down at the baby's crib. She reached in.

    "Daddy!" She let out a terrifying scream.

    I dropped the phonebook and ran to the back practically stumbling over Jimmy who stepped out in the hallway. I ran into Tina's bedroom. The pale lifeless baby was in the crib partially covered by a blanket. His dry gray eyes stared blankly. I pulled a crying Tracy away from the crib and held her face to my chest as I pulled her down the hallway. I grabbed Jimmy on my way down the hall and took both of them to the living room. "Sit here." Both were holding me so tightly I had to practically force them down on the sofa. "Don't move." I picked up the phone and called 911.

    "911. What is your emergency?"

    "I need an ambulance, the police, the baby's dead...my wife...I mean ex-

The Kitchen Dance

wife, Tina. I don't know where she is." I was shocked and so shaken up I could hardly speak. Then I suddenly realized Joule may be in danger. "I have to go. I have to call someone," I said without thinking.

"Could you please stay on the line, sir?" The operator continued in her monotone voice.

"No! I have to call someone. Tina may be after her." I hung up the phone and hit redial again forgetting Joule's number was not the last number I dialed.

"911. What is your emergency?" It was a different operator.

I quickly hung up the phone then dialed Joule's number. I still got her voicemail message. I turned away from my children and took the handset to the kitchen. "Joule! Get out of the loft! Go to the diner! It's Tina. I think she's killed her baby. She might be looking for you." I hung up and called her cell phone. There was no answer. She must have left it in the car.

* * * *

Joule

When I returned to the loft, I discovered that in my haste to leave I forgot to close the garage door and the access door to the warehouse stood wide open. I hesitated getting out of the car until I noticed nothing in the garage was disturbed. I pulled my phone from my purse and pressed 911. When the operator answered, I gave her my name and address and explained my situation. He informed me he would send an officer.

I got out of the car and looked around. Neither the locked storage cabinets nor the van was tampered with. I examined the doorknob but saw no damage. I tried to trace my steps upon leaving the night before and I could not recall whether or not I closed and locked the door. I turned on the florescent lighting and a bright blue wash of light filled the warehouse. I cautiously looked around. Allen had moved the supplies, tools and equipment to the workshop at the lake. There was nothing in the large space except for the steel supports too narrow to hide behind. I had locked up Roosevelt's room when I cleared out his things, so the only place to hide was the laundry room. I hesitated at the bottom of the stairs and looked at the small warehouse door, undecided if I should stay or go to the diner. I took the stairs up to my loft. It was just as I left it: locked.

The phone was ringing inside. I quickly unlocked the door and ran for the phone in the kitchen.

"Hello."

"Joule!" Allen yelled over the phone. "When did you get home?"

"Just now. I just walked in the door."

"You need to get out of there, call the police and go straight to the diner.

Tina is not here and, Joule, the baby is dead."

A sick feeling spread into my chest. "What? Allen, what did you say about the baby?"

"I think either Tina or maybe Joe killed the baby. She's gone and the phonebook was open to the pages with your name and address."

"Oh, my God, Allen, I don't know what to say. What should I do?"

"Get out of there, Joule."

Then I remembered there was a spare key in the laundry room downstairs. That is when I looked down on the floor and noticed a shadow blocking the light, casting over one of my relief sculptures. I turned, startled to find a woman I did not recognize. "Allen!" I shrieked too horrified to think.

"Joule! Is it Tina?" Allen shouted over the handset. "Get out of there!"

The woman approached me and revealed a large butcher knife in her gloved hand. I panicked, threw the phone at her, striking her in the face as I attempted to run past her towards the door.

* * * *

Allen

I could hear the thud of the handset as it hit something and rattled around like it landed on the floor. I screamed in the phone. "Tina! No! Tina!"

The kids began to scream.

"Oh shit!" I yelled to the kids. "Shut up! Shut up!" It was doing no good to yell at the phone or the kids. I could still hear the scuffle going on in Joule's loft. I hung up and counted silently to five trying to get myself together. The kids continued to whimper. I dialed 911.

"911. What is your emergency?" The operator answered.

"You have to get someone to…" I grabbed the phonebook and searched desperately on the opened pages for Joule's number and address. I'd been there many times but never noticed an address.

"Sir?" The 911 operator spoke calmly. "We have received three calls from this number in the past five minutes. Do you have an emergency?"

"Yes! Tina, Tina Brooks, my ex-wife, I think she's killed her baby and is now after my friend, Joule, J-O-U-L-E Dalton. I just called her. Tina is there! It's a warehouse with a loft apartment." I read off the address to the operator.

"Sir, I'm sorry but that is not our jurisdiction," the operator told me.

"Look, you've got to help her. Tina is there! I think they were fighting! You've got to get someone over there! And get someone over here! The baby is here."

"Sir, we have already dispatched a unit to your address. Please remain on the line until they arrive." The operator maintained her cool, controlled speech. "I will forward the information about your friend, sir."

I paced around the room holding the phone. I saw a neighbor coming out of his trailer and handed the phone to Tracy. "Stay on the line! Don't hang up!" I called out to the neighbor. "Hey! I need to use your phone! It's an emergency."

The neighbor walked back into his trailer and came back with his handset. I tried Joule's number again but the voice mail picked up with Joule saying she was on the phone.

The police pulled up.

* * * *

Joule

I stumbled past Tina and crashed into one of my relief sculptures. Blood, from a wound it tore in my side, stained the white artwork. Tina ran for me and made another stabbing motion with the bloody knife. I was able to grab her hand and we struggled for control. I smashed Tina against one of my relief sculptures and banged her hand against a protrusion until she released the knife. I kicked the knife towards the door. Tina pulled her hand free from my grip and punched me in the face, shoved me aside, and went for her knife. I was able to tackle Tina just as she grabbed the knife. The impact caused Tina to lose her grip and the knife skidded across the floor, making a clattering sound as it fell down the steep staircase.

Tina flipped over and began kicking me, blocking the way out, and the only direction for me to run was towards the back part of the loft. There was no time to close the massive sliding bedroom doors, and the lock was more for privacy than protection. I ran for the fire escape. I looked back. Tina stood there at the loft's entry door watching me. I climbed out the window as Tina stomped down the warehouse staircase. I stopped on the fire escape landing. I could hear her running down the metal stairs to the warehouse. There was no place for me to go if I ran down the fire escape. It led to the alley and I would be trapped between a chain link fence and Tina. I climbed back in the window. I could run for the loft door and lock her out. I shut the window and locked it. I ran to the front door.

Tina reached the door before I did.

I ran back to my bedroom where now I wished I had built a real door. I ran inside the closet instead. I pushed against the door with all my might because it had no lock.

Tina pounded on the door.

"What do you want?" I yelled through the door.

"I want you out of our lives!" Tina screamed at me.

Suddenly it was quiet. I placed my ear against the door but could not hear anything.

"Tina?" I called out.

Slam! Tina banged something against the door. The sound and force of the blow sent me to the closet floor. I jumped up and pressed myself against the door. I heard something heavy crash against the closet door again. I could feel the blow as it slammed the door against my back. I grabbed for all the clothes I could reach from off the rod and piled them up under my feet to help block the door. Tina kept banging on the door and screaming obscenities. I was finally able to pull down the rod that ran the length of the walk-in closet and brace it on top of the pile of clothes between the closet door and the back wall. I looked around the closet and found the stepladder and then remembered the access door. I positioned the ladder, a bit unsteady on the pile of clothes and climbed it only to discover I was not tall enough to climb up inside the panel.

Slam! A crack appeared on the closet door. I positioned the small ladder in hopes of accessing the top shelf on Daniel's side. *Slam!* The crack widened. *Slam!* A hole appeared in the door.

Tina looked in through the hole.

I hit her in the face with a stiletto heel. Tina reeled back holding the bloody gash on her forehead then shoved her fingers through the hole and yanked away a piece of wood. She reached her hand inside groping for the doorknob. I took a whack at her hand with the heel of my shoe.

Tina finally retreated.

I listened carefully and could hear Tina in the kitchen fumbling through the drawers. I climbed the wobbly stepladder and attempted precariously to climb on the shelf and get inside the attic space.

Tina was not what I expected. For some reason I envisioned her as a petite woman with light brown or blonde hair but this Tina was taller than I was and outweighed me by at least fifty pounds. Her over-processed blonde hair was razor cut close to her round face. Her acrylic nails were painted a bright green. Her pillow like breasts strained at the straps of her cheap bra that showed through her thin t-shirt. She was the most frightening thing I had ever seen. The fact that I could remember those details when my life was in danger amazed me.

I fell off the ladder again. Frantically I piled more clothes and repositioned the ladder on the pile. This time I made a successful attempt using the ladder and the shelves to climb inside the access door. I used the tip of my toes to kick at the stepladder. It tumbled over under a lower rack of pants and skirts. I

The Kitchen Dance

replaced the panel serving as an access cover quietly behind me just as Tina looked through the hole in the closet door.

I heard her struggling with the closet door again. She turned the door knob and pushed hard enough to release the latch. She shoved and banged against the door until I could hear the sound of something cracking as the rod slipped from its brace and burst through the sheetrock on the opposite wall. I could hear Tina swearing as she put her weight into shoving the door against the pile of clothes.

"Oh, you're a smart one," Tina snarled.

I could hear her in the closet now. I realized she could see the stepladder and probably had seen the access door. I could hear her doing something with the ladder. I quietly pressed both my hands on the access panel preparing to use my weight against it to prevent her from opening it. Too much weight and I could fall through. It sounded as if she were attempting to climb the ladder but was having the same problems I did gaining access to the door. She was way too heavy to hoist herself up the way I did. There were sounds of her grunts and shuffling clothes and then it was quiet.

I thought she had left the closet.

I looked around the dark crawl space. The only light was a vent at the end of the warehouse illuminated by a street light outside. The only other way out, except for falling through the suspended ceiling tiles, was to cross the span between the support wall of the walk-in closet to the entry closet support wall which would make access to the elevator shaft or loft entrance easier. The drop ceiling would not support my weight and the only possibility was to hang from the I-beams which were too high over my head for me to reach or, if I could locate the vertical supports and spread out my weight, I may make it across the ceiling grid. I listened for Tina. Nothing. Slowly I lifted the access door. The light from the closet spilled into the dark crawl space. No Tina. I saw a flashlight on the lower shelf. I leaned out of the access door and reached for it.

Tina came screaming into the closet. She waved her butcher knife, duct taped to my broom handle, and swung it at me. I was able to grab the light just as Tina slashed my arm. The blow knocked the flashlight from my hand and smashed into Tina's face. Tina screamed and grabbed her face, her nose, probably broken, bleeding profusely.

There was limited light but I made my way across the top of the drop ceiling supports, searching for adequate support. The thin brackets creaked and bent under by weight. I missed a support causing my foot to crack through the suspended foam tile.

Tina probably heard the commotion because she ran into the living area and began stabbing at the ceiling where my foot broke through the foam tile. I tried to get away but she could hear my movements and continued to drive the butcher knife through the ceiling.

I was able to climb on a wide sheet metal plenum strapped to the support beams by galvanized plumbers tape. I braced my legs where the flex duct protruded in several directions, like spider legs across the loft's attic, to avoid the knife as it pierced the ceiling. Broken pieces of foam ceiling fell from the grid as Tina continued to stab at me. I felt the coiled tube crushing beneath my weight and I realized the thin structure used for airflow was not sturdy enough and I tried to move. The sickening sound of the plenum collapsing ensued.

Tina heard the sound and stopped stabbing. I could see her through the holes she punctured. She was smiling up at me. Blood trickled from her nose and formed rivulets around her teeth.

I slid off the plenum, making my way across the flexible duct, and quickly made my way to the top of the loft's side wall just as the plenum and all its spidery robotic legs collapsed through the ceiling beneath me. I was dizzy from my blood loss and the unbearable heat that was trapped in the crawl space above the loft.

Tina, covered by bits of foam ceiling, cowered as the duct and pieces crashed down on top of her. The plenum missed her and the lightweight flexible duct did little harm. Tina got back up, adjusted her damaged weapon, and listened for my movements.

I was watching her from my position along the double studded support topping the perimeter wall of the loft. I could barely move on the three and half inch wide span of wood attached to the steel support beams. I tried to catch my breath and considered my options. I could feel the blood pumping from the slice in my forearm with every frantic beat of my heart. If I did not do something fast I would bleed to death.

One choice would involve getting to the area above the other closet without breaking through the ceiling. If I could brace the door to keep Tina out I could kick through the sheetrock wall and insulation in order to squeeze through a fourteen inch wide hole above the shelf. This would gain access to either the elevator shaft or the landing just outside the door, depending on which wall I could kick through. I could not remember if the elevator was up or down. I tried to think. If the elevator was up I could not break through the metal sides. If it was down I could climb through the work panel on top of the elevator but the doors were jammed. Would I be able to get them open? The elevator shaft was out.

Tina began screaming, cursing and stabbing at the ceiling again but she did not find me. I had to think fast. I considered the loft's entry door. The door to the loft was still open, but Tina would be able to get to me before I could get down. There was one other chance. I could fight.

The Kitchen Dance

With most of my weight on the studs, I kept my balance with one arm and leg stretched out over the flimsy drop ceiling supports. I did not realize blood from my side and arm injuries were dripping on the porous ceiling tiles.

Tina went silent and I could hear her walking around the living area, obviously listening for me. I noticed the sticky blood pooling under my arm. A bright red spot of my blood was soaking into the spongy tile.

The blood soaked through and revealed itself on the ceiling tiles. Tina must have seen it because she stabbed at the ceiling. I screamed as the blade just missed my hand. I began crawling as fast as I was able across the suspended tile between the rafters as pieces of the flimsy material broke away, springing rays of light into the crawl space.

Tina continued to cram the blade through the tiles, just missing me. I made it to the area over the entry closet. The corner of the support walls gave me a protected place to sit momentarily. I was covered with sweat, blood, tiny pieces of ceiling tile, and bits of insulation. I tried to catch my breath but the air above the loft was unbearably hot and sweat stung my bleeding wounds.

I listened for Tina and heard some commotion in the kitchen, then silence. I looked around the ceiling and thought about dropping down over the entry door to my loft. It was only an eight foot drop.

Thump! A piece of ceiling tile flipped up and Tina's head popped up through one of the holes in the ceiling a few feet away from where I was positioned. She pulled her homemade weapon through the hole and began stabbing at me. I kicked at the knife and was able to knock it loose from the broomstick.

Tina pulled back her weapon and attempted to secure the blade with the torn duct tape to the end of the broomstick while I made for the area above the door. She realized what I was up to, jumped off the bar stool and ran for the main door. She stood on the stair landing waiting for me to climb above her.

I did not make it to the door. I fell through the ceiling tile as soon as I left my perch and landed with a painful thud on the inside of the doorway. I gained my wits just in time to shut the door in Tina's face as she lunged for me with her broomstick bayonet. The butcher knife stuck into the door between the doorknob and jamb blocking the locking mechanism.

Tina struggled to free the wedged knife. I could hear the commotion and reached for the table next to the closet. I positioned the table like a battering ram. Just as Tina yanked the knife free, I opened the door tossing Tina off balance. She began to fall backwards and I took the thin table and shoved it at her, causing her to lose her balance and tumble down the steep metal stairs. I stood at the top landing and gaped down at Tina sprawled limply on the lower landing of the steep staircase.

Geri G. Taylor

* * * *

Allen

I stood in the kitchen and watched one of the paramedics standing in the hall. The trailer was filled with strangers. The kids were scared. Two men dressed in dull sports coats with dark pants came in the door and spoke with the policeman who was the first to show up at the trailer. A man and a woman wearing vests carrying tackle boxes and cameras struggled past the man blocking the narrow hallway. I could hear several voices talking at once, mixed in with the sounds of Jimmy's soft crying.

The bigger of the two men wearing the sports coats came into the kitchen with me. "Are you Mr. Brooks?"

"Yes, sir."

"I have a few questions I'd like to ask you, Mr. Brooks." He spoke calmly. I turned away from him and looked in the refrigerator for juice or something to get for the kids. An expired jug of milk and a half bottle of formula was the only thing left to drink. I found a plastic ice tray in the freezer. I washed out two glasses and made the kids a glass of water, all the while my mind was wandering back to Joule. I feared it was too late and I knew this night was far from being over.

I noticed the paramedics were quiet, and I looked up as they brought Joey's little body zipped into a small white bag only a couple of feet long. He looked tiny on the stretcher and I felt my stomach turn over. I was hit with an overwhelming sadness. I choked up and found it hard to breath, causing Jimmy to cry even harder as we watched Joey being taken away from us to the ambulance. I looked at Tracy whose eyes were wide with terror. I set the glasses of water on the coffee table and sat on the sofa between them and pulled each of them close to me.

The coroner came out next. He didn't speak. He walked past us like we weren't even there. When one of the paramedics opened the door, I could hear talk coming from a group of nosy neighbors who showed up to gawk around our trailer already teaming with police. When the coroner followed the paramedic out the door and closed it, the trailer was quiet again.

The man came from the kitchen flipping through a few pages of a small notepad he carried in his hands. "Mr. Brooks, I'm Detective Grafton. I need to ask you a few questions." He found a blank page. "You phoned 911 regarding this incident?"

"Yes, I did." I could tell this man was going to drag through this. My heart began to pound with anger and frustration.

The Kitchen Dance

"You found the infant's body?"

Tracy gasped and I looked over at her terrified face. "He has a name!" she cried out. "His name is Joey!"

"Yes." I took my arm from around Jimmy and held Tracy's head against my chest trying to calm her down. "I found the baby in his bed." I thought the less she had to do with this the better.

"You said the mother of the child," he continued, flipping his notebook back a few pages, "a Tina Brooks, your ex-wife, killed the baby?"

"I don't know. I may have said that. I was pretty shaken up when I found him…" I trailed off. "I was worried about a friend of mine." I looked down at my children. "Officer—"

"Detective Grafton."

"I'm sorry, Detective," I apologized. "Do my children have to be here for this?"

"Daddy, no!" Tracy begged. "Please don't leave us."

"Okay, baby." I held them closer.

The detective pulled a sheet of paper from his sports coat pocket. "Yes. I have in the operator's report you notified 911 regarding another incident at a separate address."

"Yes. I've told you and about a half dozen other officers already. Has anyone gone up there?"

"Mr. Brooks, that is not our jurisdiction but we are having someone look into it."

"Like hell you are! Tina was there. That was over an hour ago! For all I know, Joule is dead," I yelled at the detective causing the kids to cry again. "God!" I hugged Jimmy against me. "I'm sorry, kids! Look, officer."

"Detective," Grafton corrected me.

"Whatever. I need to get these kids out of here. Are you through with us?"

"I have a few more questions. You gave us the time you arrived and found the body, excuse me, Joey, and where were you before that?"

"Could you just let me take my kids to my parents and check on my friend, Joule?" I asked.

"I want Tracy here to speak with my partner. He has a few questions for her. Where would you be more comfortable, miss?" Detective Grafton asked Tracy. "I have a girl about your age. She's very smart. I'm sure you are, too." He tried to talk to her gently.

"She's fine right here with me," I told him, wrapping my arm tighter around her shoulders.

"She'll be close by, Mr. Brooks." He motioned for Tracy to come along with him.

She pulled away from me and stood up on her own. She willingly followed Detective Grafton outside. I stood up and lifted Jimmy into my arms and set him on my hip and followed them out. Grafton handed her off to the other detective, introducing him as Williams, who took Tracy and sat with her on a bench on our front deck.

Grafton steered me back in the trailer but left the door open and positioned me so I could see Tracy. "What time did you get home?" he asked.

I checked my watch. It was already a quarter 'til seven. "Around five."

"Where were you before that?"

"My parents' house most of the day, before that, at Joule's." I told him. "We spent last night at Joule's cabin on the lake."

"And who is Jule?"

"J-O-U-L-E Dalton." I felt my energy being sucked out of me. Nothing was being done about Joule.

Grafton wrote down her name in his pad and continued to interrogate me. I struggled to focus and when he was finished, I forgot the questions he'd asked along with the answers I'd given.

"I think that's all for now." He looked back at his partner who gave him a nod. "I may want to call you and ask you to come down to the precinct."

"I'll do whatever you need," I offered.

"Where can you be reached?"

"I don't know. There's an answering machine here." I tossed my head back towards the kitchen. "If I'm not here I'll call in and check the messages."

Grafton handed me his card.

I pocketed the card. Tracy came back to me and slid in under my free arm. I wrapped it around her and held her to my heart.

Grafton and Williams pulled away in their car and the rest of the police officers followed. I looked out over the crowd of neighbors held back by the officers. They looked at me and the kids with a combination of fear and pity. I shut the door, closing them out.

I coaxed Tracy to sit on the sofa and put Jimmy beside her. I picked up the phone and tried Joule's number. Her voicemail picked up. I tried her cell phone. No answer. "Damn." I sat between the children. I felt dizzy. I rolled the handset around in my hands. I could not stop the tears of both fear and frustration in my eyes. I did not want the kids to see me break down. I wiped my eyes against my sleeve and called Joule's loft again. Her voicemail answered again. I hung up. "Get in the truck, kids."

* * * *

Joule

The Kitchen Dance

"911. What is your emergency?"

"Hang on." I looked at my handset and read the caller identification. Brooks, Allen & Tina appeared on the screen. I was tempted to change lines but decided not to because a call from their house meant Allen and the kids were still there and I could call them back.

"I'm sorry." I don't know why I apologized to the operator. "I had an intruder. She has fallen down my staircase and I think…" I looked down the steep staircase at Tina. "She's dead."

"We have already received a call from the sheriff's office regarding this address and have dispatched a unit to your address. Please remain on the line until an officer arrives."

I heard the sounds of sirens. "I hear them now."

"When the officer arrives, please give him your phone for verification."

"I can't let them in. I can't get downstairs. She's blocking the stairs," I told her. "Wait." I grabbed my keys from the drawer of the thin table on the floor of the entry landing, the one I used to shove Tina away from me. I made my way with the phone to the back of the loft, opened the window in my bedroom, and climbed down the fire escape. The phone crackled in my ear the farther I got away from the unit. "Are you still there?" I asked the operator.

"Yes, Ma'am, but your connection sounds weak."

"I see them now." I waved at the officers and showed them the phone. One of the officers met me halfway and took the phone from me to speak with the 911 operator while the other officer waited for me to open the small warehouse door. The other officer unclipped his holster and positioned his hand around his gun. With his flashlight in his other hand he entered the warehouse in front of me.

"She's over there." I turned on the warehouse light. "On the stairs."

The officer rounded the corner to the staircase. "Ma'am, there's nobody here."

I looked around the warehouse terrified. "Check the laundry room." I pointed to the small room.

The officer drew his gun and pushed open the door to the small room. No Tina.

"And this other room?" The officer asked about Roosevelt's room.

"It's supposed to be locked," I told him.

The officer checked the knob. It was locked. He looked around the warehouse. "Anywhere else, Ma'am?"

I looked at the garage entry door. She could have made it out the door but I never heard the overhead door open. Then again, I had not been listening for such a sound. I looked up at my loft entrance.

The officer took the stairs towards the loft. "Stay here, Miss." He radioed his partner who came in the warehouse and stood in the open doorway.

I suddenly felt dizzy and nauseous as my knees buckled beneath me. I fell in a heap below the staircase. As if in a dream I became aware of a man's voice calling for an ambulance and felt the sharp stinging sensation as he patted my face.

"Ma'am! Ms. Dalton? Are you still with me?" His voice was firm yet kind as I tried to focus my eyes on the young officer before me. That was when I remembered that I had left the overhead door wide open.

* * * *

Allen

I parked close to a police car and got out of my truck. "Stay in the truck," I warned the kids. "Lock the doors! I'll be right over there!" I pointed across the street at the two officers in front of Joule's warehouse.

My stomach was sick from all the stress built up inside me on the three hour long drive to the city. "I'm looking for Joule Dalton," I told the officers. "She's the lady that lives here."

"She's gone," the taller of the two officers told me. "They took her away in an ambulance a couple of hours ago."

"Is she alright?" I almost choked.

"We don't know, Sir, we weren't here when they took her," The shorter officer said. "We were called back here by the guy who has the diner down there." The officer nodded his head towards John's diner down the street. "He reported there was a strange woman hanging around the warehouse and we thought it might be the suspect."

"Did he describe her?" I asked.

"Yes, sir," The shorter officer answered. "She's a blonde, short hair, average height."

"That's Tina!" I exclaimed.

"Are you Mr. Brooks?" the taller officer asked.

"Yes, I am."

"Sir, we'll need you to—"

Suddenly the kids were screaming.

I looked back towards the truck. The kids were leaning forward in their seat straining to see me. Suddenly, a dark form appeared by the driver's side window of the truck.

"Mommy!" I could hear Jimmy's voice muffled by the closed windows and could see him reaching over to unlock the door. Tracy looked frightened when the interior light of the truck cab came on as soon as the door opened. A bloody Tina climbed in and tried to start the truck. The engine tried to turn over but didn't. She tried again. I ran towards my old truck as fast I could. The truck started as I ran towards them and Tina peeled away.

"That's her!" I yelled back at the officers. "She's got my kids!"

The taller officer got in his car but was too late for a successful pursuit.

I ran over to the other police car and could hear him announce over the radio a full description of my truck. "And she's with my two children. My daughter, Tracy, she's twelve and my son, Jimmy, is six."

The officer added this to the description.

"We're putting an Amber alert out on them. We will contact you as soon as we find them, sir."

"Look, I don't have a cell phone," I told him hopelessly.

"I should give you a ride to the police station." The officer opened one of the rear doors of the patrol car for me to get in.

"I need to get to the hospital," I practically begged. "I need to see Joule first."

"So we can reach you at the hospital?"

"Yes, sir," I assured him.

The officer pulled away in the patrol car and I headed down the street to John's diner.

"Allen!" Gail called out as she ran to embrace me the moment I walked in the diner. "Oh, my God! I am sorry about Joule. Is she doing alright? Wait!" She held me at arm's length. "What are you doing here? Oh, my God! Is she—"

"I don't know," I cut in. "I haven't seen her."

"We saw them take her off in the ambulance." John came from behind the counter. "She looked pretty bad, Allen. Do you know what happened?"

"I don't know." I felt sick to my stomach again. "I need to call a cab. My-Tina-my kids," I stammered.

"Here, Allen, sit down." Gail tried to guide me to a booth. "I'll get you some water."

"No. I'm okay." I sat in the booth anyway. "I need to call a cab. I've got to get to the hospital."

"Are you okay to drive?" John asked me.

"What? My truck-Tina," I started stammering again.

"Wait a sec." John went behind the counter and reached under the cash register. He came back and handed me a key to Joule's flat. "She left this with me a while back, you know, in case Roosevelt got locked out or something. Just take her car. I'm sure she wouldn't care."

I ran back to the loft and, when I got inside, I was shocked by the amount of blood and destruction. I found her cell phone and the keys to the Jaguar. Bracing myself behind the wheel I drove that car as hard as I could all the way to the hospital.

When I entered the emergency room, Joule was drowsily fighting sleep. By the light over the hospital bed, Joule looked beaten up badly and her voice was weak. "Did they find Tina?"

I lowered my head, shaking it slowly.

"They gave me something for the pain." Joule sounded tired. "It's making me sleepy. I don't want to go to sleep. I want to be awake."

My stomach still ached and the stress made me feel exhausted. I could hardly stand. I fought the tears welling up in my eyes. I turned away from her and peered out the blinds of the window overlooking the rocky roof of another part of the hospital. I could see the skeleton of a pigeon on the roof lit up by the open blinds of the windows below me.

"Allen?" Joule asked.

"Yeah."

"We were happy weren't we?" she said weakly.

"Yeah. Very happy," I managed to add.

Joule took in a deep breath. "It was the happiest I have ever been." She breathed out softly.

"Me, too."

"Do you think we will ever be that happy again?" she asked.

"I don't know." I lost the battle with my tears. My voice croaked like a tired and sick old man. "I don't know. I just don't know." I looked over at Joule. Her eyelids lost their battle to stay open. She had fallen asleep.

* * * *

A phone rang and I was startled from sleep, slumped in an uncomfortable hospital chair. Joule stirred. The phone rang out again and I realized it was the phone by Joule's bed and I fumbled to answer it. "Hello."

"Is this Allen Brooks?" a man's voice asked.

"Yes." I fought to wake up. "Yes, it is."

"Mr. Brooks. This is Detective Richards. We've found your children."

"Where are they?" I bolted straight up.

"We located them at a convenience store and they are in transit to the precinct." Richards told me.

"Are they alright?" I asked.

"Yes, sir. They appear to be okay. Sleepy, but unharmed."

"Okay. I'll meet you there at the precinct. Uh, detective? What about

The Kitchen Dance

Tina? Their mother, did you find her?"

"No, sir."

"What about the truck?" I asked the detective.

"No, sir. Apparently Tina Brooks stopped for gas. The store attendant informed us Mrs. Brooks brought the children in with her to prepay for gas and left them in the store to purchase soft drinks. She filled the tank with gas then pulled out and left them there. Whether intentional or not, we don't know."

"I'm worried about Joule. Tina may come here to the hospital."

"I'll send an officer to look after Ms. Dalton. Your children are going to want to see you as soon as possible," Detective Richards told me.

"Yes, of course, I'll be there." I closed the phone and stood up and stretched out my aching back. I leaned down over Joule and whispered, "Joule." She barely stirred. "I will be back soon." I kissed her forehead and left her there, sleeping.

Chapter Twenty-One

Allen

I arrived at the police station and asked an officer behind the desk for directions to where my kids were. He took me to the elevator and I followed him until we found an office where my kids were waiting. When I walked in, Tracy and Jimmy were sitting together in one of the two chairs across the desk from a guy in a suit.

"Daddy!" the kids yelled in unison but did not get up. They were not sure if they were allowed to get up or not. I went to them, got down on my knees and pulled them out of the chair into my arms.

"Can I take them home now?" I asked the man.

"Not back to the trailer!" Tracy protested.

"No. We'll go back to Grandma's." I tried to calm her down.

"Mr. Brooks, I am Detective Richards. We need to ask you a few questions before you leave."

"Please, my kids need to get to bed. I've got to get them to my parent's house," I protested. It was nearly two in the morning.

"Could you meet me here tomorrow?" Richards asked.

"Of course, when?" I was relieved to be getting the kids away from here.

"Why don't I call you?" Detective Richards offered.

I gave him Joule's cell phone number.

I took the kids out of the station and buckled them up in the backseat of the sports car.

"Daddy?" Jimmy asked as I started the car.

"Yeah Jimmy." I pulled away from the curb. The Jaguar wanted to leap out from under me.

The Kitchen Dance

"Mommy said you left us for Joule," Jimmy whimpered.

"No, Jimmy, that's not what happened. Let's not talk about this right now."

"But Mommy said we were going to be a happy family again. But Joule—" Jimmy continued.

"Shut up!" Tracy interrupted. "You don't even know what you're talking about!"

"She said this was all Joule's fault," Jimmy argued with Tracy. "It's Joule's fault Joey's dead."

"That's a lie. Mom is nuts!" Tracy screamed at Jimmy. She looked up at me calmly. "She told me she didn't know about the baby."

"What?" I asked Tracy.

"Shit-for-brains here asked her why she killed Joey!" Tracy told me.

"Oh, my God." I was bewildered. "Jimmy?" I looked up in the rear view mirror at Jimmy sitting behind me in the backseat.

"She said she didn't. She told us the baby was with Joe! Joe took Joey last night. Is our brother with Joe, Daddy?" Jimmy asked innocently.

"No, Stupid! He's dead. Our little brother is dead! She killed him!" Tracy screamed. "Our mother killed him!"

"Tracy!" I yelled at her even though I did not want to. I knew she needed to let it out but not like this and in front of Jimmy.

"What if she comes back for us?" Jimmy became hysterical. "What if she wants to kill us, too? What are we going to do, Daddy! She's going to kill us because you left her!"

I pulled over to the roadside and stopped the car so hard the children rocked forward, restrained by their seat belts, and then slammed back against their seat.

"Daddy!" Tracy yelled at me.

"Now listen you two!" I was angry. I turned around in my seat and I shouted at them. "This is all very confusing! I did not leave your mother for Joule. Your mother left me for Joe! Do you understand? She made me leave!" I took a deep breath and tried to calm down. "I love you both. You are my family! But I love Joule, too! And I wanted us all to be a family! I don't know what happened. I don't know why this happened but bad things do happen." I turned to face the front and tried to calm down. "Boy, did a lot of bad things happen." I caught eyes with Jimmy in the rear view mirror. "But, people can get through bad things and still have very good lives. We need to think about having good times." I turned to face them. "So, Tracy, enough of the name-calling and Jimmy, don't believe everything someone tells you."

"Not even people I know?" Jimmy was confused.

"Not even people you know." I was just as confused.

"Not even you?" Jimmy kept on.

I wanted to say not even me. Even I couldn't bear the burden of the truth. "Look, Jimmy, this is going to be very hard. What happened to Joey was sad. I will try to be as honest with you as I can. But you're only six-years-old. I think you need to be spared from some of this."

"What about me, Daddy? Are you going to lie to me?" Tracy asked me in her sassy preteen way.

"I don't know, honey. I'll do my best not to."

I turned around and looked at the long dark road ahead of me. We sat there in silence for a few minutes before I put the car in gear and pulled back onto the road.

* * * *

Joule

I saw Allen walk towards me down the hallway toward the detective's office. He looked surprised when he saw me standing with Philip just outside the detective's door.

"What are you doing here?" he asked me as his hand slipped around my cheek to the back of my neck and he kissed me just shy of my mouth. He offered his right hand to Philip who gladly shook it.

"Detective Richards called me. He wants to ask me a few questions. He told me you were coming in. He told me a detective named Grafton wanted to meet you here."

"I could have picked you up at the hospital." Allen slid his hand down my arm and wrapped his fingers around the forearm of my uninjured arm and gave me a gentle squeeze as if hugging me might cause me pain.

"Philip was at the hospital when I was released so he brought me here. I did not want you to have to drive in. Richards told me about Tracy and Jimmy. Where are the kids, now?"

"They're with my parents."

"You drove all the way there and back?" I asked him with pity and concern.

"No, they met me. We're staying at a hotel."

"Are they okay?" I asked.

"They were still asleep when I left them."

"Did you tell your parents?" I asked with concern. "About everything?"

"Yes." he answered flatly.

"I'm sorry." I could not think of anything to say that did not sound like a

The Kitchen Dance

cliché. "I can't imagine what they think of me."

"There not blaming you, Joule."

"Oh, Allen. You look exhausted."

"I was up most of the night. I've probably only had a couple hours of sleep."

"You should try what the nurse gave me. I think I'm still asleep."

A man walked out of Richards's office. "Good. You're both here." He motioned to another detective to join them. "Mr. Brooks, you remember Detective Williams?"

Allen nodded.

"Ms. Dalton, I'm Detective Grafton and this is Detective Williams. We are with the sheriff's office." Neither man extended their hand in a polite effort at a greeting, obviously noticing my right hand was resting in a sling.

"Tina Brooks was found early this morning and we brought her in for questioning," Detective Williams greeted us by saying.

Allen and I exchanged relieved looks.

"We released her about an hour ago."

Our relieved looks quickly morphed into concern.

"Ms. Dalton, Detective Williams and I will be asking you some questions," Detective Richards stepped out of his office and informed me.

Allen gave me a quizzical look before we were taken into separate interrogation rooms.

* * * *

Allen

Grafton asked me to be seated on the opposite side of a table in the center of the room. He turned a camcorder around to face me and pressed buttons. He set a microphone attached to the camera by a long thin cable on the table in front of me. Another detective came in the room.

"This is Detective Clinton." Grafton introduced the detective from the city's police force. "We'll be conducting this interview together if you don't mind."

"No. I don't mind." I fidgeted with the zipper on the jacket I was wearing trying to decide whether or not to take it off.

Clinton spoke in the microphone announcing the date and time and everyone's name in order to record it. "Mr. Brooks. You are not under arrest. This is simply an interview. You may discontinue this conversation at any point. Detective Grafton and I will need to ask you questions we feel are pertinent to our investigation." Detective Clinton informed me.

"Okay."

"And you understand you may stop this interview at any point and you are free to leave?" Grafton reminded me as he leaned over the table.

"Yes, I understand." I had nothing to hide.

"I need you to take us through the past forty eight hours." Clinton took a seat across the table from me. Grafton leaned against the wall beside the door.

I looked at my watch. It was a new watch Joule had bought me. It was a few minutes past three in the afternoon. "Well, Friday, at this time, I just got home. The kids were alone in the trailer. They told me they were alone since they got home from school."

"When you say kids, you are referring to…" Clinton checked his notepad. "Tracy, age twelve, and Jimmy Brooks?"

"Yes," I replied. "My kids."

"Where was the baby?" Clinton continued.

"Jimmy told me Tina took the baby with her."

"Did you look for the baby?" Clinton continued.

"What do you mean?" I asked.

"Did you look for the baby anywhere in the home?" Grafton interrupted.

"No, my son said Tina had him with her."

"So you never verified whether the infant was present in the home or not?" Clinton asked.

"No." I felt my eyebrows creasing. I never thought to look.

"Jimmy is how old?" Clinton asked.

"Six."

Clinton scribbled something on his notepad. I looked back at Grafton feeling confused and a little uneasy.

* * * *

Joule

I asked Philip to wait when Detective Williams asked me to follow him into a separate interview room where Detective Richards was setting up a video recorder. Williams guided me inside the room. Richards stopped fiddling with the video recorder and pulled a chair away from the table and offered me the seat. I noticed two files on the table.

Both Williams and Richards stood over me as Richards explained the procedures of the interview. I had been interviewed before. Grilled would be a better expression. After Daniel's murder, I would guess more time was spent interviewing me than was spent searching for the men whose description I so precisely detailed.

The Kitchen Dance

"Ms. Dalton. Where were you at approximately 6:00 last night?" Detective Richards took the seat across the table from me.

"I was home," I replied.

"And where is your home?" Richards pressed.

"At my warehouse. I have a loft apartment." I gave him the address.

"According to the report you gave the officer at the scene, you encountered Tina Brooks on your premises."

"Yes." I sighed deeply still lethargic from the pain medication I took earlier. I was already bored with the formalities. I knew how slowly this could progress.

"Are you alright?" Williams seemed concerned. "Can I get you some coffee or something?"

"I'm fine," I humored him.

"Had you spoken to Mrs. Brooks prior to this encounter?"

"Not really. I answered the phone when she called for Allen. I never spoke to her though."

Williams picked up the other file and flipped through the pages. "Ms. Dalton, according to Mrs. Brooks, you invited her over to your loft."

"No, that's not true," I protested.

Williams showed Richards the report and the two men took a moment of my time to compare the two reports.

"You indicated she attacked you?" Richards added as more of a statement than a question.

"Yes." I remembered from my last interrogation to keep my answers brief and not to elaborate unless asked.

"According to Mrs. Brooks, you attacked her. She says here you shoved her into the wall and hit her in the face with a flashlight and you threw some sort of sheet metal structure at her then pushed her down your stairs."

"What? No, that is not how it happened!" I exclaimed with shock. "Look at me." I held out my injured arm and lifted my shirt high enough to reveal the bandages over my sliced ribs. "She did this to me."

"According to Mrs. Brooks, you did these to yourself." Williams scraped a metal chair across the floor and positioned it at the end of the table.

"What? How? She had a knife! She brought it with her for Christ's sake! She came after me first and stabbed me here." I pointed to my bandaged arm. I was feeling cornered all over again. I felt the adrenaline slipping into my bloodstream as if hot lava was being injected straight into my veins through a massive syringe. I could feel my heart beat faster and my head growing light as my thoughts grew cloudier than the medications from the night before had caused.

"The only knife we found in your loft had your prints on it, but none belonging to Mrs. Brooks."

"That could have been one of my knives. But she had another one. I'm telling you she brought it with her. She probably took her knife when she left my loft. What about the broom and the duct tape? Did you see that?"

Williams looked over at Richards who checked over the report without looking at me. "According to Mrs. Brooks, you used this to destroy your loft. She said you were ranting like a lunatic when she arrived."

"No! I can't believe this! That woman is crazy! She killed her own baby!"

"According to Mrs. Brooks, the baby was left in the care of the baby's father. She was not aware of the baby's death until the police located her this morning."

"Well? Did you talk to the father?" I did not dare to get caught up in the previous accusations. I was too angry to think clearly.

"No, Ma'am. We have not been able to locate him as of yet." Detective Richards informed me.

I reached for the file. "What else did she say?"

Williams put out his hand to block me. "Ms. Dalton, according to Mrs. Brooks, you were interfering in the possible reconciliation of her marriage. When she asked to talk with you, you invited her over. When she arrived, your loft was already damaged, you were bloody, and you attacked her."

Bewildered, I rested my elbow on the table and buried my face in my hand.

"She said you came after her, attacked her, and pushed her down your staircase, knocking her unconscious. She indicated here in her report when she came to, you were no longer in the building." Richards flipped the page of the report.

"She said that?" I questioned her eloquence in such a detailed description of her fantastical version of the event.

"No, I'm paraphrasing," Richards informed me with a sarcastic expression on his face. "She's gone into a great deal of detail about the encounter."

"Let me see it." I reached for the file again but was prohibited.

"She wanted to file assault charges against you but she was too distraught over her baby's death to do so at that time. She plans to return with her attorney later this afternoon," Williams warned me. "You or your attorney can get a copy of the report when she files her complaint."

I looked at the detective, one then the other, expressing ultimate shock and disbelief.

* * * *

Allen

"When was the last time you saw the baby alive?" Grafton asked.
"That morning," I mumbled behind my hands.
"Mr. Brooks, could you please speak in the microphone."
"Friday morning." I raked my hair back with my fingers and spoke directly and clearly into the microphone while Grafton referred to his notes. "But I heard him Friday night, over the phone. He was crying," I suddenly remembered.
"And what time was this?" Clinton asked.
"Around eight or eight thirty."
An officer tapped on the door, opened it and motioned for Grafton. He spoke to the detective quietly in the hall then Grafton returned to the interrogation room.
"Mr. Brooks. Joe Calvechio, the baby's father, was just brought in. He says he did not have the baby Friday night or Saturday and his alibi appears tight."
"Then you need to find Tina."
"We'll be bringing her back in for more questioning. For now, I have some more questions for you."

* * * *

Joule

"It's starting all over again." I pressed my palms against my eyes.
"What is starting, Ms. Dalton?" Williams asked.
"You're accusing me, aren't you?" I pulled my palms away and waited for my eyes to refocus. "Do I need to contact my attorney?"
"Let's just say, had Mrs. Brooks been at the bottom of your staircase, she would have been the third dead body we've found at your home in the past couple of years."

* * * *

Allen

"We could never prove she had anything to do with her husband's death but we never found the men who supposedly killed him. We can't help but be curious, Mr. Brooks, why she hired you, a homeless man, much like the two homeless men who she reported killed her husband. The next thing you know we find Roosevelt Graham dead in her warehouse.

"He died of a heart attack," I argued.

"A heart attack that may have been caused by a stressful situation like an attempt by someone to take his life? You were staying in the warehouse at the time of Mr. Graham's death, were you not?"

"Yes, I was in the loft." A sickening fear began to creep up my spine and sharp pain stabbed behind my eyes.

"Were you sleeping with Ms. Dalton?" Clinton asked me.

"No, on the sofa."

"I think what Detective Clinton means is, were you and Ms. Dalton romantically involved?"

"No. Not then. Not at that time." I thought after I said it. I probably should not have added the last part.

"It just seems convenient the people who may be getting in the way of her happiness tend to end up dead," Williams added mocking me.

"Joule loved Roosevelt and she would never do anything to hurt him."

"Yet she put the warehouse up for sale less than a month after his death."

* * * *

Joule

"Is that where Mr. Brooks comes in? Did you hire Mr. Brooks to kill Roosevelt Graham so you could sell the warehouse and move back out to the cabin? Old Roosevelt didn't add to the curb appeal did he?" Detective Richards accused me.

"I want to call my lawyer," I declared. "This interview is over!"

* * * *

Allen

"So with Mr. Graham, your ex-wife, and her baby out of the way, you and Ms. Dalton were free to pursue your own interests. You would get your kids. Ms. Dalton could sell her warehouse and add to the money from her inheritance and her husband's life insurance policy and all of you could live happily ever after. But, why you? Why would she want to run off with you? You have nothing. Something tells me she'll just get rid of you as well," Grafton ragged on me.

I was stunned speechless. I raked my hands through my hair. How did these guys know my business? What all had I told Tina during the past couple of weeks. How had she found a way to use all this against me? I could not sort it out fast enough. "I don't understand any of this," I admitted with defeat.

"Would you like me to call you a court appointed attorney or did you think Ms. Dalton was going to pay for your legal counsel?" Grafton kept up with his ribbing.

"Am I under arrest?" I asked.

"Not until we find sufficient evidence, Mr. Brooks. But we're looking into it."

"Then I guess this so-called interview is over." I stood and zipped up my jacket.

Grafton and Clinton released me from the interrogation room. I saw Joule with Philip in the hall and could tell by her expression she was just as confused and unhappy as I was. Philip put his arm around her shoulders and started walking her away from me. I wanted to catch up to them, talk to her, hold her and tell her she was still asleep and I was delirious from the lack of it and we were only dreaming this. But I knew I could not. I went up to her slowly catching them as they waited on the elevator. And then I started thinking, remembering, and doubting everything.

"It's not going very well," I told her. "Is it?"

"I think it's best if you stay with your parents." Joule stepped in the elevator. Philip blocked me from getting in with them and the doors closed in front of my face.

I stood in the empty hall staring blankly at the elevator doors. I could not put forth the effort into pushing the button. Who was this woman? Was I such a bad judge of character that I could not have seen that Joule was capable of attacking Tina, hurting Roosevelt, even murdering her husband? My first wife had thrown me a curve ball with her shopaholic addiction and my second wife, Tina, had turned against me and our marriage as well. Was I that big a fool not to see where this was going with Joule? All the negative thoughts I ever had about why Joule would ever be interested in me gnawed their way like worms in a corpse destroying all the good in our relationship. Did she just use me? Is she trying to set me up for Roosevelt's death? Is she lying about Tina? Was she anywhere near our trailer today and was she capable of killing a baby? Joey? Just to get what she wanted.

A woman stepped in front of me out of nowhere. I never heard her coming down the hallway but her hand reached out and pressed the elevator button. My heart jumped when the doors opened. Somehow I feared Joule would be standing there. But she wasn't and the woman stepped in the empty elevator and turned towards me. She was an older woman, dressed in a dark suit and white blouse wearing glasses that reflected a glare so I could not see her eyes.

Her mouth was tense with concern as she waited alone in the elevator for the doors to close.

I went back to the detective's office. Detective Grafton was alone in the interrogation room making some notes in the file. I knocked on the door. He closed the file when he saw it was me and tucked his pen in his breast pocket before opening the door.

"I want to know about Joule's husband's murder." I insisted. "Why do you think she did it? And tell me why you think she'd let some old man she hardly knew live with her? God! She even fixed up this nice room for him. I don't see how someone would go to all the trouble just to kill them years later."

"Please sit down, Mr. Brooks." Grafton said a little too calmly as he guided me to the chair and closed the door.

"Hell, no!" I hissed. "This is...how do they say it...off-the-record? I'm not going to let you video or record this conversation. I need some answers and I think you owe it to me."

"Mr. Brooks." Grafton was quiet and condescending. "Are you having doubts about Ms. Dalton's integrity?" A slight smile slid up his face and it made me feel sick and angry. "Please, Mr. Brooks," he pulled the chair away from the table. "We'll just talk."

"Oh, you're good." I admitted. "For a minute there, you had me thinking. Now I know this is just your game. I see how you are trying to manipulate me, dancing me around this little room trying to get me where you want me and to say what you want me to say. I'm not here to sit down and answer any more of your questions. I'm here to get answers. I want to know why you accused Joule of killing her husband."

"I'm sure you know, Mr. Brooks, that in similar cases, it was usually the spouse that committed the crime." Grafton took the seat he had offered to me.

"But Roosevelt was the witness."

Grafton gave me a sarcastic look. "Corroborating a story and being an eye witness to a crime is a totally different bird." Grafton played with the file like he was going to open it. "Roosevelt said he heard the gunshot and walked in to see Joule holding her dying husband. A weapon was obviously used but never found. With no concrete evidence we could not arrest her." Detective Grafton gave me a hard look. "Tell me, Mr. Brooks, does lack of evidence mean a person is innocent."

"Joule has a good character. She works hard. She's generous and she volunteers at a soup kitchen." I defended her.

"Oh, yes." Grafton was smug and acted as if he had a personal grudge against Joule. "She has quite a resume and plenty of character witnesses to support what a nice person she is." Grafton gave me a cool look. "Sit down, Mr. Brooks, or I will tell you no more."

I yanked the seat away from the table and plopped down crossing my arms over my chest trying to keep a grip on my anger.

"You see, Allen. May I call you, Allen?"

I did not answer.

"Ms. Dalton is in the business of sales. Sure, she's an interior designer but let's face it, everything is about selling. I'm trying to sell you something right now. I'm using tactics of manipulation to get from you what I want. When dealing with someone like Ms. Dalton, we detectives know we have to tighten up our game." Grafton leaned back in his chair and created a mirror image of how I was sitting. "You, on the other hand, are a bit easier to read."

"Are you saying I'm stupid or something."

"No, Mr. Brooks, just uninformed."

I stood up and smoothed out my clothes. "You know, Detective, I may be walking around with blinders on but I believe I have a pretty good grasp of who Joule is. You're just shooting birdshot in the air hoping it will hit something, but all your tiny little efforts are falling to the ground. You must be feeling stupid right now because you're wrong about Joule. Joule took me in when I had nothing and asked nothing from me in return. She took good care of Roosevelt and it just sickens me to hear you say anything against her. She would never do anything to hurt him or anybody else." I made my way to the door but turned around before opening it. "I admit it. I was standing out in that hallway thinking 'Man, I don't have women figured out.' But that's not true of Joule. I may not play your games or dance your little dance but I understand relationships and, if anything, I do know why my marriages failed. I'm a simple man but I'm not an ignorant man. I trust Joule with my children and my life. And I know Tina was not well—mentally, and I believe she went after Joule, and Joule did whatever she needed to do to protect herself. And little Joey." I shook my head, the grief finally setting in, and I found it hard to catch my breath. "God, I hope you'll stop wasting time creating lies and start finding the truth."

Chapter Twenty-Two

Joule

    I returned to the cabin after a few days with Philip and Elaine. I was putting the photos and mementos, still spread across the table, back in the box. I opened the city's newspaper I brought with me and cut out an article titled "Mother Kills Infant during Postpartum Episode". I put the clipped article on top of the photos and closed the box. Another box of memories, I thought, to add to the boxes filled with pictures of my parents and family, now gone, my life with Daniel, over two years past, and now my life with Allen and his kids.
    The phone rang. I looked at the caller identification read West, Philip & Elaine. "Hello." I tried to answer it as if I had not read the caller I.D. and as if I did not know who was calling.
    "Joule, what are you doing?" Elaine replied as if it had been a long time and we just needed to catch up.
    "I'm just cleaning up the cabin." I kept up the ruse. "I was working on a new scrapbook before all this happened," I finally disclosed. "Now, I'm just—" I trailed off. "What are you doing?"
    "Joule, Allen called me." Elaine went straight to the point. "He said you weren't returning his calls."
    "That's right." I propped the handset on my shoulder and took the box and the scrapbook to the closet in my new bedroom, placing them on a high shelf in the closet.
    "I think you should talk to him, Joule."
    "I just don't see how this can work out, 'Laine. His ex-wife will always be a part of our lives. Every time I see these scars on my arm and side I think about her attacking me. How can I look at those children and not remember? How can they look at me and not think about what happened? What if the kids

blame me for what happened to their mother? And the detectives! All the horrible things they accused us of doing? Of killing Roosevelt? Not to mention the lies they told Allen. It's just been too much."

"I didn't say it would be a breeze," Elaine tried to placate me. "If nothing else, I can attest to how easily people can be misjudged. Just because someone is rich, it does not mean they are greedy or snobby. Just because a husband is murdered does not mean his wife killed him. Just because a man has no money does not mean he is worthless. Allen is a good man and a good father. You, Allen, and those kids are going to have to heal the wounds and live with the scars regardless. Why not heal the wounds and live with the scars together?"

I could not respond. I was choked up and not ready to share. I could feel my voice being rung out of my throat like a dishrag and I was about to scream but no sound or words could come out. So many things I shared were used against me and I could not tell anyone how I felt about it, not even with my best friend.

"Joule, he says he loves you and I know you loved him."

I could not respond.

"Joule?"

"Yes," I managed to muster, but it sounded more like a bark from a small, yappy dog than a word.

"You'll make new memories, good memories, and great memories! And in no time, all these great times will fill your scrapbook. I know you would do whatever you could to give those children a happy home to grow up in. Promise me you will at least think about it. Okay?" Elaine pushed.

I still could not answer. The tears stung at my eyes and I sat down on the sill below the large windows and looked out over the lake. It was hot outside and I thought about how the kids would have loved an afternoon dip in the shallow waters around the dock.

"Joule?" Elaine tested to see if I were still on the line.

"Yes." I breathed out letting her know I was still available.

"It is just like your cabin on the lake perched on the side of a hill. Just because something looks precarious doesn't mean it's not sturdy."

"Right out of college I had this boyfriend, Saul. Did I ever tell you about him?"

"I don't think so."

"Anyway, we met in college and he followed me to graduate school. We were together about three years then one day he just left. No note, nothing."

"I remember now. You lived in that warehouse with several other artists."

"Yes, that was him." I let the memory of that year flow over me like warm water. I had no scrapbook of those days, no photographs, no news clippings, yet the memories both good and bad remained as vivid as if they just occurred yesterday. "Losing my parents and Daniel was traumatic, and Roosevelt's dying was heartbreaking. Still, to have someone doubt you is a pain like no other. I work hard at my job always trying to do my best work. I volunteer at the soup kitchen and I try to be kind and considerate to the less fortunate because, Elaine, 'there but for the grace of God go I', and I want so much for everyone to have a home, a satisfying job, and food to eat. So when those detectives start asking me those outrageous questions and accusing me again of killing my husband, having something to do with Roosevelt's death and—" I could no longer hold back the sobs, "when they accused me of attacking Tina, I realized that everything I thought I was meant nothing if others were so easily led to falsely judge me."

"Joule, Philip and I never thought you did any of those things." Elaine cried through her sympathetic response. "No one who knows you ever doubted you or blamed you."

"But I saw the look in Allen's eyes, for that brief second, when Philip and I were getting in the elevator, I saw doubt."

"Joule, please. Allen was just as shaken up as you were. He was exhausted. His children had just been taken from him and left at a convenience store. I'm sure the detectives gave him the riot act as they did you." Elaine pleaded with me. "Please, just talk to him."

"I used to think it was fate Allen and I met. When he showed up in Daniel's coat, I thought he had come along to replace Daniel; to fill in for him in a way. Do you know what I mean?" I continued to look out at the white hot sky reflecting off the silver water. "Even his name, Allen, so close to Daniel. Allen. Daniel. Funny, don't you think that I would even think that?" I did not give her a chance to answer. "He was nothing like Daniel. Totally opposite."

"But that is why you needed him," Elaine tried to console me. "Daniel was a handsome man and an outstanding architect. I can see how you loved him. Although there were times when I did not see how you could stand him, but all men are that way honey," Elaine added with a little laugh. "It's a separate road, I know. Same coat, different man. Same Joule, different life."

I wiped my nose and smiled to myself. I was so grateful to have such a wonderful friend like Elaine. It should not matter what the rest of the world thought about me or the stories they fabricated on misinformation. This precious person was always there for me. "What about your nice-looking Stephen Croft?" I volleyed. "I thought for sure you would jump right back into fixing me up with him."

"Yes." Elaine laughed. "There is that."

Epilogue

Allen

    I would never have guessed a year ago that I would be a member in a huge crowd, each looking for their respective loved ones in a line of college graduates. Somewhere in the group dressed in academic regalia gathered for their commencement exercises in the school's assembly center, was my son. The list of names in alphabetical order was announced by a professor wearing a throw pillow on top of his head and a robe with more strips of fabric and sashes than the West's living room windows. I craned my head to look over the six foot four man who was half as wide as he was tall who chose the seat in front of me. When the speaker finally reached the name James Allen Brooks III, I stood up for a better look. My son crossed the stage and received his diploma. He turned to the audience and waved as if he could see me and I waved back.
    He'd been a gift to me in a way. It was like an offering to make amends for something. Joule hoped it would make up for how, in some way, she had wronged me. I never blamed her for any of this. Instead, I blamed myself. It was her forgiveness I needed and I'd nothing to offer her in return.

* * * *

    Cheryl had called me. She told me James, or Buddy as she still called him, was nearing the end of his summer session and was up to his neck in finals. She did not feel it was a good time for me to see him. It was bad enough life had given me a pretty good kick in the ass. Now my first ex-wife was calling me out of the blue telling me how I couldn't see my oldest son. I hadn't even asked. I just assumed he wrote me off. With all the confusion of Joey's death and Tina's sentencing I rarely thought about my firstborn. After the incident with Tina and little Joey, I immediately moved the kids to my parents' house and put the trailer up for sale. Eventually, I sold it to the trailer park manager for little to nothing but at least it was no longer my concern. Since I purchased it before I married Tina, I was able to pocket all the money and the kids and I moved into an apartment near my parents. I was relieved the divorce was finalized a couple of months before the incident and I did not have the burden of making any decisions on Tina's behalf. I could leave it up to her parents and her attorney. I had suffered enough. For now I was planning a future with just me and my kids.

The investigation ruled Joey's death a homicide but did not have sufficient evidence to charge Tina with first degree murder. Joule agreed with the state prosecutor to drop her attempted manslaughter if Tina took the guilty plea of killing little Joey for reasons of insanity. Joe Calvechio pushed for her to spend her life in prison. I testified for Tina's sake because, according to her psychoanalyst, she was suffering from postpartum psychosis. She had always been temperamental but even I believed she lost control. Tina's commitment into the state run psychiatric facility for a minimum sentence was upsetting for the kids. I was upset because she could get out in a few years. Jimmy would still be a minor and she could press for his custody. I could not think about that now. I had already forced the kids to see her on her few permitted visitations. I could only manage one crisis at a time. That is why I was surprised when Cheryl called.

"Your friend, Joule, called," she told me. I was surprised that Joule was able to find her, let alone be willing. But Cheryl would like Joule, I realized. They both liked nice things except Joule was willing to work for them. "She told me about what happened and how your kids just lost their little brother and now might be a good time for them to get to know their big brother," Cheryl added. "I agree with her, Allen. I know you hate me but don't you think it is time we bury the hatchet and get along for Buddy's sake?"

"I never hated you, Cheryl."

"You're kidding, right?" Her voice came out with a nervous laugh. "After all I put you through? I thought you would never want to speak to me again."

"Is that why you ran off?" I didn't know if I should be angry or respond with the same nervous laugh. "Because you thought I was mad at you?" I chose the nervous laugh.

"Allen. I was just a kid. I did not know how to manage money. I wanted everything I saw," she confessed. "I'm sorry I put you, put all of us, through that." She waited for my response but I had none. "You hated me didn't you?"

"No," I answered flatly. "Not for the debt but maybe because you took James away from me." I was honest.

The Kitchen Dance

"You were busy with your new family." Cheryl let her jealousy surface.

"Tracy and Jimmy keep me very busy. But there was always room for James and we could have been friends, Cheryl."

"We still can. It's not too late." I could tell she was filled with emotion.

We agreed we would get together after James's exams. I called Joule. I wanted to thank her and I wanted her to be a part of it.

* * * *

I was sitting with my parents, Tracy, Jimmy, Cheryl, her husband, and Cheryl's parents. Cheryl and I looked at each other and smiled approvingly. She looked good dressed in fashionable clothing. Her multicolored blonde hair was stylishly cut short and flipped up in the back. She was slim and firm and her tanned face looked a bit stretched over her skull. Her husband, a meek man with thin red hair and blotchy skin, may have been hard on the eye but he was a friendly man who certainly kept Cheryl in the lifestyle she had always wanted.

My parents stood up from their seats to allow Joule to squeeze past them and take the empty seat beside me. She waited below the stage to take pictures of James with the other flash happy loved ones, who flowed in a similar line of alphabetical order as their photographic subjects, wanting to capture the moment.

After the ceremony I shook the hand of James, the graduate, and then embraced him. He looked more like me than I could have ever imagined. Joule joined us and I pulled her into the hug while Tracy and Jimmy gathered around us.

"Congratulations, son."

"Thanks for coming," James said.

"I wouldn't have missed it." There was much I had missed. I could do nothing about that now and there was no point in dwelling on it. We had our future to look forward to. I turned back to Cheryl and her husband and smiled.

Hugs and congratulations continued as Joule took her camera and began photographing the group until another graduate approached.

"Let me do that," he offered.

"Yeah, Joule." James motioned for Joule. "Come get in the picture."

"Thanks." She smiled at James but I knew what was coming. "I'm just here to take pictures."

* * * *

Joule

I was enjoying a few minutes to myself in the cabin. A combination of compact discs randomly played a selection of music. The sunlight streaked through openings between the branches and leaves and danced across the dining table where I pressed the photograph from James's graduation on a page in the scrapbook filled with other precious memories shared with Allen and his children. Adhered to the pages of the thick book were only good memories. Tucked away in a box were the others where they existed somewhere in the back of our lives, but they did not define us. Time and healing faded the scars but did not remove them. We were all better people for having survived it, and the burden we bore lighter for having carried it together.

I stuffed the book in a box with a label bearing Allen's address. I set it on the counter between the kitchen and dining area and I was looking in a cabinet for a glass when Elaine came through the front door.

"Hel-loo, Jou-elle," she sang as she came in quickly greeting me with a hug. "Just look at what the cat dragged in." She announced Stephen Croft as he walked in the front door.

"Oh, Elaine." I shook my head in mocking disbelief.

Philip soon followed carrying a bag I recognized from the bakery.

"Hello, Stephen." I crossed the living room to greet them.

"Did you know Stephen was the engineer who inspected the foundation for the addition to your cabin?" Elaine seemed overjoyed. "We didn't know until we came down your drive. He knew Daniel."

"Really? It's a small world."

"Not that small," Stephen greeted me. "I've done most of the inspections for your firm's construction projects."

Philip intervened, "Come with me, Stephen, and I'll show you the finished renovation." And the two men quickly passed through the living room to the deck on the rear of the cabin.

I returned to the kitchen. "This is awkward."

"I knew if I asked, you'd say no."

"You always know what is best for me. Don't you, Elaine?" I collected a stack of colorful plates from the cabinets, the Fulper Pottery plates I now used every day.

Elaine reached for the scrapbook in the box and turned back the pages revealing photos and mementos of Allen's and his family. "Why are there no pictures of you?"

"I thought it might be better for the kids if they remembered the good times they had here and not necessarily remember me."

"Oh, Joule." Elaine put the book back in the box. "Is this really what you want?"

"Yes. You know, I'm okay." I reached in the refrigerator and pulled out

The Kitchen Dance

the steaks and a head of Romaine lettuce. "He's working now. It's a good job. And the kids are doing much better. We'll keep in touch but, we both know, accept, we just can't be together." I took the lettuce to the sink and began washing it. "You know, Allen is a great dad and he needs to just be a dad for now and probably for a long time. I love him enough to respect that." I looked out the window watching Philip and Stephen descend the long staircase to the lake. "And he loves me enough to let me move on."

"Can I help you?" Elaine came to the sink and took the head of lettuce from me and began breaking off the leaves.

"I went to see her." I reached behind Elaine to get a bowl.

"Who?" Elaine shook the wet lettuce leaves.

"Tina."

"What?" Elaine dropped the leaves in the sink and dried her hands on the towel.

"She wrote me a letter to apologize. It was short and to the point saying how she had been ill—mentally, since the baby—Joey, was born. She was dealing with the grief of breaking up her marriage. At least she finally owned up to that. But when Allen moved on, she just could not bear it any longer. She said she did not know what happened. It was an uncontrollable rage."

"I'm just flabbergasted." Elaine shook her head in disbelief. "Why didn't you tell me you were going to see her? I would have come with you."

"It was something I had to work out for myself. I didn't tell Allen until after I spoke with her." I nudged Elaine away from the sink and took over the washing of the lettuce. "Her psychologist set up a visitation and she and I just talked."

"Were you scared?" Elaine tore off a few paper towels from the roll handing them to me.

"No. I wasn't at all. I felt it was something I had to do and I'm glad I did." I laid the lettuce leaves out on the paper towel and dabbed them dry. "She didn't look at all like the woman who attacked me. She greeted me like I was an old friend or her sister. She was so relieved I actually came to see her. She is still terribly distraught about everything she did and I don't know how she will ever forgive herself. She believed I could never forgive her."

"But you did." Elaine put the lettuce in a bowl and began washing a vine-ripened tomato from the Fuhrmans' garden.

"Of course, I did." I put the bowl of lettuce in the refrigerator. "And when I was leaving, she wanted me to hug her."

"And you did." Elaine pulled me into a hug. "You are such a nice person, Joule." She released me from her embrace. "You know, he's a nice guy, too." Elaine referred to Stephen.

"I'm sure he is." I returned to the refrigerator for some beers. "Let's take these down to the boys."

* * * *

Philip and Elaine returned to the cabin while Stephen and I watched the evening sun dance on the waves across the lake. "I like to fish," Stephen admitted as he took a drink of his beer. He turned toward the cabin. "The addition looks great."

"Did it pass your inspection?"

"Absolutely."

"Do I?"

Stephen laughed. "You know, Elaine."

"Boy, do I." We clinked bottles. "I know she's told you everything about me and what happened with Allen."

"It is a long drive out here." He nodded. "But, listen to me. I do know a lot about you. But there is something you need to know about me. Not all guys come with a lot of baggage. I've never been married. No kids. And the worst thing my parents ever did to me was not buy me a giant Mickey Mouse doll at Disneyland. Even when I lay on the ground in front of Cinderella's castle and pitched a fit in front of all those people who gathered to watch Tinker Bell do her thing. It was devastating."

"So, you were quite a bratty child?" I said sarcastically.

"No, that was just last year," he replied matter-of-factly and gave a sly smile.

"Ha! Ha! Ha!" I gave an obligatory laugh but then smirked with sincerity.

"I can be as big a jerk as the next guy and I travel constantly with my job. It is difficult to date someone, let alone marry, have kids…" he trailed off, "but I'd like to have dinner with you tonight, if you don't mind, and we'll just see how this goes, because you know Elaine is not going to let up until she gets results. You know, we do have a lot in common. At least it's a start."

"I know and it's a date." I slipped my arm into the crook of his and we walked up the steep staircase stopping just short of the expansive deck overlooking the lake.

"It looks precarious but it's a good foundation." Stephen regarded the cantilever supports.

I smiled up at Stephen. He was definitely an attractive man. Even though Elaine would take all the credit, this was a relationship I wanted to pursue.

We returned to the kitchen to find Philip and Elaine bumping into each other as they busied themselves around the kitchen trying to find what they needed for our evening's feast.

The Kitchen Dance

"Where do you keep the garlic press?" Elaine asked as she inspected the drawers.

"I thought you had a big platter?" Philip searched a cabinet just over her head.

"In the cabinet above the refrigerator," I told Philip and, "I don't have a garlic press," I told Elaine as I dug in the refrigerator for a jar of chopped garlic.

"Can I help with something?" Stephen joined the kitchen dance.

"Yes. You can butter the bread from the bakery. And here," I reached around Elaine to retrieve a roll of foil. "Wrap it up and we'll stick it in the oven. Can you turn on the oven?" I asked Philip who was standing at the range peppering the steaks. I fished a knife for the butter and a spoon for the garlic from my utensil drawer at Stephen's waist then bumped into Elaine as she crossed with the tub of softened butter I kept on the stove.

"There are too many people in this kitchen!" Elaine laughed as she bumped Philip.

I stepped back and took it all in. "There are never too many people in a kitchen," I replied as I took her hand and spun her around like a ballerina amidst all the chaos.

The kitchen is not just a room; it is the heart of the home often filled with friends and family, hard work and fun times, too many people and absolute solitude, old habits and new experiences, comfort and cravings, tears and laughter, fights and embraces. And it is the one place in our home and our community where we all can gather together to nourish our bodies, and in the kitchen, we dance.

About the Author

I wrote, actually, drew my first storybook during my preschool years about a troll who lived under a bridge, as trolls tend to do, in an unkempt cave. One day, a cute little lady troll came along and changed his life completely. He fell in love and allowed her to transform him into a kind gentleman who lived in a clean and lovely home, albeit still under a bridge, as trolls tend to do.

In many films, writers are stereotypically portrayed seated at their uncluttered desk inserting a fresh sheet of paper into their typewriter and then staring dismally at the glaring white emptiness of the page before them. I rarely look at the blankness before me with dismay. The stories are always there. I just wish I could type as fast as the story unfolds and not make so many typos. Even though the tap-tap of old-fashioned typewriter keys are a melodic symphony to a writer's ear most writers these days open a word processing program on a laptop and hit "file" then "new" and their fingers dance to the dull clicks of their keyboards. Either way, I love that sound!

My life as of late has not been ideal for writing and the characters of my stories nag at me like those in Luigi Pirandello's *Sei Personaggi in Cerca d'Autore (Six Characters in Search of an Author)* at the most inconvenient times wanting to know why their stories have not been written. I enjoy performing on stage and the process of acting in films but I owe it to my characters to return to the dull clicks of my laptop because I am the only one who can write their stories. I look forward to other people reading them.

http://g2taylor.intuitwebsites.com/
http://creativedazewithgeri.blogspot.com